Rainbow by Moonlight

Rainbow by Moonlight

Loletta Clouse

Chicory Books
Knoxville, Tennessee
2009

Library of Congress Control Number: 2009931984

Published by Tennessee Valley Publishing

Order **Rainbow by Moonlight** and other exciting books by **Loletta Clouse**.

Wilder—An epic tale of power, strife,and romance in the East Tennessee coalfields of the 1930's.

The Homesteads—A bittersweet story of hope and determination to build a new way of life in the rugged mountains of East Tennessee during the 1930's.

Mallie—A story of love and redemption set in The Great Smoky Mountains in the era of the logging boom.

Available from:
    Chicory Books
    PO Box 31131
    Knoxville, TN 37930
    1-865-693-5678
    www.chicorybooks.com

Cover inset black and white photo from the James E. Thompson Collection used by permission of the McClung Historical Collection.

Printed and bound in the United States of America.

Rainbow by Moonlight

Thank you God,
sometimes it takes a miracle.

Among the many miracles of my life
I count my family and friends who have indulged me
with their generosity, support and good humor.

With special thanks to Timothy Jenkins.
I relish your kindness.

August 6, 1920

Dear Mother and Father

    I have only a moment to dash off a bit of correspondence to let you know I arrived safely in the town of Sevierville. My trip was without mishap with some minor delays as one might expect coming all the way from Chicago and changing trains in Knoxville. I was well cared for by the porters and red caps who were in all regards courteous and helpful. I was directed by a kindly gentleman as to where I might find a meal of excellent quality when we were delayed in Lexington. Moreover, I passed the time most pleasantly with a widow of some refinement who was going to visit her grand children in Knoxville. Therefore, you see, your fears of a young woman traveling alone were much exaggerated.

    Dr. Bishop, who is a professor at Murphy College, and his wife were waiting for me upon my arrival at the depot. They showed me great hospitality, as did their daughter Evelyn who met me at their home. Miss Bishop teaches at the Pi Beta Phi Settlement School and her family regularly hosts the new teachers when they arrive. They appear to be people of some intellect and we passed a pleasant evening of conversation.

    Miss Bishop has arranged for us to be brought by car to Gatlinburg and delivered to the school tomorrow. I will write at length when I know more of what my teaching duties are to be. I am most excited to meet my students and to see the place I am to call home for the next year. Do not worry, for I am well. I will finish now, as I must have this letter ready for the morning post.

Your loving daughter
Claire

Chapter 1

Four days ago, Claire Blackburn had been sitting in her family's parlor in Evanston, Illinois, the favored daughter of a well-to-do family and the most unlikely person to be relieving herself in a field of ragweed on the side of a dusty mountain road. Popping up out of the bushes, she adjusted her slim skirt. She felt exhilarated by the boldness and the ordinariness of the act. It was symbolic of her new life. Each day would present challenges that would be daunting in their newness before they became commonplace.

Ever mindful of where she stepped, for Evelyn Bishop had cautioned her about snakes, she found herself thinking that her mother would find this even worse than dangerous. She would find it all very unladylike. Smiling boldly, she walked the short distance back to the Model T.

Claire had hoped for the sake of decorum to make it to their destination but too much coffee with her meal had forced her to confess her predicament. Evelyn had then unceremoniously announced it to their driver, Mr. Andy Huff who was a prominent citizen of Gatlinburg. Claire had considered hurrying off to be done with it hoping to keep some of her dignity intact, but Evelyn had insisted upon standing watch instructing her as they went on the wisdom of being alert to snakes lurking in the tall weeds. Now Evelyn jumped back into the car without a word with Claire following closely behind her.

"Let's be off, Mr. Huff," Evelyn said matter-of-factly as the man sat staring modestly ahead.

He took off without another word.

Claire sat back against the seat a self-satisfied grin tugging at her lips.

All day the sky had been clear blue. The sun had burned off the morning fog and left the air still and quite warm. The mountains lay ahead, ridge after ridge of random deep green peaks shrouded in a blue mist. Deep valleys ran between each high mountain hiding worlds of flowers, plants, trees and multiple species of wildlife that had thrived there for millions of years.

Moreover, each valley held a world of people who had chosen a life of isolation and austerity. The thought enthralled Claire as it had from the moment she had first heard of the Great Smoky Mountains. She had known from the beginning that her decision to teach at an isolated mountain school would be the most important one of her young life. One from which she would be unable to turn back even as fear and desolation had almost overcome her the night before as she stood on the platform of the Sevierville Depot with her valise of books at her feet, the train pulling away with a mournful whistle. A group of men sat idly whittling a pile of wood shavings at their feet. They stared at her as she stepped down from the train. They spit their tobacco into the dirt and continued to watch her as she craned her neck hoping to spot the Bishops. She pretended not to hear as they discussed her manner of dress and the fact that she was traveling alone. A shrunken brown skinned women in a bonnet passed by giving her a hard look from tired and rheumy eyes. Finally, she spied the Bishops and they swooped down upon her with warm greetings gathering her into their carriage like a lost chick. Claire never confided her relief.

"The road will be getting a bit rougher from here on out," Evelyn Bishop observed, just as the Model T sank into a rut.

Claire's teeth clicked together and her head bounced against the roof of the car. The surprisingly smooth gravel road they had traveled for the last seven miles played out replaced instead by a narrow path of ruts and boulders.

Mr. Huff had picked the women up just after a delightful noon meal at the Bishop's home. Claire found their home quite charming and comfortable but as pleasant as her stay had been, she found that as they sat talking in the parlor, she was eager to get to the mountains. It struck her, that the room was not unlike the staid, and overly warm rooms of many of her college professors at Wellesley. Delighted by their intellect and pleased by their interest in the Pi Beta Phi School where Evelyn had been a teacher for some time, she had plied the Bishop family with endless questions until she felt quite ashamed of herself. They seemed to take it in stride as they had entertained many of the young women who had come to teach.

"It will be like this for the next nine miles till we get to Gatlinburg," Evelyn said, "but I'm thinking it won't be as bad today as it gets. We have not had rain in some days."

The cadence of Evelyn's speech was slow and meandering and Claire had to wait until the words had fully settled upon her to catch their meaning. With each train stop, going south the patterns of speech had changed each time slowing and stretching out like a cat in a windowsill.

"I'm sure I will be fine," Claire said. She wondered how many times she would utter that statement in the coming year as she tried to convince herself and others that it was true. Her intent was that in time, she would prove herself and there would be no need to ask. Proving herself was not something new. It was something she had been doing for most of her life

"Why, of course you will be fine. I have made this trip plenty of times. And I'd say you are every bit as strong as me." Evelyn said with a reassuring smile.

The first thing that always struck people about Claire was her strength of character. She had an air of confidence about her that people often remarked upon. They assumed that she was bold and fearless before she spoke a word. At only five feet two inches tall, and slight of build, it was something she had worked hard to cultivate. Recalling the tenacity with which she had broken down her parents, convincing them to let her try this year at the settlement school, how could she deny it?

"It has been quite a pleasant journey so far," Claire offered, afraid that she had been absorbed in her own thoughts and had not been a proper traveling companion. Evelyn merely nodded. She was no doubt lost in her own thoughts. Two years before she had been made Head Resident for the school, a job filled with endless responsibilities.

For the first part of the trip, they had traveled on such a nice road that Claire had foolishly assumed the whole journey would be that way. She was still adjusting to the change and this new road was providing a challenge to her pleasant mood.

The day was brilliant, shining, and warm and the passing scenery kept Claire alert. She did not want her eyes to pass too quickly over any one sight. She wanted to pause for a while at each new setting to drink in the experience and to ask what manner of bird made such a high pitched trilling, or about the insects whose overlapping melodies filled the air, or the wildflowers whose pungent aroma came in heady waves. She dared not interrupt the trip, she thought, with the silliness of a schoolgirl that wanted to remember this first trip into the mountains.

The car jolted suddenly sending Claire once again bouncing against the rooftop. The road ahead seemed impassible to Claire and she could only hold on and wonder at Evelyn's words that it could be "a bit rougher."

They sat crammed together, Claire, Evelyn and Mr. Huff in the front seat of his Model T, the back filled with her trunk and valise. Perhaps, their being wedged so tightly together served to keep them all from flying out at each new jolt, she thought.

Mr. Huff, she learned, owned the Mountain View Hotel where hunters, anglers and vacationers found food and lodging in the mountains. He had also been helpful in getting the Settlement School in Gatlinburg. Now his hotel entertained frequent visitors to the school as people from all over came to see what was taking place there.

In 1910 when the women of the Pi Beta Phi Fraternity had first scouted out Gatlinburg as a possible location for a school, it was little more than an open space between the mountains. The town, such as it was, consisted of six homes, a one-room schoolhouse, two churches, a general store and a blacksmith shop. There was no organized government except for a local sheriff and a letter carrier. The county school board operated largely one-room schoolhouses with little funding and community support. The residents were suspicious of government and generally unwilling to come together in support of civic projects.

What Dr. May Keller, a settlement school pioneer who came on behalf of the Pi Beta Phi Fraternity, learned on her visit was that the small village of Gatlinburg held a secret. Up every creek and recess in the mountains lived communities of people. Over two hundred families filled the mountains all with children in need of an education. It had taken considerable effort by Dr. Keller and anyone she could enlist to help her convince the community that the Fraternity wanted nothing more than the opportunity to bring a school to Gatlinburg. They suspected her of being a Mormon or worse a Catholic bent on bringing some strange religion to their children.

On February 1912, the Fraternity leased a house, hired a teacher and opened the school to thirteen children. The community promised to find a parcel of land for them on which they would build a school but that promise was slow to come. It had been Andy Huff, along with a number of other prominent citizens, who had gathered the names and solicited the monies with which the parcel had finally been bought.

"You might want to hang on," Mr. Huff remarked laconically.

Claire who sat on the outside could only wonder how she could hold any tighter as each new boulder sent her teeth clicking and her spine popping. "Thank you, Mr. Huff," Claire said. "That certainly seems like sound advice."

"It's a good thing we didn't get rain last night," Mr. Huff said. "That's the Little Pigeon River we are following. It swells up pretty fast with a good rain coming down off these mountains."

Claire looked at the tumbling mountain stream that poured over boulders and rested in deep pools. Looking up, she thought of the first raindrops falling on the tallest peaks above her. The drops collecting into small trickles that turned into streams as it splashed over mossy rocks and between fern covered banks in its relentless drive to get to the valley floor. She searched the blue sky for signs of an errant storm cloud and was relieved to see the sky was still clear. "Does it indeed, Mr. Huff," Claire remarked.

"We most likely wouldn't be making this trip. The road floods out with a good rain."

"Does it rain a lot here?"

"That it does," Mr. Huff said with a nod of his head. "Rains even more high up in the mountains. You can be up in the mountains and a thick cloud will gather overhead. It will rain buckets and not a drop will fall in the valley. When it does rain in the valley, this road can get mighty slick."

Claire could only imagine the holes in the road filled with water and mud as the Model T struggled up and down over the meandering road. "The soil is red," she remarked.

"Red clay is in a lot of the soil around here," Mr. Huff said. He was a tall thin man with an intelligent face.

When Claire thought she could bear the torturous road no longer, the way opened upon the expansive beauty of a valley. The vistas stretched not to distant horizons but ran up the foothills of the high mountains, which circled all around like blue walls keeping out everything but the shimmering beauty. Past the cleared land, the dense green forests of red spruce and Frasier fur spread almost unbroken up the mountains until it met a bluish-purple mist. Claire could not stop the small intake of breath as she marveled at the beauty. She had often heard the expression 'love at first sight' but she had never experienced it until now. Thoughts flitted around her mind but no words came. It was like entering a magical room and closing the door behind her. It was both thrilling and frightening.

Claire had read everything the Fraternity had given her to study on the settlement school and on life in the mountains. While faithfully reading the Pi Beta Phi newsletter the *Arrow*, she had run her fingers over the pictures of the browned parched faces of the women in bonnets and plain dresses. What she had in common with them, she could only wonder. She had been given a reading list to prepare her for mountain life, which she had read earnestly even on the train ride. Nothing in her reading, however, had prepared her for the beauty of the Great Smoky Mountains.

In her heart, she wanted to be useful but all the while, she had kept her less noble reasons for coming to herself. Moreover, to whom could she speak of her need to have a life that was her souls own doing. A woman could have artistic affinities as was her nature, but to tell her parents that she wanted to pursue a career as an artist, to travel abroad to study and later to set up her own studio would have transgressed against every belief they had of what a respectable woman of her class was to do with her life. Therefore, she had couched her need for freedom into a proper feminine role by proposing to go into the mountains as the bearer of culture and social good.

Mr. Huff pointed to a moderate size green frame building. "That hotel belongs to me," he said.

Claire thought the building, though unremarkable, was rather nice. She was pleased to discover that there were such accommodations in town and she wondered if her parents might visit her someday. The village was quite small with only a few houses visible, although in the distance she could see plumes of smoke rising from what must be homes tucked away in the clear green mountainsides.

They drove some further distance along the road where several buildings sat on a knoll. Directly behind the houses lay a garden, surrounded by more cleared land and beyond that was forest.

Stopping in front of one of the buildings, Mr. Huff got out and quickly unloaded her trunk. "You'll come have supper with us at the hotel when you get settled."

"I'd be delighted Mr. Huff. Thank you for your kindness," Claire said. She barely had time to thank him before he hopped into the car and drove off. She straightened her skirt and dusted off her blouse wondering how she must look after her ride.

"This is the teachers' cottage," Evelyn said. "It's where you will be staying."

The cottage was a lovely frame house with two floors and a porch that ran the length of the house. Thick vines grew up the porch supports and on each side of the steps were big flower boxes filled with nasturtiums and chrysanthemums. On the porch sat a rocker and several straight-backed chairs. Claire thought it was altogether pleasant and inviting. In her mind, she had pictured something far more rugged and primitive and she felt almost disappointed to see that it was not unlike a summer cottage. Feeling sheepish at her thoughts and fearing that Evelyn might have read her mind she said, "It's really quite lovely."

Suddenly three women rushed down the steps of the cottage. Evelyn introduced the older woman as Aunt Lizzie Reagan. She was thin, gray haired, and her skin was brown and scored from the sun. "Aunt Lizzie helps us here at the school."

"I am so happy to meet you. I am Claire Blackburn."

Aunt Lizzie nodded shyly. "Pleased to meet you."

"And I am Miss Abbey," the thin woman said, stepping forward. "I am here from Chicago visiting the school."

The third woman was a tall buxom woman with a pleasant face and thick red hair springing loose from its hairpins and curling softly around her face. She came forward and unexpectedly hugged Claire.

"I'm Tessie Moore. I have been so looking forward to you coming since we first got your letter."

"Thank you, Tessie. You are very kind," Claire said. She was not one given to overt gestures of affection, as even her family did not often embrace. Nonetheless, she was genuinely touched by such a warm welcome.

Tessie's already bright smile widened.

Together the women herded her up the steps and into the dining room where the table groaned under the weight of the most delicious smelling meal Claire could imagine. She realized that she was ravenous and asked only to wash up from her dusty journey. When she returned, the women fell upon the food with great appetite, eating and chattering like a nest of baby birds.

"I teach school in Chicago," Miss Abbey said between bites. "I've been here for a week and then I'll be returning home tomorrow for the new school year."

Claire nodded her mouth full of fried chicken. She had never tasted anything so delicious. She had filled her plate with fresh tomatoes, potatoes and chicken with gravy hardly knowing what to eat next.

Miss Abbey seeing her dilemma continued, "They are doing such wonderful things with the children here. This week some of the girls learned how to can fruits and vegetables. They are dear girls and not nearly as mountain-like as I had thought in the beginning. In fact, they are all quite eager to learn. I am not saying it is not different here. It is a far different place from Chicago. I can tell you that."

"I am sure that is the case," Claire said pleasantly. She thought of all she had read and heard about the mountain people. Her reading list had described them as everything from shiftless, backward and lazy to noble descendents of pure Scots-Irish stock trapped in time by mountain isolation. She wondered where in the truth lay and she was eager to find out.

"Of course, I haven't actually been up into the mountains," Miss Abbey continued. "It's so far to walk to the homes of most of the families."

Claire was struck by the thought that any one could travel so far and have so little curiosity about this strange new world about them.

"I am fortunate to have more time here, Miss Abbey. I look forward to the opportunity of meeting as many families as possible," Claire said politely.

Miss Abbey blinked repeatedly. "Yes, of course. You are most fortunate."

Claire quickly tiring of Miss Abbey looked across the table to the cheerful Tessie and asked, "What do you teach, Tessie?"

Tessie, whose plump cheeks were already rosy from the August heat, turned a deeper red as everyone turned toward her. When she spoke of the children, however, her face lighted up. "I teach spelling and writing to the little ones. I like teaching the younger ones best. The young ones are the most loving little things. And you won't believe how earnest and hard working they can be."

"I am sure they are a delight," Claire said sincerely. She wondered if it might be Tessie who drew them in with her irrepressible nature.

Tessie stood up and started clearing the dishes. "Here let me help you," Claire said. As she cleared the plates, she turned to Mrs. Reagan. "Thank you for that wonderful meal Mrs. Reagan. I can't remember when I have eaten so much."

"I'm glad you enjoyed it. You can call me Aunt Lizzie. Everybody does."

"Thank you Aunt Lizzie."

"Don't worry Aunt Lizzie," Tessie said over her shoulder, "we will clean up."

"I'll leave you to it then," Aunt Lizzie said. "I'm going to sit out on the porch where it's cool."

"I'll join you," Miss Abbey called after her.

"Some people are not cut out for this," Tessie said to Claire. "If you can't wash dishes, you got no business being here." Tessie's voice never lost its sweetness but she said it loudly enough for Miss Abbey to hear.

As Tessie washed the dishes, Claire dried them. They worked together as though they had done it many times. "How long have you been here, Tessie?"

"I came last fall."

"And you plan on staying another year?"

"Oh, yes. I can't leave my little ones," Tessie said with a radiant smile.

"What made you decide to come to the settlement school?"

"Well, I always knew I wanted to teach. I have three sisters and two brothers. They are all younger than me so I guess I grew up teaching little ones."

"Where did you grow up?"

"Outside of Bloomington, Indiana. My daddy is a Baptist minister. He and Mommy encouraged me to always be of service to others."

"So they encouraged you to come here?" Claire said, trying to hide her surprise.

Tessie nodded. "They didn't want me to leave home of course, but they knew it was for the good of the children here. They have even been to visit me once."

"They must be very proud of you."

Tessie blushed and waved away the compliment. "You want to take a little walk and cool off some before dark?" she asked as she put away the last of the food.

"I would love that. It is warm here in August."

"The days can be so hot your clothes stick to you, but the nights cool down."

They walked down the front steps waving to Aunt Lizzie and Miss Abbey but not inviting them along. "That is the boy's dormitory," Tessie said pointing to the house next door. And the house next to it is the girl's dormitory."

"Do all the students stay in the dormitories?"

"No, some live close enough to walk. The school found out early on that many of the little ones who so wanted an education lived too far away to walk every day. And even if we sent for them they couldn't survive a ride in a jolt wagon everyday."

"What is a jolt wagon?"

"That's the name they give to farm wagons. But it is a pretty good description for what happens when you try to travel on any of these mountain roads."

Just the thought brought memories of the day to mind and Claire put her hands on her hips and massaged the small of her back with her thumbs. "How many children stay in the dormitories?"

"Oh, sometimes we have so many children we put cots in the hallway. The number depends on the season. Many of the children are needed at home to bring in the crops and help out with chores."

"That must make teaching very difficult."

"We work around it," Tessie said smiling. "When having enough to eat depends on getting the crop in, it can be difficult convincing parents that it is just as important for the children to learn to read and write as it is to harvest corn."

"Yes, I see what you mean," Claire said.

"Let's walk down Pi Phi Lane."

Claire gave her a questioning look.

"It's a path back of the cottage that goes up through a thicket of trees. The school owns thirty-five acres and it goes up to the top of that mountain. The path winds along through it."

"Thirty-five acres?" Claire asked.

"Oh, don't worry. We won't walk it all tonight," Tessie said smiling.

Claire could see a cabin beyond the property, surrounded by a cleared area and then a cornfield. "Does everyone here grow corn?"

"They plant it up every hill and dell," Tessie said with a chuckle. "Where I come from, the land is so flat the cornfields stretch for miles. Here the fields run up the mountainsides."

They strolled on comfortable in the silence. Dusk gathered around them and the sound of insects swelled into an evening chorus. Suddenly, without warning a yawn slipped from Claire's mouth. "I do so apologize," she said. "The fatigue of my trip seems to have overcome me."

"Oh dear, I am sorry, Claire. I forgot you have had a long day. Let's go back and I'll show you to your room," Tessie said turning on her heels with a bounce.

"I think I am going to have to get used to long days around here."

"You'll do just fine."

Claire smiled to herself in the growing dark. "I am looking forward to it, Tessie," she said and knew at once that she meant it.

When they got back to the cottage, Aunt Lizzie and Miss Abbey had disappeared from sight. Following Tessie upstairs to a sparsely furnished room, she was surprised to find her trunk waiting.

"I had one of the boys bring your things up," Tessie said proudly. "The room is all yours until we get another teacher."

"You are so kind," Claire said. "I will just unpack a few things tonight."

"There will be plenty of time to do that tomorrow. It's Sunday and you can sleep late. If you want, I will come by and get you for church? They are having a revival."

"I'd love that. Thank you."

Tessie reached out and gave her an awkward hug. Her body was as soft and warm as a goose down pillow. Claire, who normally was slow to warm to other people found herself taken with Tessie's pleasant nature.

"I'm so glad you are here. I know we are going to get along," Tessie said as she slipped out closing the door behind her.

Claire let out the breath she felt she had been holding for days. Slipping from her dress, she hung it up so the wrinkles from the trip would fall out. She might have to make her clothing last, since she was not sure yet how she was to get her laundry done.

Opening her trunk, she took out her nightgown and pulled it over her head. It felt soft and comforting. The familiar feel made her think of home. She unpinned and took down her long dark hair as fine and straight as silk threads. As she brushed the glistening locks, she realized that even her scalp ached from the jolting ride. Still, she brushed her hair a hundred strokes. This at least would please her mother, she thought. Then she took out her pens and paper to remind her to write a letter to her parents and her sister Lenora in the morning. Her mind swirled with what she would tell them about the drive up in a Model T, Tessie and Aunt Lizzie and the wonderful meal. She rubbed her neck and felt the day's journey in every muscle. Lying down on the bed, she thought she might rest for just a time before she finished unpacking. It was her last thought until morning.

Chapter 2

Claire awoke with a start. Opening her eyes, she felt herself float back from a world that she had been wandering in her sleep. Reaching out her hand, she ran it across the bed, grabbing onto the sheet to ground herself. Her mouth was dry and the room was warm. She sat up and looked around trying to place her surroundings. Clothes lay strewn about the room and her trunk sat open on the floor. She remembered now that she had been unpacking when the wave of fatigue had washed over her. Days of putting on a brave front with her parents, traveling alone without even a female companion, meeting so many new and different people and the bone-rattling trip to Gatlinburg had drained her of any reserves.

The sudden realization that she had spent her first night in the mountains brought her wide-awake. Springing out of bed, she walked to the small dresser and looked at her face in the mirror. She was not unattractive even with the night's sleep still clinging to her face, the blue gray shadows of fatigue serving only to highlight her round dark eyes. Her beauty was something she took neither pride in nor credit for much to her mother's dismay. Men turned to look at her and even women sometimes gave her jealous glances but she was not interested in the kind of suitor her looks attracted and had already rebuffed several. "If I can not have a husband who admires me for my intelligence, my strength and abilities, I will have none at all," she had announced with certainty to her beleaguered parents. Her mother had clasped her heart in an all too familiar gesture while her father had simply gone to the porch for a smoke.

It was, after all, nineteen-twenty and women were pushing themselves to the foreground everywhere. The war had employed women to make munitions, drive trams, work as nurses and even serve in the WAAC, the Navy and the Red Cross. They had gained a new freedom and respect and soon women might even have the vote.

The sheltered, submissive, genteel Victorian lady had given way to a new active, capable and confident woman.

Quickly brushing back her long dark hair, Claire pinned it into place with practiced ease. A familiar routine in what was to be her very unfamiliar new life. Her room at the teachers' cottage was clean, simply furnished and worlds away from her life growing up in Evanston.

Claire's father, reserved and stodgy by nature, was a banker and businessman of considerable influence. His role in Claire's life was to provide her with the best home and access to the finest families in the best social circles. The rearing of two daughters left him confounded and he preferred to leave the general matters to his wife. Her mother Josephine, a tiny whirlwind of boundless energy, had dedicated her life to her husband, to her children and to her church. Her mother had interceded with her father when Claire had wanted to go to college winning him over when she explained that many young women from the best families were now going to university. It was a decision, Claire feared, they both came to regret as more often than not on her visits home she spoke endlessly of the plight of women and the need for women's suffrage.

Her mother was not a progressive woman but she was possessed of a strong sense of duty to the poor and less fortunate of society. Nevertheless, when Claire had brought up her intention to go south and teach school at the Pi Beta Phi Settlement School in the Great Smoky Mountains, her mother had reacted as though someone had struck her on the head, sitting down hard and sharp in her chair. She sat stunned for some time before finding her voice. The South she argued, especially this place some called Appalachia was not safe for a woman alone. The people were primitive and ignorant at best and worse they had no desire to better themselves. "People still die of typhoid from filthy living conditions," she protested as though Claire had asked to go on a foreign mission to darkest Africa.

Claire clinched her jaw to keep from speaking and watched the dust play in the light from the parlor window. It helped to block out her mother's heavy sighs.

Her mother went on to ask, "Why can't you be an easy child like your sister." It had been her mother's battle cry for as long as

Claire could remember. It was the way her mother rallied herself against what she called the 'willfulness' of her younger daughter.

It was a conundrum, Claire agreed. She did not mean to be willful and could not in fact see it that way. It was simply who she was. It pained her that her mother could find that so objectionable.

"Surely you would have me go where I am needed," Claire argued piously. "Is it not our duty to help those less fortunate?" she added, shamelessly throwing her mother's own words back at her. No one believed more strongly than her mother did that it was her duty as a woman of means to cure all the social ills of the world. Josephine had fussed and chattered about wringing her hands for days. While her father, having long since absolved himself of the responsibility for his younger daughters' revolt against a conventional existence, could only shake his head and go back to reading his paper. In the end, her parents had consented to one year. Then she would be expected to come home and find a suitable husband as her sister had done.

Claire had spent the last four years attending college at Wellesley studying art. Upon leaving her beloved college, she had discovered that there was no place for her or her art in the world. Even though she studied harder than any one in her class, the world she discovered, was unprepared for a woman artist and her work was dismissed as trifling and of little substance, no mater what subject she chose.

Despite over one million women having proven themselves during the war by doing every job from assembly-line work, to delivering coal, to nurses in overseas hospitals, Claire found that now her options were limited to teacher or stenographer.

It was at college that she had first heard Miss Eleanor Kingsley from the Pi Beta Phi women's fraternity speak on the settlement school established in the Great Smoky Mountains. To honor their founders on their fiftieth anniversary, the Fraternity had searched the country for a place most in need of a school and had discovered the small mountain village of Gatlinburg. They had established a one-room school at the junction of Baskin's Creek and the Little Pigeon River. It had grown despite many hardships surviving even through the war years. Now with the war over, the school was poised to make great strides. The school was in need of teachers. "Not just ordinary teachers, however, but women of uncompromising spirit, extraordinary intellect and an ability to cope under the harshest of circumstance," Miss Kingsley proclaimed. "The settlement school curriculum requires an active participation in the community. You must live among the people you intend to help in order to win their hearts and their minds."

Claire listened with great interest to the many challenges the school faced. Many of the children suffered from poor nutrition and disease. Hookworm ran rampant among the children who seldom wore shoes except in winter. Their homes were often dark and crowded with whole families sleeping in the same room and often the same bed. They lived far from the school and could not walk the four or five miles one-way each day. Adding to these problems, the families, even when they wanted to see their children educated, could not spare them from work in the fields or homes. Many of the families were reluctant to trust their children to the influence of outsiders, people they viewed as foreigners.

The woman then issued a challenge, "Do you think you could go into this isolated mountain community and be an example to these people and to raise them up out of their poverty and ignorance to a new way of life?"

Claire had not realized until then how deeply she had been searching for some place where her education and intellect might find expression. To go to such a foreign place, to help change young peoples lives was heady stuff. Admittedly, up until that moment, Claire had not shown any interest in the kind of charity work to which her mother and sister Lenora had so dedicated themselves. Lenora, practical and efficient, had followed their mother's example caring for her two sons while active in the church.

It was impossible to go to Wellesley without acquiring knowledge of the changing roll of women in society. Claire was aware of Jane Addams and all the work she had done at Hull House in Chicago and the work that Lillian Wald had done in New York's Henry Street Settlement. They had chosen to live there in the neighborhoods with the people they proposed to help. She even had some vague knowledge of settlement schools as a classmate of hers had gone to the Hindman School in Kentucky where she had taught for two years.

It was common for her classmates to go off for mission work, for it was a message often repeated by her professors that educated women had an obligation to society.

Claire had resisted the message that it was somehow a woman's duty to mend the broken fabric of society but she felt inexplicably drawn to this far away place in the mountains. If teaching was to be the life left open to her, then let it be in this most challenging of places, she thought. She had begun her preparations immediately to take up her position as teacher at the Settlement school and now as she glanced about the room, her clothes so carelessly unpacked the night before, she could hardly believe that in three short months her life had taken such a turn.

Shaking out her gray dress, she hung it up thinking how practical it was and that it might serve her well in the coming days. Next the gingham dress, a favorite and a gift from her sister. The sight of it gave her a pang of homesickness and she remembered her promise to write her sister a long letter. She had always been close to Lenora even though they were so very different. Lenora was down to earth and not given to dreaming or whimsy but she tolerated this in Claire, up to a point, as older sisters were inclined to do. Consequently, Claire was willing to share some of her feelings with her sister for Lenora's advice was always practical and uncluttered by emotions. Even so, she did not share all of herself as Lenora was not one given to doubt or introspection.

Putting her underclothing and stockings in the dresser, she caught sight of her face again in the mirror. Being petit with fine bones and fair skin, she had worked hard to be taken seriously throughout her life. No one could guess that beneath her practiced bravado and refined aloofness lay a longing for understanding, a longing to express all the tumbled dreams that haunted her. She always felt that she was standing on the edge of her life and she longed to plunge headfirst into it.

The light from the window was growing brighter and the room even warmer. Deciding that Tessie might come for her at any minute, she hurried about unpacking. Taking the books from her trunk, she put them on the small desk by the window. Pulling back the curtain, she could not resist looking out at the shimmering green mountains.

She was as surprised by the beauty as she had been the day before. None of her reading about the mountain people had prepared her for the mountains themselves. Hungry to get out her sketchbook, she imagined wandering the mountains, climbing to some crest and setting up her canvas. Could she capture such rugged beauty and would the world accept such bold paintings from a woman, she thought.

She had wondered many times before coming south what manner of people chose to live in such isolation and hardship in the mountains when they could so easily live elsewhere. Were they seeking the promise of a new life in the mountains or merely fleeing a civilization that had no place for them. Seeing the radiance and majesty surrounding her explained a great deal but surely even these people could not claim to tame these mountains, she thought.

A knock at the door brought Claire back from her revelry. "Yes, I am awake," she called.

"Claire, it's Tessie."

"Come in, Tessie. I'm decent, if not properly dressed."

Tessie tucked her head in shyly before opening the door further and greeted Claire with a big smile. No one could call Tessie pretty, but her face dotted with freckles and green eyes sparkling, was awash with kindness.

"Tessie, you dear, you must have let me sleep far too late. The sun is up and it appears we are going to have a beautiful day," Claire said.

"I thought you might need your rest after your trip. Did you sleep well?"

"Wonderfully, thank you. I was sure I would not be able to sleep at all, I was so keyed up, but I don't remember a thing after I put my head down."

"I'm afraid you missed breakfast. Aunt Lizzie is not one to hold a meal but I saved you something in the warming oven. I thought you might want a bath first."

"Oh, Tessie, you are a love."

"Well," Tessie stammered, reluctant to accept such praise, "as soon as you are dressed and had your breakfast we will head off to the church for the revival. There should be quite a crowd there today."

"All right, Tessie. I will hurry along. I feel terribly guilty that you must watch after me so. I don't want to be a bother." It was in fact, her most sincere wish that she not be a burden.

"Claire, you are not to fret about such a thing. It takes a few days to find your way around here that's all."

"Thank you, Tessie," she said relieved. "And Tessie..."

"Yes."

"What is a revival?"

"You have never been to a revival?" Tessie said incredulously.

"I don't think Presbyterians have revivals," Claire said pondering the matter.

"Well, then, it may take some explaining and I may not be that good at it even if I am a preacher's daughter," Tessie said chuckling.

"You make it sound exciting," Claire said.

"People come from miles," Tessie said raising her hand as if to confirm her words. "They walk mostly, starting before daylight, some hiking eight or nine miles. Then they stay with local families as they are mostly related by blood or marriage anyway. A circuit rider preacher comes for a week and holds the services. Sometimes on Sunday they have two or three services."

"And what goes on at these services?" Claire asked intrigued.

Tessie cocked her head to one side and put her hand on her chin. "That is something you may have to see for yourself."

Chapter 3

The White Oaks Flats Baptist Church was a white clapboard building with a small steeple and bell. A crowd milled about the yard collecting in groups to visit. There was a stir in the crowd and they turned to stare at Tessie and Claire as they walked the road to the church.

"Good morning," Tessie said warmly as she passed each group. "This is Claire Blackburn the new teacher," she announced to everyone.

Claire nodded and smiled to each group as they passed by. She tried not to notice as they looked her over from head to toe and discussed it amongst themselves.

"Aunt Wilmer," Tessie said as they approached a tiny, stoop shouldered woman in a plain gray calico dress. "How are you today?"

"I reckon the good Lord seen fit to give me another day."

"And isn't it a beautiful day at that," Tessie said cheerfully. "Did you walk all the way here?"

"No, I rode my mule Amos," Aunt Wilmer said matter-of-factly. "He's blind like me but he knows the way."

"Aunt Wilmer, this is Claire Blackburn. She's new at the school."

"Are you married?" Aunt Wilmer asked without hesitation.

Claire was quickly learning that any unmarried or widowed woman was called "Aunt" regardless if they were of any relation. "No, ma'am I'm not married," she said graciously.

"I can take care of that for you," Aunt Wilmer replied earnestly. "I know a man on Fighting Creek is a lookin' for a wife. He's a might older but he's got his own place."

"I appreciate that Aunt Wilmer," Claire said with bemusement. "I am not ready to get married just yet."

"You're not ugly is ya?" Aunt Wilmer asked. "Cause if you are, we can work our way around it."

Claire blushed and found she was speechless.

"She's quite pretty, Aunt Wilmer," Tessie said, stepping in to save her.

"You are like all them womenfolk at the school. I don't reckon there's a married one in the bunch."

"I suppose everyone is too busy teaching the children," Claire offered.

"I thought to myself when I first heard of what you'uns was doin' that's some quare women in their store-bought clothes and their fine way of talkin'. But when I got to know'em though I come to admire what all you'uns was tryin' to do."

"Thank you so much," Claire said at last.

"We had better be going Aunt Wilmer," Tessie said.

"You change your mind, young lady. Miss Tessie here knows where to find me."

"Thank you for the offer," Claire said. "It was nice meeting you."

A small gathering of men clustered by the front door parted to let them through.

"Mr. Wheeler is there room for us inside," Tessie asked as they reached the door.

"They've got'em packed in there today, Miss Moore. That's for sure. Don't you worry none. My wife is settin' up front with the younguns and she'll make room for you. You just go on in now."

"This is Miss Blackburn. She has come to teach."

Mr. Wheeler nodded as the other men looked on with obvious curiosity. "You're a little bit ain't you," said Wheeler.

Claire merely smiled. She was not accustomed to such straightforwardness but she found she was not offended. After all, it was something she had heard all of her life in different ways. Her sister Lenora who topped her by two inches was fond of saying that what she lacked in size she made up for in stubbornness. Tessie saved her from further scrutiny by pushing her forward through the church doors and into the aisle.

The blast of heat and the rank odor of sweat almost knocked her off her feet. She had to stop herself from reeling backwards. Up the center of the church ran the aisle with pews made of rough-hewn lumber, each about ten feet long on either side. More pews, pushed against the walls, were filled to the last inch with worshipers, and those who could not find a seat stood where they could find space.

Tessie headed boldly to the front where Minnie Wheeler sat holding a baby. Several younger children clustered around her. When she saw the women, she scooped up the two-year-old sitting next to her, holding baby and child with ease. Without hesitation, Tessie sat down pulling yet another little girl onto her lap. She motioned for Claire to join her.

Easing her way between Tessie and the other children, Claire sat down and smiled at the three other children who filled the pew. The oldest was a girl of perhaps nine or ten who looked away shyly when their eyes met.

The preacher had not stopped talking from the moment they had entered the room. His bellowing voice roared above the congregation as he stomped up and down growing ever more frenzied with each turn. His fiery black eyes scanned the rap congregation pinning some of the children to their seats like bugs. Sweat ran down his face and dripped from his chin as he flailed his arms about. With practiced flair, he ripped the handkerchief from his pocket, mopped his face and then flourished it about using it to emphasize his words.

To Claire the preachers words all seemed jumbled together, but she could gather his sermon was an impassioned plea for the souls of the wayward to see the error of their ways. She looked around her at the mesmerized crowd. The men who all sat on the opposite side of the church nodded in solemn agreement. The children sat big eyed and rigid on the hard pews as though a mere fidget might cast them into the fire and brimstone. Some of the women rocked and waved their arms about in the air looking up to the ceiling as though the words were raining down on them. Others appeared about to faint and Claire could only wonder if it was the sermon or the heat that was affecting them.

When the preacher ended his sermon, his voice, hoarse from his two-hour long effort, softened as he gave an invitation to the unsaved to come to the mourner's bench at the front of the church. A group of adults who had been sitting on a bench at the front stood up and began to sing a hymn. Several small children, including the young girl who sat next to Claire, got up, went down, and knelt on the bench. Mothers all around the church began to weep and call out with joy that their children were saved. Claire could not help but stare and she turned to look at Tessie who had her hands together in prayer and was smiling sweetly as though it was the most gratifying of experiences.

Then suddenly, it was over. The deeply engaging and familiar ritual that had bound them together into something greater than themselves was over. The emotion and drama that had filled every corner of the room seemed to evaporate in an instant. Folks stood up, patted each other on the back and started filing out of the church. Children with angelic, tear-stained faces now chased each other around the room laughing.

"You'll come and eat dinner with us," Minnie Wheeler said.

"Why thank you Mrs. Wheeler," Tessie said. "That is very kind of you. Are you sure we won't be any trouble."

"We'd be proud to have you," she said solemnly. "You know where we live. Just follow the crowd." With that, she gathered her children about her like a brood of baby chicks and hurried them out the door.

The women followed, Tessie speaking to each one and introducing Claire at every opportunity. Claire's head swirled at all the new people and she wondered how she would remember them all.

As they walked up the road toward the Forks of the River community, Claire saw a tall, dark-haired man ahead of them. He was holding a little girls hand, talking gently and smiling down at her. Suddenly, the little girl broke away and came running throwing herself at Tessie. She wrapped her arms around Tessie's skirt and then just as quickly released her grip and backed away shyly. She stood looking at the dirt, the heat rising in her cheeks.

"Why Emily," Tessie said gently, "I am so happy to see you. You look so pretty today."

Emily looked up, a smile spreading across her face. Thick blond curls framed her small eager face. Awash with curiosity, her blue eyes took Claire in from head to toe before she caught her looking back and turned to tuck her head into her shoulder shyly.

The man came striding toward them and softly put his hand on Emily's head. "I hope she didn't mess up your dress Miss Tessie. She was searching you out in the church and I reckon it got the better of her when she spied you walking."

"Oh, I'm just pleased to see Emily," Tessie said. "She is looking well. Has she had a good summer then?"

"My ma takes good care of her," he said simply.

"Were you at the revival?"

"I brought Emily and Ma down. Emily don't get to see a lot of her cousins except now and again."

"Oh, Mr. Morgan, this is Miss Claire Blackburn. She will be teaching at the school."

"Pleased to meet you, ma'am," Mr. Morgan said, tipping his hat. "You can call me Shade, most folks do."

"Shade, that's an unusual name," Claire said.

"Reckon, you got a point," he said politely. "My given name is John. I am named after my grandpa but I got two uncles and three nephews named John. A lot of names here in the mountains get used over and over. The names get passed down. So I'm known as Shade John."

"How are the other men named John known?"

"Well, there's Blacksmith John and Fighting John and Broom-maker John."

He seemed to find some humor in the telling of it for a grin pulled at his lip. Claire wondered if he could be putting her on. "Oh, I see," she said, "but why do they call you Shade?" He looked suddenly uncomfortable at the question and Claire began to regret her boldness.

"When I was a youngun, I was puny for a long time. My ma would put me under the shade of a tree so's she could get her work done. So my brothers took to callin' me Shade."

His voice was strong and clear and he stood with his feet firmly planted, his shoulders squared on his six-foot frame. His angular face held dark eyes set far apart, heavy brows and a straight, thin nose. There was something guarded and brooding about him and she found his looks more interesting than handsome but she had to admit he had done well to get over the 'puniness' of his childhood. "I like it," she said honestly.

"Well, we had this little Billy goat. Ma used to tie him to the tree too so's he could watch after me. I reckon my brothers let me off easy by not callin' me Goat John."

A hearty laugh burst from Claire lips and then threw her hands to her mouth. Shade's face showed little expression but she caught a glint of humor in his eyes. "I would say you were indeed lucky," she said with a warm smile.

"Emily we better get on and let these ladies be," he said. "Nice to meet you Miss Blackburn."

"Call me Claire," she offered.

"Nice to meet you Miss Claire."

"Good to see you again, Miss Tessie," he said, turning to go.

"I hope you are going to let Emily attend school this year, Mr. Morgan," Tessie called after them.

Shade stopped and stood for a moment. "Well now, we'll have to see," Shade said turning slightly. "Ma's teaching her some and she's still young."

"She's so smart and she wants to go to school."

Emily looked up and searched her father's face.

"Won't you think about it? I will take good care of her I promise."

He seemed pained by her words and continued to offer excuses. "She's a big help at home. I don't know that I could do without her just now."

Claire looked at Emily's smooth shining face. With her blond hair and blue eyes, she did not favor her father so Claire could only assume she looked like her mother. She was no more than seven or eight but she had a presence about her that made her seem older. Claire was sure she needed to be in school and she could not understand her father's hesitation.

Emily looked from her father to Claire. She said nothing but there was a longing in her little face. Then she looked again to her father, an unspoken sadness passing between them.

"You know I am beholden to you," Shade offered.

"Its Emily I'm thinking about, of course," Tessie persisted.

"I'll think on it then," Shade said. "We best get along Emily before all the foods gone."

"We'll be up to call on you soon," Tessie said.

"You're welcome anytime," Shade said with a nod as they walked away. "Ma would be pleased."

They walked on in silence for a while until Shade and his daughter were out of sight. Tessie seemed lost in thought her face screwed up. "Mr. Morgan is an important man in the community," she offered finally. "He owns a farm up Roaring Fork. And he has a tub mill where folks from around bring their corn to be ground."

"He seems quite nice and his daughter is beautiful. He seems reluctant to let her go to school. Does he have something against girls getting an education?"

"Oh no, he has always been a big supporter of the school. He knows everyone and he's respected, so when he speaks well of the school people listen."

"So why doesn't he want his daughter to go to school?"

"He's just not ready to let go of her yet."

"That seems odd given his support."

"His wife died last year," Tessie said, at last. "He's still in mourning."

"Oh, I am sorry. What happened?"

"She died in childbirth. The Spanish Influenza had left her too weak. Lost the baby too."

"Oh my, I didn't realize the influenza had made it to this isolated place."

"Oh yes, we had quite a few cases. What with sickness all over, we had not a doctor or nurse to help out."

"You were here?" Claire asked.

Tessie nodded.

"Oh, yes of course, I had forgotten. But weren't you afraid?"

"I am ashamed to say I was. I had nursed my brothers and sisters through measles and such but I had never been around anything as frightening as the Spanish Influenza. None of the teachers had."

"What did you do?"

"The teachers all did what they could. They cooked and cleaned and kept the children."

"Is that why he said he was beholden to you?"

"When they were all sick, Shade, his wife and mother, I took Emily to stay with me at the school."

"That was very kind of you."

"No, it was nothing really. Mountain folks do not ask for help you see. Neighbors just come when they are needed without having to be asked. When they hear a neighbor is sick they come, milk the cow and feed the livestock. They gather firewood and cook for the sick until they are better and can do for themselves. Then they go home until they are needed again. It is a wonderful thing the way they help each other.

However, at that time there were just too many folks sick, so when Shade Morgan asked me to care for Emily, I was pleased to do it. I knew it cost him to have to ask for help and I was honored he trusted me.

Claire could hear it in Tessie's voice. She could hear the joy and pride she felt in serving these people of the Great Smoky Mountains when they needed her.

"It helped, you know," Tessie said.

"What do you mean?"

"The school will be getting a nurse soon. The Fraternity has approved one. The school has been asking for a nurse but the influenza epidemic convinced them we needed someone here. What with all the children needing inoculations against infectious diseases like diphtheria and smallpox we need a nurse here all the time. Moreover, there are all manner of cuts and scrapes and broken bones."

Claire thought it a wonder that one nurse could handle such a world of needs. "What have the people done for medical care?"

"A doctor comes up from Knoxville now and again. Every community seems to have a woman who helps out delivering babies and treating ailments with home remedies, herbs and poultices of her own making."

"How do you think they will accept a trained nurse coming?"

"It changed the way some of the people here felt about the school and the teachers when we were so willing to help out during the epidemic. Some of the folks who had never really been keen on having us here came to see us in a different light because of what we did to help out."

"You mean they no longer see us as strange women in store bought dresses?" Claire asked.

"Well, we will always be that, but now we are 'their' strange women in store bought dresses," Tessie said with a hearty laugh.

Claire laughed too as she thought of what a strange day it had been. The noon sun was making her dress stick to her in a most uncomfortable way and dust covered her shoes but she felt alive and happy as they walked down the road. Her stomach rumbled and she realized that she was famished. She hoped they too would arrive before all the food was gone.

August 8, 1920

Dear Lenora

It is Sunday evening and I am sitting in the living room of the Teachers' Cottage that is my new home. Aunt Lizzie, who helps with the housekeeping and Tessie a fellow teacher and new friend, are rocking away on the front porch. It is the custom to spend evenings on the porch, as it is cooler there. I must tell you about the little straight back chairs that are on the porch and scattered all about the house. I am sitting in one now and it is most comfortable. They are made here in the mountains all by hand and without nails. They are fitted together and even the legs are made without machinery. You would find them most attractive and quite unusual. They sell for $1.25. Let me know if you would like some, as it would greatly benefit the families.

I have had only the briefest time to myself since arriving. I am sitting here by lamplight, as the cottage does not have electricity. Evelyn Bishop, our director, is looking into a Delco generator that might soon provide us with electric lights. We do have, much to my relief, indoor plumbing. Furthermore, Tessie has assured me that one of the young girls will wash my clothes to earn money for school and that I might expect them to be returned to me in fine condition. Therefore, that is another problem solved.

You will be happy to know that I attended church today. It was a lively event and quite different from home. A local family invited me to dinner, which is the noon meal here. It was quite a distance to walk, something to which I must become accustomed. There were so many people that we had to wait while young girls hurriedly washed the dishes to allow enough plates for everyone. I met many of the children who attend the school and their parents. They were all most kind and made me feel welcome.

Later we went back to church for a special singing at three o'clock. They called it Sacred Harp Singing and it is a mountain tradition. They have a most peculiar way in which they sing the musical notes. It is in a cappella, four part harmony, the voice being considered the musical instrument or the Sacred Harp. It was quite uplifting to hear such unusual harmonies done at the top of their voices. I know with your love of music and your years in the church choir you would have found it most unusual but enjoyable.

Tomorrow I will visit the school and see my classroom for the first time. I am very excited and I know I have made the right choice in coming here. I know it will be a busy year. Much progress has been made here thanks to the hard work of so many who came before me. It is very inspiring and I feel I must do my part.

Give my love to the children. I miss all of you fiercely. Please write, as I will look forward to news of the family.

Your loving sister
Claire

Chapter 4

Claire backed out of the supply closet, her hand covering her nose. Dust filled the room and she tried unsuccessfully to hold back the sneezes but they escaped rapid fire.

Tessie came up behind her laughing. "I should have warned you. No one has cleaned the supply closet in a while."

"I can see that," Claire said, blinking back the tears in her eyes. They had been cleaning the school all morning. The school was a large white frame building with classrooms on each end and a larger room in the middle where the children assembled in the mornings for devotion.

Claire had swept and dusted the classroom where she would be teaching among other subjects writing, grammar and geography. She had put her desk in order and numbered the new textbooks the children would use when school started the next week. Together she and Tessie had mended the older textbooks. The children had to buy their own books, so many of them bought used books if they were available. Now, with that done, she was tackling the closet where all the school supplies were stored.

"Let me help you," Tessie offered.

Tessie liked to clean and she was making sure they did a proper job of it. Claire enjoyed neatness and organization but she was not as eager to tackle the entire school in one day, however much she enjoyed Tessie's company. They both reveled in discovering what others had deemed important enough to keep, trying to decide what purpose it served and then when they could not, tossing it in the trash. Spying what looked like a pile of twigs Claire reached tentatively back into the deepest part of the closet and gently pulled it into the light. It appeared to be a bird's nest made of mud and sticks. Inside were acorns, and a variety of seedpods. "Do you like my new hat?" Claire asked, holding the nest above her head.

"Oh, you are the envy of the school," Tessie squealed. "How do you stay ahead of the latest fashions?"

"It is a gift. How can I deny it," Claire said, her nose held high.

They laughed like school girls while Claire moved the nest about as though trying different poses.

"I see you found my nature lesson," a voice said from behind them.

Claire looked out to see Agnes Ward coming toward them carrying a small basket. She immediately sat the nest back in the closet and looked at Tessie with a sheepish grin. Tessie turned away to contain her laughter. They both then turned solemnly to greet Agnes.

"That is the nest of a barn swallow. As I am sure you know, the barn swallow likes to attach its nest of mud and twigs to the side of a rafter high up where the chicks will be safe. I hope you weren't intending to throw that away."

"Oh, no Agnes," Tessie said sincerely. "We would never do that."

Agnes taught the middle grades and was sober and industrious by nature. She attacked each task that morning with boundless energy and efficiency. Claire was sure she taught her classes with the same intensity and she was glad they had been caught in time before the nest was tossed.

"Oh, I do hope you two are at a stopping point," Agnes said. "I was so hoping you would walk to the Riley place with me. I brought along a picnic for us to eat along the way."

Tessie picked up a stack of papers and was nervously clutching them. She smiled at Claire. "Why Agnes that's a grand idea," she said.

Much to Claire's delight Tessie put down the papers and began to dust off her skirt and clear the cobwebs from her hair. She was eager to get outside into the fresh air. "Who are the Rileys?" Claire asked.

"These hills are full of Rileys as you will soon discover," Agnes chortled. She had a birdlike quality made more pronounced by the way she bobbed her head as she spoke. "Today we will visit Al and Mary Riley. Their cabin is only two miles up the road and we can rest half way and have a pleasant meal," she said pointing to the basket.

It would be Claire's first adventure into the mountains and she was excited at the prospect. She was also very hungry. Her appetite was hearty for every meal since she had arrived in the mountains and she wondered if she would soon have to let out her dresses.

They walked up Pi Phi Lane and struck off toward Baskin Creek when they reached the road. The day was bright and sparkling and Claire felt exhilarated. *Like a child let out of school,* she thought and smiled to herself. All around her in the fields and woods wildflowers bloomed. She was learning the names of some of them from Agnes who seemed to know a great deal about the local plants.

"This one with orange flowers spotted with brown is the Spotted Jewelweed. Hummingbirds are especially attracted to it. My favorite of this variety is the touch-me-not. They have seed pods that when they mature, explode when they are touched."

Agnes sounded like the teacher she was, patiently instructing her student, but Claire was grateful for she had so much to learn. "Agnes, how is it you know so much about the local plants when you have been here such a short time?"

Agnes paused, her head bobbing and then dropping on her chest before she looked up again. "My father is a scientist. He puts great stock in intellectual debate. He wanted a son but to his grave disappointment, he had only me. I made up for that by reading every book in his library. I made it my mission to be prepared to debate him on any subject he chose. I think in doing so I developed a quite extraordinary memory."

Claire was unprepared for Agnes' rather personal explanation. She realized that she had been holding her breath and she exhaled slowly. "I am grateful to be the beneficiary," she said kindly.

Agnes said simply, "Thank you. I find it serves me well as a teacher."

Claire had shared with no one, not even her sister, how unsure she felt about teaching her first classes. Her letters home to her family were like notes to a distant aunt full of pleasantries withholding all of her doubts and fears. She wanted to ask Tessie and Agnes if they had felt any such doubts when they first arrived but she was hesitant to reveal herself.

"This oddly named plant is Joe-Pye weed," Agnes continued. "It got its name, or so it is said, from a New England Indian herb doctor who had cured typhus with it. I do not know the truth to that story but the mountain people use the native plant remedies as well for a variety of ills." She paused and turned to Claire. "When you get an opportunity to meet one of the Granny women, you will find their knowledge fascinating if sometimes disturbing."

"The Granny women are the mountain doctors," Tessie answered before Claire could ask. "Most of the women use a Granny woman to deliver babies and treat the sick. They have never had anyone else to call on."

"And who are these women?" Claire asked.

"They are neighbor women who have trained themselves to make tonics and teas for coughs and upset stomachs and poultices for wounds and cuts," Tessie explained. "The mountain people send for them and put great faith in their advice, taking whatever potion offered with unwavering trust."

"The mountains are a dangerous place it seems," Agnes said, "and so the Granny women perform a service born of need. Burns are a common thing especially with the children because the cabins have open fireplaces on which they do all the cooking. They work and play outside without shoes so they are subject to all types of parasites especially hookworm. Farm work is done with axes, hoes and other dangerous tools. One hears everyday of someone being kicked by a mule or bitten by a poisonous snake. Of course, sanitation and hygiene is abysmal so an injury might become septic and fatal."

"The mothers get no care before or after the baby comes," Tessie said. "And there are no inoculations for the baby or checkups.

"That is why we are so pleased to be getting a trained nurse for the school," Agnes added.

"Yes, Tessie was telling me. She is certainly going to be busy." Claire marveled at how the mountain people had learned to survive so much sickness and misfortune by using whatever they had at hand. She wondered how they would accept a trained nurse.

"Oh look Claire, its pokeweed," Agnes said pointing to a tall plant. Clusters of deep purple berries hung from each plant.

Claire reached out her hand to pick a berry from the cluster. Agnes grabbed her wrist.

"You can't eat them," she said gently. "They are poisonous."

Claire pulled back her hand.

"I have found its best not to eat anything unless I ask Aunt Lizzie," Agnes said. "That's how I learned to save myself from stomachaches or worse."

"I'll remember that," Claire said feeling foolish.

"The early settlers used the pokeweed berry for ink," Agnes said unperturbed. "You see in addition to using plants for medicine, they used all kinds of plants for dyeing. They dyed yarns and cloth using alder bark, rhododendron leaves and even walnut hulls. You will see later when you see some of the coverlets the women have made. And the baskets they make from honeysuckle vine and willow bark are dyed with plant infusions."

The admiration for the ingeniousness of the people was obvious in Agnes' words. Claire had more questions, but she was afraid her companions would grow weary of her endless curiosity.

They came to a mountain cabin where an old toothless woman sat rocking on the front porch smoking a pipe. She was as brown and wrinkled as a dried apple doll. Agnes called out a greeting. The woman stared at them, nodded and continued to rock without speaking. Agnes did not seem offended but continued to wave as she walked on up the road.

"Why didn't the woman speak?" Claire asked at last.

"Some of the older mountain people are very reserved. It takes a while for them to get to know you. When I first started coming up here, she wouldn't even nod."

"How long have you been coming up here?"

"Every two weeks or so for the last year."

"When did she start to nod," Claire asked.

"It was a month ago this week," Agnes said thoughtfully.

Claire marveled at Agnes' understanding of the woman and her willingness to persevere for the small reward of a nod. She wondered if Agnes had gleaned that too from her relationship with her father. It made Claire wonder if she would ever tame her own grand expectations and her fiercely wild impatience.

They turned off into the trees and onto a narrow footpath. Claire looked up the steep slope and realized there was no relief from the endless rocks. Her feet felt bruised through the thin soles of her shoes and she chided herself for not having put on sturdier ones, but there was nothing to be done about it now. She was happy when Agnes spied a lovely place by a stream and sat the picnic basket down.

Water spilled over mossy rocks forming clear pools. The sun searched the forest for an opening shooting down shafts of light. On the surface, water striders floated making tiny dimples in the pool and casting their shadows on the bottom as gnats and other small insects buzzed overhead.

Tessie sat down just as a chipmunk scurried from beneath a laurel. He sat up, looked at them suspiciously, then grabbed a seed and hurried away. They laughed at the antics, frightening the sparrows overhead. The birds sounded the alarm and flew out of the trees in unison. The women laughed again that their little picnic could have caused such a commotion.

Claire sat down on a flat rock completely entranced that such a quiet little world could be so filled with life. She took off her shoes and put her feet into the cool stream watching as tiny minnows and salamanders scattered in alarm. Frogs leapt from the opposite bank and she felt bad for disturbing their tranquil day. The stream bank was dotted with tiny bluets trembling in the most gentle of breezes. The roots of laurel exposed by endless water passing on its way to the valley were like fingers clinging to the bank.

Claire was content to drink in the tranquility and beauty of this timeless place. In hundreds of more years the boulder on which she sat might wear away, but yesterday, today and tomorrow had been the same for generations of mountain people. It occurred to her, that she and her kind were now suddenly bringing change to the mountains.

Claire pulled her feet from the stream, dried them on the hem of her skirt and eased on her shoes. Agnes sat nearby on a mossy log busily unpacking their lunch. Behind her was a large shrub six feet high covered in clusters of seedpods. Birds feasted on the seeds scattering as much as they ate. It made Claire wish she had brought her sketchpad and pencil and she vowed to bring them the next time.

In her next letter, she would ask her mother to send her a Kodak so that she might take photographs.

Agnes handed her a napkin. Wrapped inside were two biscuits left over from the morning breakfast, one oozing blackberry jam and the other filled with slices of bacon. Aunt Lizzie made the blackberry jam from berries that grew wild all around the mountains. It was delicious with the fresh churned butter made from the milk they got everyday from the cow the school owned. They even added the milk to their coffee and it was rich and sweet.

Claire had eaten three biscuits that morning with two cups of coffee. She simply could not get enough of them. Any thought that her time at the school would be bleak and monastic had vanished with that first biscuit. Finishing the last bite, she scooped the jam from the corner of her mouth with her tongue and savored the tiny morsel. She noticed that Agnes sat primly on the log picking at her lunch, Tessie and Claire at her feet like children. Agnes offered them a pear for dessert. Claire knew they were hard and green for she had tried them the night before, still hunger overruled and she took one. She sat nibbling on the pear as her eyes took in the scenes around her as though she were putting them on canvas. How lovely it would be to steal away and paint, she thought.

"Claire," Tessie called.

Claire looked at Tessie who had a bemused look on her face.

"We have been calling your name," Tessie said laughing.

"You were daydreaming," Agnes said. "A penny for your thoughts?"

Claire felt herself grow warm. Her companions were kind and charming and she felt guilty that she was dreaming of being alone. "It is just so beautiful here," she said simply.

"Then you must go with us on a real adventure," Agnes said.

"We are planning to go camping over night in the mountains," Tessie said excitedly.

"I have never been camping," Claire confessed.

"Neither have we, but we have found a local man, Wiley Oakley, who can take us."

"Have you met him?" Claire asked.

"I have not yet had the privilege," Agnes said as though she was awaiting a formal occasion. "He has quite a reputation for his knowledge of the mountains. Hunters and fishermen from Knoxville, Nashville and other cities have been seeking him out for a number of years because he knows the best places for trout, deer and wild boars."

"I can assume we won't be hunting," Claire queried.

"You are quite right," Agnes agreed. "However it seems he also knows every plant and animal species in these mountains. He has been walking the mountains since he was a young boy. That's why they call him the Roaming Man of the Mountains."

"What an unusual name," Claire mused.

"They say he is quite good-natured and a marvelous storyteller," Agnes said.

"Then we would be most fortunate to have him as our guide," Claire said. She was beginning to discover that just as some of the mountain people were shy and reserved an equal number were congenial and sociable. She thought suddenly of Shade Morgan. She had watched him that day at the Wheelers as he went purposely about the crowd his square shoulders thrown back. Occasionally he would put his broad hand on a man's shoulder, swapping stories, and a laugh. Then he would move on, kneeling next to an elderly woman seated in a chair, leaning in close. Each time he was greeted warmly, each person reluctant to have him leave. Proud and confident, he was not what she expected from a mountain man.

"It seems that most everyone here has a descriptive name in addition to their given name. How do you keep all of the children sorted out when you get them in your classroom?" Claire asked.

"Oh, at first, it can be quite the challenge," Agnes admitted, "but you will do fine, I'm sure."

"Yes, fine, I'm sure," said Claire somewhat wearily. "I do think that I would enjoy going camping."

"Then we shall have a great time," agreed Agnes. "But we must head on up the way to the Riley place if we are to make it back by dark." She neatly refolded their napkins and placed them back into the basket. With determined strokes, she brushed the moss from her dress then picked up the basket and put it on her arm.

"Is that one of Mary Riley's baskets you carry?" Claire asked.

"Yes, isn't it lovely," she said, holding it out for Claire to examine. "She makes them from willow and some from oak splits. She learned to make them from her mother and she has taught her girls."

"Do a lot of the women here make baskets?"

"The people here either grow or make everything they need. There is very little money to buy anything. What they don't make they barter," Agnes said. "There are few jobs, although some of the men work in logging or sell tan bark."

"The school found out early on that if we were to help the children we would need to help their families," Tessie said. "The school looked for ways to supplement the farming they did by providing a way they might make money."

"They discovered that many of the women made exquisite quilts, hand-woven coverlets and blankets and created lovely baskets. They hit upon the idea of offering their goods through the Fraternity. When people buy the goods they are not just getting a lovely item but they are doing good for the mountain people. And the women can stay home with their children and still make money."

"You should see how proud these women are when they can make a little money for the family. The children too come to school better dressed and in some cases better fed," said Tessie.

They walked on until they came to a stone and log structure. The bank had been dug out around a spring, shored up with rocks and a house built over it. The four walls were made of rough-cut logs and the roof covered with wooden shingles. "Would you like to get a drink at the springhouse?" Tessie asked.

A spout hewn from wood came out of the back wall. Water poured from the spout into a trough and ran down spilling onto the rock floor forming a small pool, which overflowed and drained out an opening in the rock wall. Tessie put her hand under the trough and scooped a handful of water into her mouth. Claire followed her lead. The water was sweet and delicious.

"The water comes from a natural spring. It stays cold so they use it to store food."

"This is my very first drink from a springhouse," Claire said laughing with delight. She looked up to see a small girl about six years old walking down the path toward them. She was barefoot and her gingham dress, two sizes too big, hung loose on her wiry frame. Her biscuit colored hair, combed and freshly plaited, fell to below her shoulder blades in one pigtail.

"Good afternoon, Miss Dealie," Tessie said.

The child stopped suddenly in her tracks and stared at them. Then she seemed to regain her composure and with the self-possession common in mountain children she spoke, "Ma's been lookin' for youns." It sounded like an older sibling scolding a younger brother or sister. The women all laughed. Dealie looked offended, her tiny brow forming into a furrow as she thought it over.

"Why thank you Dealie for coming to tell us," Tessie said graciously. "Why don't you run and tell her we are on our way."

"Yes, ma'am, Miss Tessie," she said full of self-importance. She turned on her heels and ran back up the path.

They turned to the right up a narrow path and topped a small rise not more than a hundred yards from the springhouse. The cabin sat in a clearing just ahead of them. It was really two rooms in front with a kitchen added to the back. On the porch built across the front of the cabin sat Mary Riley and her girls working. Mary looked up, nodded to the women, and called out a greeting. She stopped her work long enough to push back the hair that had fallen into her face and smooth the wrinkles from her dress. Then she went back to weaving her basket. Dealie sat on the porch leaning against the rustic handrail looking proud for having carried the word that the women were coming. An older girl sat around a wooden-hooped churn, her sturdy arms pushing the dasher up and down. Although her dress was drab and worn, she had sewn a small white collar on it and her hair was neat and newly brushed.

The yard was hard packed dirt swept clean of weeds, leaves and sticks. Chickens ran freely about the place and scattered squawking as the women approached. The place, though weathered, had a scrubbed, well-kept look about it.

"Good afternoon, Mrs. Riley," Agnes said. "Mrs. Riley, I brought Miss Tessie and Miss Claire with me. They are both teachers at the school. I think you know Miss Tessie."

Mary Riley looked up, her tired face crinkled in a half-smile, but her fingers never ceased their work weaving the basket she held in her lap. "Come on up and make yourself at home. I've been looking for you to come any day. I've about got your baskets ready, Miss Agnes," she said. Her voice was slow and halting.

"That's wonderful, Mary," Agnes said.

"Frannie here has been helping me. She's getting to be a good hand to help."

For the first time, Claire noticed a young girl no more than ten sitting on a stool next to the cabin weaving a basket. The girl did not speak but cast an anxious glance toward them. Her brown hair cropped off just below the ears clung to her small face and her faded shapeless dress was too big for her thin frame, but her hazel eyes were intelligent and questioning. Claire stepped to the edge of the porch and looked at the basket she was weaving. It was perfectly shaped and neat. "You are doing a very nice job on that basket, Frannie." The girl looked down at her hands, but mumbled a shy thank you.

"Martha Jane, that butters done," Mary Riley said without looking up.

The older girl took the churn she had been working so vigorously and went inside the cabin. Mary Riley invited the women to sit with her on the porch as she continued to work. Claire took a seat in a straight back chair similar to the ones at the school and she wondered if Mr. Riley had made them. Agnes took the stool that Martha Jane left behind and Tessie sat on the porch step.

"Mrs. Riley, I think your baskets are beautiful. Agnes tells me you made the one we carried our picnic in today and I admire it greatly."

"I never seen'em as pretty till Miss Agnes brought it to my mind. We always just made 'em cause they was needed."

"I would love to know how you do such beautiful work," Claire said.

The woman's expression was utterly blank for a moment then she continued to work. Claire wondered if Mary Riley had heard her or misunderstood what she had said. She felt awkward and was unsure what to say next.

"They's not so much to it once you learn," Mary Riley said in her halting speech. "The first two or three you make most likely won't have no shape a'tall but when it comes to you it's the simplest thing. I've made a heap of baskets. I've used honeysuckle, willow, oak splits, most anything I could get. My mama taught me when I was just a youngun."

"I would love for you to show me," Claire said. Again, the woman gave Claire the same blank expression but this time she gave a slight nod. Then Claire looked at Mary Riley's gnarled hands and realized that she was showing her how and that she had been showing her all along. Suddenly, it came to her that her rapid-fire questions must have made Mary Riley uncomfortable. Just as Mary's slow speech and long silences made Claire uncomfortable.

Her excitement about coming to the mountains, tinged with the apprehension she felt at encountering this vastly different culture, made her wonder how one ever came to fully understand and accept another culture. Consciously, she let go of her thoughts and began to study Mary's patient work. She noted too, that the mountain woman's expressionless face had visibly softened lost in handiwork.

"How long does it take to make a basket like this?" Claire asked.

The woman pondered the question for several minutes as though she had never given the subject any thought before now. "A good while," she offered at last. "The weaving is simple but the shaping takes some knowing. Every basket has its own special shape according to how you mean to use it, eggs, garden truck or berry picking."

Martha Jane appeared in the cabin doorway holding a crock in the crook of her arm. Claire could feel her eyes roaming over her. "I like the way you done your hair up," she said.

Claire's hand went to her head, smoothing back the wayward tendrils. She had not given her looks a thought since early that morning when she had dressed for the day. It was a wonder what she must look like after the morning at the school and then the hike up. Still she thanked the girl.

"Ma, I'm going to take the butter to the springhouse."

Mary nodded.

They all watched as Martha Jane walked languidly away.

"She's foolish about some boy," Dealie said throwing her tiny hand to her hip.

Claire tried not to smile at Dealie's confident manner, which she found endearing. Her bold proclamation, however, she found shocking for it was difficult to imagine that Martha Jane was old enough to be thinking about boys.

"Dealie, hush now," her ma said.

Dealie crossed her arms and let out a frustrated sigh but said no more on the subject. Then just as suddenly, she sprang from the porch scattering the startled chickens that had been quietly pecking for worms in the yard. The women watched as childlike Dealie began to spin until she was too dizzy to stand, only to fall and stand up again.

Mary finished the basket and held it up shyly for everyone to see. "This basket will outlast all of us."

The women exclaimed their admiration and she covered her face with her hand but she was obviously pleased.

"How many do you have finished?" Agnes asked.

"A dozen," she said proudly. "It took most of the winter. I can't make as many when summer comes for working in the garden."

"You did wonderfully well," Agnes said.

"I want to thank you Miss Agnes for selling them for me. I never thought nobody would give me cash money for my baskets. It's done me a world of good to be able to get the girls some things they needed."

"I am happy to do it," Agnes said.

"Now, I've got some pinto beans and corn pone. Come on in and eat," Mary said kindly.

"That's really nice of you," Agnes said, "but we carried along a picnic and ate it by the creek on the way up."

"Stay awhile and visit anyhow," she said.

"We did stop to have a cool drink from the spring," Claire said, not wanting to appear ungrateful. "It was so good after our long walk."

"Well, I'm glad you enjoyed it," Mary said genuinely pleased. "You are welcome to all you can hold."

"Thank you, Mary," Claire said.

"We really need to head back," Agnes chimed in.

"You don't need to hurry off. Stay and set a spell," Mary urged. "Frannie go in and get some of them walnuts and a bit of corn pone for these folks."

Frannie jumped up and came back studiously dividing her goodies equally among the teachers.

Tessie had told Claire that "visiting" was a big part of mountain life and that a certain amount of socializing was expected. One could not appear to be in too big a hurry or risk offending the host.

Claire looked at the food in her hand and thought it an odd combination, but when she tasted them together, she was pleasantly surprised. She had no trouble finishing every bite. "That was delicious," she said sincerely. Mary Riley's grooved face broke into a simple grin, a gesture that warmed them both.

"We would love to stay longer," Tessie said at last, "but we have a world of work to do back at the school. Maybe we can stay longer next time."

"Frannie go in and get them other baskets," Mary said. The girl got up and went in without a word.

"I'll help you Frannie," Claire volunteered. The cabin was sparse, the walls made of hewn logs notched at the ends, but the bare puncheon floors were scrubbed clean. Beds filled the front room. Clothes hung on pegs above the beds. The kitchen was at the back through a narrow door. A large wooden table filled with seats for five sat in the center of the room on the bare floor. A black pot hung on a hook in the massive open fireplace at the far end of the room. Between the wall and the corner hung iron skillets and two well-worn dishpans. Below them sat the churn with its wooden lid and dasher that Martha Jane had so recently used to make fresh butter. In the corner was a small cabinet similar to one at the teachers' cottage. Aunt Lizzie called it a pie safe and it was used to store food away from flies and other "varmints." Overhead on wooden beams hung strings of dried beans and field corn still on the cob. Several wooden meal and flour bins sat under a crude wooden shelf near a tiny window.

As they gathered up the baskets, Claire stopped what she was doing and took a moment to pin her hair back in place. She could feel Frannie looking at her, watching her movements, examining her clothes, but when she met her gaze, the young girl could only look down at her bare feet.

Claire, whose mind had stalled on the meagerness of the family's existence, suddenly picked up on the conversation outside. Agnes was asking Mrs. Riley if she had talked to her husband about the girls attending school. This had been their true purpose in making the trek up the mountain. She could hear Mary Riley say, "my man's puzzlin' on it now and I was fixin' to name it to him again."

Looking at the young girl who stood before her in a faded calico dress, eyes quick and alert, she asked, "Would you like to go to school?"

"I can make myself useful," Frannie said proudly.

"I'm sure you could. You are already a good hand to make baskets."

"I can cook and do wash, hoe corn better than my mama and I can ride our ole nag, Mae, like a man," Frannie said earnestly.

Claire could only look at Frannie's thin shy face and wonder at a desire so strong it had driven her to plead her case so boldly.

Frannie looked at Claire, tears pooling in the corners of her eyes. "I won't be no trouble," she added, sucking in a short sobbing breath.

Instinctively, Claire went to her knees and wrapped her arms around the girl's slender body. When Frannie buried her head in the bend of Claire's neck, her heart turned over in her chest. "Well, we will just have to see what we can do, won't we Miss Frannie." She could feel the girl shaking her head and the feeling vibrated down her spine and into the soles of her bruised feet.

Chapter 5

Frannie sat across the supper table as her pa chewed his food, intent on his meal, his black eyes barely visible under brushy eyebrows. Her pa had his hard ways with all of them and at times, those eyes had frozen her in place. She knew he was painfully shy around anyone that was not kin and that most of his solemn nature came from his being hard of hearing.

In an unspoken agreement with her ma, who would once again tonight bring up school to her pa, Frannie had done all of her chores without being asked, even slopping the hogs which she hated. It was not so much the smell, as their loud greedy noises and the way they threatened to break through their pens to get at whatever food she carried in her bucket. She gathered the eggs from every nest even those hidden in the woods and she was careful to watch for snakes. Not wanting to give her pa any reason to be in a bad mood, for he often questioned her about her chores, she even carried kindling in for the morning fire. Tonight he seemed content to listen to her ma talk about the teachers' visit.

"They was three of 'em Al," her ma said, her voice unnaturally high. "They walked all the way up here from the schoolhouse to collect baskets."

"I was the one fetched'em from the springhouse," Dealie bragged.

Martha Jane gave her a squint-eyed look.

Al nodded but continued eating.

They all knew he doted on Dealie and tolerated her ways better than he did the other girls. Dealie was the only one who could talk her way out of a chore or coax their pa from one of his moods. She could even get their pa to halfway talk about how he had met their ma and how they had courted. Like all children, it was something they were curious about but he always told Frannie and Martha Jane to hush up when they asked about it like it shamed him and then he would get mad and run them out into the yard. He would not get mad when Dealie asked, but would look sideways at their ma and grin. Sometimes he would tell the smallest tale, like how he had seen her at church wearing a blue gingham dress or how she was so shy she covered her mouth when she laughed and it was a full year before he had seen if she had any teeth.

They never begrudged Dealies' way with their pa, being too caught up in the magic of it. "Lordie Mercy," he would say sometimes when Dealie asked him questions and then he would turn to their ma and say, "What's to come out of this child's mouth next." He would even surprise them at times by laughing aloud at his own memories. "I ain't thought of that in years," he would say. "Ain't it quare how plain it comes back to a fellow." Even if he never told the memory, those were the best times.

Dealie had almost drowned in a swollen spring creek when she was three years old and had spent the better part of a week in bed, after which her folks acted as if she was made of glass. If Frannie had been the jealous type, she might have resented Dealie, but instead, she was inclined to baby her like the rest.

Mary hesitated.

"They was dressed fine and had their hair all done up," Martha Jane jumped into the silence. "You should hear 'em talk, Pa. They sound fine like…."

Mary shook her head.

Martha Jane's voice trailed off. She crossed her arms but held her tongue despite looking miffed.

Frannie was glad to have Martha Jane hushed. She had come close to kicking her under the table for gushing on about the teachers in front of their pa. She had hardly been able to catch her breath being so close to Miss Claire, who was so beautiful and stylish. It had been hard to resist reaching out to touch her fine clothes. Even though she had spent the afternoon alone imitating her speech, she had the good sense to keep that to herself.

"They're real nice womenfolk. They didn't act like they was better than us. They made over them baskets like they was something special," Mary said trying to hide her pride. "And they was not above drinking from the springhouse and eatin' what I offered 'em," Mary rushed to add.

Al stopped in mid-chew to ask, "Did they pay you for them baskets?"

Mary nodded. "They took 'em all. They say folks from all over want to buy them. I never dreamed."

"What did they give you for 'em?" Al asked, holding up his hand to cut her short.

Frannie watched as her Ma's shoulders dropped and she hunkered down. Pride was not a trait well tolerated by her pa. It was all right to make baskets for berry picking or collecting vegetables from the garden, but just talking about the beauty and skill of it could make folks think you were getting above your raising. Sometimes when it was just Frannie and her ma, sitting on the front porch working away with white oak ribs, they talked about what they could do to make the baskets more shapely or the best way to hammer out the knobs and rough places to make them better looking. Even if her ma still spoke of her baskets as "simple homemade" affairs, she appreciated the skill it took and the praise it had brought her.

While they sat making baskets, her ma told stories of what her mother's life had been like where there had been no neighbors for miles, no store bought cloth, and only occasional oil for a lamp. Panthers squalling out in the night like they could pounce through the roof. Then she would always end her stories by saying, "Your pa has give us a good life here on Baskin's Creek. We have not done without a bite to eat and a place to sleep but I vowed and declared early on that my girls would have a better life." Then she would press her thin lips together and nod to herself as though to reaffirm her promise.

"They give me seventy-five cents a piece for the small willow reed baskets. It holds about a quart. I had five of them. And they give me a dollar for the willow darning baskets. I had three of them. They give me a dollar and a quarter for the half bushel white oak splits and I had four of them."

"I declare," Al said.

"We got enough to buy a milk cow," Mary said.

Frannie's heart sank. A milk cow was something they desperately needed since Daisy, old and bony, had died last spring. They had been trading eggs with a neighbor for milk ever since. Still she could not believe all her hard work making baskets was about to go for a cow instead of the schooling she had dreamed of all those months. Hadn't her ma promised the teachers that she would name it to her pa again and now here she was prattling on about a cow?

Her pa pushed back from the table and stood up. Reaching into a bowl on the wooden shelf behind him, he took out his pipe, carefully packing it.

"One of the new teachers has offered to pay for Frannie's schooling," her ma said casually.

Her ma had said it as though it was of no real importance. That everyday such an offer came their way and they were free to pick and choose at will. Frannie's heart caught in her throat.

"Girls get to the dishes," her ma said. They all three jumped up scattershot and began clearing the table. They dared not look at their folks.

"I don't take charity," her pa said. "I can pay for my girls to go to school." Without another word, he strode outside with Mary close on his tail.

The girls could hear the soft rumble of voices as they washed the dishes. They worked quietly catching each other's eye with each rise and fall of their folk's conversation. Their folks were working out the details of the girl's futures only a few feet away from them on the porch and it left all three of the children breathless.

Frannie could not take it in. Just like that, she was to go to school. Her whole world had turned on those few words. She realized that her ma had been shaping the story all along, making it into something her pa could find acceptable. He could provide for his girls without the charity of some stranger, she heard him say repeatedly. She wondered if one of the teachers had offered to pay for her schooling or if her ma had simply said it knowing her pa would never stand for it.

The girls waited until the voices had died down before they poured out onto the porch. Dealie headed out into the yard to catch the last light. Pa had whittled a ball and cup out of mountain laurel and she spent hours learning to swing the stick with one hand so the ball would drop into the cup without touching it with the other hand.

Frannie sat on the porch step and leaned back against the rough post watching the half moon rise, feeling the beauty of the sky, wondering if anyone could understand what was in her mind and her heart. It seemed like her thoughts were always swarming like bees only they never could settle down. Especially, like at dusty-dark when she would be sitting out on the porch and she felt like crying inside for no reason. She could not talk about such things not even to her ma and certainly not with Martha Jane who sat now unbraiding her hair and combing it with her fingers.

Her dream was to be a teacher, maybe travel to strange places and meet all kinds of people. Maybe nobody she knew felt the things she felt. It seemed everybody she knew talked about crops, cooking, washing or sewing. Even her ma who dreamed of her girls schooling never thought beyond it.

It could not be helped this dream she had no matter how lonesome it made her feel. Now the whole world was opening up. She hugged her sides and wondered if she had imagined it all. She closed her eyes for an instant, overcome by the thought of it. Then her eyes popped open. Had her pa not meant what he said? She shifted around to study her folk's faces in the soft evening light. Their faces gave away nothing. The silence stretched out. Just when Frannie was on her second helping of doubt, her pa stood up. Her gaze followed him upward.

He rubbed his chin as though puzzling a moment.

"Frannie gal, I think we got time before dark to rive us some more oak splits," he said. "Your ma will be needin'em to make baskets."

She looked at her ma who simply rocked a little in her chair and waved her on with her hand. Frannie jumped off the porch and ran toward the woodpile knowing now that she had not dreamed it. When she looked back, she thought she saw a slight crooked grin on her ma's face.

Chapter 6

If there was one thing Shade Morgan had learned in his thirty years on earth, it was that life did not go in a straight line. If it did, he would be kissing his baby boy's head before heading off to the tub mill that morning. He would be taking pleasure all day in the thought of coming home to his wife Sarah, who would be smiling from the porch, her palm to her forehead as she wiped the heat from her face from the supper she was cooking. But there would be none of that, there would only be his daughter, Emily, running to greet him. At least there would still be Emily, he thought.

Shade was headed out to meet Hiram Bradley who sharpened the millstones for the tub mill that Shade's family had operated for generations. Many of the families up Roaring Fork brought their grain for him to grind. Taking a toll of a bushel of grain for the use of the mill provided enough cornmeal to last the year even if Sarah had insisted they grow their own corn "to be safer than sorry."

He was born a practical man and nothing in his life had served to change that but he had loved his wife and sometimes it wore him out missing her. Grief popped out on him like clammy sweat on a feverish man every time he thought he was getting over her and tried to test himself.

Shade and Sarah had grown up less than a mile apart and he could not remember a time he had not known her. He had first noticed her fishing with her pa when she was eight years old and he was ten. She was sitting on a rough cliff of rocks holding a homemade pole with a sinker hammered from lead. Threading a thick red worm on her hook with the same skill he had later seen her use to stitch up an axe wound on his leg, she looked up at him with a satisfied grin. She was soon pulling out the most beautiful brook trout he had ever seen. However, it had been the glint in her eye, a kind of self-assured sparkle, which

55

had closed the deal. He had made up his mind right then to have Sarah as his bride.

It had been one of the wisest decisions of his life. They had married when Shade was eighteen and Sarah was sixteen. His folks had built them a tiny cabin not two hundred yards from their own. Working in unspoken tandem, they had made a home for their little family. Sarah was a hard worker, cooking, washing and ironing without complaint and hoeing the garden, even when she had been pregnant with Emily. She put by enough food each summer to get them through the winter, while making quilts by lamplight after a day of chores.

His ma said the way of the Lord was not for him to know. She was right about that for he had seen black hearted scoundrels get by with less suffering while good folks were laid low by burying half a dozen of their family. Every cemetery up every hollow was filled with tiny headstones one after another from children lost. His ma had suffered the loss of her husband four years ago. Shade's pa had dropped dead plowing the field for spring crops as he had done every year. That was when Shade had built the frame house and moved her in with him and Sarah. His ma had also suffered a burden no mother should have to bear, the loss of two children. His older brother had gone hunting and tumbled down a ravine, his leg broken in three places. The cold had taken him before they found him. Diphtheria had swooped in one winter and grabbed his other brother Caleb carrying him off swiftly in its sharp talons. It had been Shade who had been marked for death at birth, small and sickly with a cry like a mewling cat his ma said and yet here he stood tall and strong. It was a puzzlement to him.

Shade's suffering, he would be the first to admit, did not make him special. It was to his way of thinking that if folks could see their lives straight up from beginning to end fewer ones might be willing to take it on for fear they could not bear up against it. In truth a man did not know what he could bear until it was laid at his feet. He had prayed, begged, and bargained with a God deaf and blind to his appeal that he could not live without Sarah. Now here was Sarah dead and he still alive.

He could see Hiram pulling up in his wagon and he waved a friendly greeting. Shade was as fine a carpenter as lived in the mountains. He had learned from his pa and improved upon it. When he built a cabin, the logs were hewn smooth, the corners tight. He could repair any piece of farm equipment and his neighbors sought him out for the rocky land was a hard taskmaster. He was always looking ahead, learning new skills and picking up ways to better himself. He had managed to get hold of a portable steam powered saw and taught himself to build a frame house trading it in for the 'weaner' cabin that he and Sarah had moved into after their wedding. Then he had used the logs from the cabin to build a sturdy barn.

The making and upkeep of grindstones, however, was a job best left to a man with special skills and Hiram was the best around. It could take a man two or three days to dress a set of millstones. After turning the stones, he would have to sharpen the grooves and lands to ensure smooth milling.

"Let me help you unload them stones, Hiram," Shade yelled. He hurried to meet the wiry little man whose body was bowed from a lifetime of handling millstones twice his weight. Hiram's white beard touched the top of his bib overalls and spread out against the background of his homemade cotton shirt. Age did not seem to change Hiram. Shade had grown up and become a man and still Hiram looked the same to him as he had when he had visited his house as a young boy. He looked at Hiram's sweat stained hat and wondered if it was the same one he had worn all of his life. Somehow it gave Shade a bit of comfort to think so.

As the two men struggled with the stones, Shade was grateful for the sweat and effort it would take that day to put in the millstones. The tub mill that Shade's father had built decades before was like hundreds that lined the streams in the Smoky Mountains. The rushing water was carried from the stream down a flume to a log building not much bigger than an outhouse that fit over the narrow bank where a wheel turned the horizontal grindstones. Shade loved the sound of the water rushing down the flume, thumping onto the wheel and the almost magical whirl of the millstone. He was proud of the fine cornmeal his mill produced and the way his neighbors depended on it.

As soon as Hiram fitted the stones into place, he chuckled, his small frame rocking with merriment. "That's as good a fit as a man could expect."

"You do fine work Hiram," Shade said genuinely.

Hiram reached over and slapped Shade on the back. "Let that water loose and see what we got here."

The only light in the mill was from the cracks in the walls, so when Shade stepped out into the bright sunlight he had to shield his eyes. The September heat was working its way down through the trees caressing the leaves with fingers more gentle than August but still strong enough to make him relish the splash of water and the cool breeze from the stream when he released the flume. By the time he got back, Hiram was pouring the first scoop of grain into the hopper. The top stone turned smoothly over the bottom stone producing a finely ground cornmeal.

"Any woman could make a pone of cornbread from that," Hiram said, letting the grain sift through his fingers. "My Esther could make bread out of sawdust and it'd taste good. And they's been times when we was first married she about had to."

"She's a good woman for sure," Shade agreed.

Hiram suddenly looked serious. "You don't need to be carryin' your grief through another winter, Shade."

"You sound like Ma," Shade said good-naturedly. He was uncomfortable with the turn of the conversation but did not want to offend Hiram who was Sarah's uncle.

"I know Sarah was my blood kin but she wouldn't want you to mourn over long. She would want Emily to have a mother to take care of her."

"She's got my ma," he said. He found himself angry that anyone but he could presume to know what Sarah would want.

"I'm just sayin'…."

"I hear you, Hiram," Shade said, cutting him short.

"Well, you know as well as I do that many a man has gone lookin' at his own wife's funeral. Had you done that, I might of held it agin ya. What I mean to say is that it has been long enough."

"All I want for now is to turn my hand to a good days work. The rest will have to take care of itself," Shade said.

There were plenty of widowers in the mountains in need of housekeepers and mothers and widows in need of support. He knew that need and custom were working to force him to take a new wife.

But Sarah had been the love of his life and settling for less was a bitter pill.

Hiram shook his head in understanding. "You won't hear no more from me."

"Esther put you up to it, did she?" Shade said grinning.

Hiram looked shame-faced. "Her and your ma has been talkin'. I figured as how, I'd never hear the end unless I said somethin'."

"You done what you had to do," Shade said. "Emily is my concern now. I aim to give her a good life."

"I know you do. I know you aim to and you have. Don't you fret on what I said."

"I'm frettin' on some dinner about now," Shade said jokingly. "Let's go up to the house and see what ma's got for us."

"That sounds good to me," Hiram agreed. "I done worked off my breakfast a while back."

There was no need to ask Hiram what he owed him for sharpening the stones. They had long ago worked out a trade. Shade would grind all of Hiram's grain that fall in exchange for the work. Most mountain folks had very little money. They grew a garden for food, kept cows, pigs and chickens for meat and eggs. If they could not make it or grow it from their own land, they bartered with a neighbor for what they needed. To Shade it was the way things were supposed to be, but change was coming to the mountains. He could feel it in the air like when the southwest wind would come roaring over the mountains foretelling the end of summer. He had first felt it when the lumber companies had come to the mountains offering to pay wages of up to a dollar a day. Wages like that were different from the little money he had gotten from occasionally hauling tan bark eight miles by wagon to sell in Pigeon Forge.

Close on the heels of the lumber companies had come the families of the company owners to spend their summers in the mountains. And soon after, they had brought along guests. Andy Huff had put them all up in his home for a while until it had become too much. Then he decided to build a hotel to house them all. These folks were hunting, fishing and hiking in the very mountains Shade called home.

Now the settlement school had come, bringing a world of changes to the children. He would have to send Emily to school for he was no fool. She would have to live in a far different world than the one in which he had grown up. He could not deny her the right to be ready for it.

He thought of the young teacher, Claire, he had met at the revival. She was as beautiful as any woman he had ever seen; he could not deny that. It was the bold way she had looked him over that had struck him. It was as though her small frame could not contain her curiosity. She was a different sort of woman and he tried to picture what kind of life had made her that way.

"I seen that new teacher, the pretty one, down by Charlie Stewarts place," Hiram said.

Shade looked at him wondering if Hiram had read his thoughts and unsure that he had not spoken aloud. It shamed him that he could have another woman on his mind so soon after talking about Sarah.

"What was she doing at Charlie's place?" Shade asked casually. He went down on one knee and busied himself retying his boot. They were brown leather, every inch oiled and laced from toe to knee. He was a man known for taking care of his possessions and he was especially fond of a good pair of leather boots. He had worn these boots for going on three winters and he thought with care he might wear them another three.

"Visitin' most likely," Hiram said at last.

"Visiting?" Shade asked. He had lost the thread of the conversation.

"Them teachers do a heap of visitin' with folks."

"That's what I hear," Shade said standing up. His hands on his hips, he stretched to ease his back which had begun to ache, a fact he was not about to admit to Hiram. Still he could not help but chuckle to himself as he looked down at the wiry little man. "Emily's been after Ma to invite her teachers up to visit."

"Best I can tell, most of the younguns think a right smart of their teachers. Although when I seen this one she weren't visitin'. She was scrambling over them rocks on the creek bank like a dang mountain goat. Had one of them Kodak's them teachers is so fond of carrin' around. For the life of me, I can't figure why them young women is always taking pictures of one thing or another. I called out to her was she all right but she just waved back."

"I met her before, she seems like the type that could take care of herself."

"Well, anyway, I reckon she thinks so," Hiram said grinning. "I 'spect she'll be up your way soon enough."

"I 'spect you're right," Shade said by way of conversation.

Just as the two men stepped into the yard, Emily flew out the front door, bounded off the porch and threw herself into her pa's waiting arms. Swooping her up holding her tightly he said, "When she does come to visit I reckon I'll let Emily tend to her."

Emily pulled away, looked at her pa for a fleeting moment before she was once again full of herself, and began telling him about her morning. As he listened to his daughter, he looked back over his shoulder, the wind stirred in the trees and he thought the roar of the southwest wind could not be far behind.

October 15, 1920

Dearest Family

I was so glad to have your letter last week. I do miss all of you awfully. Please share this letter with Lenora, as I have been much too busy to write as my days here are filled from morning until late into the evenings. The pictures Lenora sent of the children were so lovely. I could kiss their faces right now. Thanks so much for the sweater as the evenings here are growing cooler. The boots and Kodak have been most useful. It is most common that I walk twelve miles or more during the week. It is a frequent request of the students that we come to visit them in their homes. In all our walks, we must cross many creeks by means of planks or logs or little bridges.

Your order of baskets was most appreciated. I hope you do not mind, as I may have to make some adjustments to your order. The mountain crafts people are not always amenable to the idea of making one item again and again and moreover farming and household chores must come before handicrafts. As with the ever-changing school curriculum, we must adjust to the needs of the people. I hope to get the baskets posted to you soon. The Post Office is in a corner of Charlie Ogles General Store, which is stocked with everything from hats to shoe polish and bluing to flour. They say that on Saturdays, the men gather and he even acts as a barber.

I do so wish you could visit and see the progress that has been made in our fine school. We now have four English classes, U. S. History, Mathematics and Latin. On Mondays and Wednesdays, my boys and girls are all gone to sewing or farm training. I love all of the sweet young girls in my classes. They are so eager to learn and their faces glow with the joy at each lesson. Oh, and if you could see how they come on a rainy day, walking all the way with their dresses simply dripping rather than miss school, your heart would break with tenderness.

The young boys present a challenge keeping them in their seats, and occupied, as they are full of energy. Another challenge faced by the school is that the children are needed at home to work. Last week we had a number of absent students because it was sorghum molasses making time. Before that, they were "pulling fodder."

We now have fifty young girls in the cooking and sewing classes. Miss Carson from Philadelphia is in to help and she is most adept at working with the older girls. Last week they made sewing bags as their first project. In addition, this week in cooking class they will make "light bread" (bread made with yeast) something most of the girls have never made or eaten as they only have "corn pone" or biscuits.

We are working hard on the Harvest Fair for later this month. The children are learning a number of songs and a short skit. It is a great deal of work but it will provide an opportunity for all of the parents to come and see what their children have learned. The mother's, many of whom have sold their handicrafts to provide for their children's schooling, will have an opportunity to display their work and win ribbons. I know that it will be well worth the many hours all the teachers are putting in on this project.

It was with great joy that we welcomed a trained nurse to the school. Miss Phyllis Higinbotham came all the way from Canada to join us. Next month the school will provide inoculations to the students. There is some hesitancy on the part of the parents, which Miss Higinbotham is working tirelessly since her arrival to overcome.

I seem always to be asking for something but the need here is so great. We are greatly in need of books for the library. Might you ask at your next Women's Club meeting?

Know that I am well and thinking of my family. I must go now as it is my turn to feed the pig. Yes I must carry a big bucket of slop past the cornfield and school house all the way to the end of our land. Now Mother, you and Lenora can have a great laugh at my expense.

Your loving daughter and sister
Claire

Chapter 7

Claire read aloud to the girls as they worked on their sewing projects. The teachers took turns in this duty and it was something she particularly enjoyed. The girls too, while intent on their sewing, seemed to enjoy the stories. Today she was reading from *Robinson Crusoe* by Daniel Defoe having chosen the book over *Jane Eyre* because she found the adventure more to her liking. Miss Carson, who was instructing the girls on their sewing, cast an occasional eye her way when she read some of the more robust passages, but said nothing.

Claire was well into the book when the girls suddenly dropped their sewing and ran to the window. Miss Carson fussed and shushed the girls, but they paid her no mind as they were quickly caught up in the ruckus that had broken out in the schoolyard. Joining the girls, Claire watched as two boys rolled about grunting and flailing at each other; dust flying in the air. This time it was a fifth grader named Leland Grady and a sixth grader named George Riley both big for their ages.

Tessie came rushing down the steps, face aflame, and hands on her hips. "Stop it this instant," she yelled.

Before Claire could give it a second thought, she dropped her book and rushed out to help her friend. Tessie was on Leland in seconds pulling him off George. Claire stepped between the two boys with her back to Leland. Tessie brought Leland around to face George and with a hail of words Claire could hardly make out, she lectured the sweaty pair.

"How many times must you boys be told there is to be no fighting," Tessie scolded. Having grown up with two brothers, it had become Tessie's unofficial job to break up the frequent fights among the boys.

"George, stand up, please," Claire said. When he stood, she noted, had he not been hanging his head, he would have been an inch taller than she was. It made her want to laugh but she dared not.

"Leland, I think you and George need to shake hands and say you are sorry," Tessie said.

They eyed each other through narrow slits but slowly Leland held out his hand and George took it. They shifted uncomfortably, kicking the dirt with their already dusty shoes.

"Now, apologize to Miss Tessie," Claire said solemnly, "for making her have to come out here when you know fighting is strictly forbidden."

"Sorry, Miss Tessie," Leland mumbled.

"Sorry, Miss Tessie," George echoed.

"You know what the punishment is for fighting, don't you boys?" Tessie asked.

They looked at her wide-eyed. Then they looked at each other and back to Tessie.

"Did you think I would let you off with an apology? You will each pull four rows of cornstalks from the school cornfield to be used for our Harvest Festival. Bring them to Aunt Lizzie and she will tell you where to store them."

The boys groaned but headed off. Claire watched as they walked side by side talking. They were once again good friends bound together by their punishment.

"I don't know if they dread their punishment nearly as much as having to face Aunt Lizzie," Claire said.

"Who will no doubt find even more work for them to do," Tessie chuckled. "I hate it that garden season is over and I no longer have hoeing to hold over their heads."

Claire laughed. "Tessie you are a treasure." Tessie usually told the boys that if they had enough energy to fight they could as well use it to hoe extra rolls of corn in the school garden. It worked without fail for hoeing was every child's most dreaded chore.

"Sometimes growing up with brothers is not so bad. You learn a thing or two about boys," Tessie said.

Tessie confessed to Claire one night as they sat on her bed drinking hot cocoa, that growing up big and gangly with red hair had been difficult. "The boys never winked at me or pulled my pigtail," she said. "The worst was that my brothers knew how it made me feel and they teased and tormented the life out of me." She wanted to tell her that being small came with its own set of burdens but she could tell by the hurt in Tessie's eyes that such a thing would not seem believable to her.

"What do you think your brothers would think now?" Claire asked.

"I think they would be proud if they knew, but I don't tell everything in my letters home," Tessie said grinning.

"Nor do I," Claire admitted. She marveled at all that had happened in the past months and how her life had changed. How could she even begin to explain it when she only half understood it herself.

"Oh, I almost forgot," exclaimed Tessie, "Aunt Lizzie is setting up the weaving loom this afternoon. Do you want to go help?"

The school had been trying to revive the almost lost art of weaving among the women of the mountains as a way of providing more income for the families. A number of beautiful coverlets had been discovered in mountain homes during the teacher's visitations. However, they soon learned that most of them had been handed down, as the younger women had given up weaving. A call had gone out to the older women to come to the school and train the younger women to weave. Claire who knew nothing about weaving was excited by the prospect of seeing it done. "I would love that. I will meet you at the teachers' cottage at three." She looked up to see the girls still standing at the window looking at the two of them. "Oh, we had better head back inside," Claire exclaimed. "I completely forgot I was reading to the girls."

They grabbed each other by the arms and tried to get out of sight before they started to laugh.

"Girls, back to our sewing," Claire heard Miss Carson say as she rounded the corner. They all scampered back to their seats twittering like sparrows.

Someone had picked up the book she had so carelessly dropped and laid it on the table. "Now where was I?" she asked. Her bookmark had been returned to the page where she left off reading.

"Robinson Crusoe is learning to make tools from the stones and the wood he found on the island," Martha Jane Riley said.

"Thank you, Martha Jane," Claire said wondering if she had been the one who had replaced the bookmark. Martha Jane was one of the most skilled seamstresses of any of the girls. She had also proven to be highly adept at cooking, canning and working in the garden. Because she was older, the teachers were working especially hard to bring her along in her studies, as they had discovered she had a sharp mind. Claire had been pleased when all three of the Riley girls had shown up to school not long after the teachers visit to buy Mary Riley's baskets. She had not expected Martha Jane but she was pleasantly surprised. Most thrilling of all had been the sight of Frannie coming up the school steps.

Claire admired all of the teachers for the way they worked so tirelessly. Endlessly dedicated and good-natured, they made her feel even more like an actor in an unfamiliar play struggling to find her role. Assigned at first to conduct the cooking classes, her bread had risen up over the pans and spilled out into the oven making a mess and stinking up the kitchen. She was then moved to sewing classes. The day the girls stitched the collar of their dresses to the armhole, Claire had at last been asked to start a drawing class. She had been both humiliated and relieved.

Even drawing classes had not been easy, for the girls had no experience. It had been difficult for Claire to break her lessons down to the most elemental parts, but her girls had made great strides.

Most of their lessons were about learning to draw familiar things like an apple on the table or a bowl. Soon, however, she had discovered Emily Morgan drawing a scene of her home place capturing with remarkable detail the cornfield running from the backdoor up the hillside, the dog asleep under the porch and the stream running nearby. Emily of the blond curls and blue eyes, whose father had come holding her hand to school handing her over like an heirloom that had been handed down through the family, was a born artist.

When Emily saw Claire looking at the drawing, she had looked stricken because she had not finished her assigned lesson. Claire asked, "Would you like to hang this up for the coming Harvest

Festival?" A smile like the sudden opening of a blossom emerged on Emily's face. Claire was struck by how deeply the need for approval cut into the souls of all people, mountain girl and foreign teacher alike.

Another wonderful thing that had arisen from Claire's art classes was that she was allowed, even encouraged, to take walks with the girls so that they might sketch. Soon she discovered she could go off alone to sketch without causing undue talk, the teachers attributing her need for solitude to her "artistic nature." She had become a familiar sight in the mountains with her khaki skirt, white waists and Panama hat and always her satchel thrown over her shoulder with pencil, sketchpad and Kodak. Claire tramped about over rocks and streams, feeling strangely at home in the mountains, accepted in ways she had never felt around people. Lured by the unknown, she was drawn to climb ever upward, the going more difficult at every turn, but determined to see what mystery lay beyond each new view.

Chapter 8

"I bought this loom from Aunt Lydia Whaley," Evelyn Bishop declared proudly.

Claire, Tessie and Aunt Lizzie had gathered to help assemble the well-worn pieces of the old loom. Evelyn stood chin in hand studying the complicated task.

"It's so big," Tessie said.

"And there are so many pieces," Claire added.

"When I was a girl," Aunt Lizzie said, "a loom and a bed was about all the furniture we had. It filled up most of the room."

"Did you ever weave on a loom like this?" asked Claire.

"When I was a little ole gal, I could weave about anything I put my mind to. It's been a 'tolable spell since then," she said with a chuckle.

"What made you give it up," asked Tessie.

"When store cloth come and it was so cheap most womenfolk 'round here begun to put their looms aside one by one till I reckon they's not too many around still in use."

"Do you think you can put this one together?" Evelyn Bishop asked.

"I think I can recollect how to put it together," Aunt Lizzie said studying the pieces. "Claire you go over and hold that piece up," she said pointing. "That's the frame. Tessie you get that notched piece. That's the heddle. That notch fits down over the frame. It is not held in place by anything more than that notch."

Claire and Tessie followed Aunt Lizzie's instructions as she led them through the complicated assembly. It was as though she could see it all in her head, recalled in perfect detail from her childhood.

"This is the beater frame and this is the harness," Aunt Lizzie said lining up each step.

"Aunt Lizzie I got the most beautiful pattern from Aunt Lydia," Evelyn said as they worked. "She called it 'Gentleman's Fancy.' Do you know that one?"

"Can't say as I do but it would be hard to out do Aunt Lydia when it comes to weaving. That woman can take it from sheep to cloth."

Claire looked to Tessie who gave her a puzzled look and then shrugged her shoulders. "What do you mean sheep to cloth?" Tessie asked.

"From sheep to cloth," Aunt Lizzie said like an incantation. She studied Tessie as if she was trying to decide if she was simple minded. Tessie squirmed under the scrutiny. "Miss Tessie, do you know why my mama took to buyin' store cloth."

Tessie shook her head.

"Because they's not many women left who is willin' to raise the sheep, shear'em, and then wash, spin, twist and dye the wool just to get to where they can have something to weave."

"I have heard so many people speak of Aunt Lydia. Won't you tell me about her," Claire said to deflect Aunt Lizzie's piercing stare.

"Aunt Lydia Whaley is one of those women," Evelyn said, stepping in to save them both, "who is a true survivor. She is a mountain woman of the old tradition. After her husband's death in the Civil War, she tended her own crops, made all her children's clothes, took her own corn to the mill and raised sheep for wool. She has patterns for weaving that are lost except in her head and she makes baskets that have been copied by all the other basket makers in these mountains. I don't think there is anything she doesn't know about getting by."

"She never remarried. Does she live alone?" Claire asked, enthralled by the courage and audacity of such a woman.

"Yes, I don't think she would have it any other way. We will go visit her someday. I am hoping that with the help of Aunt Lizzie and Aunt Lydia we can establish a weaving class for the women. So many of the women work all day in their homes and they never have a chance to socialize or to use their talents. I am sure that there are other looms stored away in barns and attics. We must be sure to spread the word as we visit."

Claire could hear in Evelyn's voice the abiding affection and respect she had for the mountain women. Her admiration too had grown for these hard working women. She had watched as Aunt Lizzie milked the cow, made butter, pickled and canned everything from the garden and much that grew wild in the hills around the school.

She was especially caught up by the notion of a woman living alone in the mountains. It seemed a silly thought to her now that she had once deemed it an act of courage to come to the mountains to teach given the care Aunt Lizzie took of them all and her comfortable room in the teachers' cottage.

"Fasten this to the bottom Claire," Aunt Lizzie said. "That's a treadle."

Not one to dally, Claire realized that even as the teachers chatted, Aunt Lizzie's mind had been on getting the loom put together. "How long has it been since you put a loom together," Claire could not stop herself from asking.

"I don't know as how I ever put one together," she said thoughtfully.

Tessie looked at Claire. "Exactly how long since you did any weaving," she asked.

Aunt Lizzie paused and ran a hand over her head to smooth her hair back into place. It was pulled back severely in a bun with little danger of a single hair escaping. Still she fussed and patted about searching for wayward strands. Then her brow furrowed, she bowed her head as though in prayer.

Claire could hear her murmuring softly. She cocked her ear trying to make out the words but she could not catch hold of them. She could tell that Aunt Lizzie had stored away her memories as neatly as she had tucked the strands of her hair. Each memory was to be searched for, caressed and put back into place carefully.

Claire and Tessie waited patiently. They delighted in Aunt Lizzie's memories and did not want to rush her rumination. Finally, Aunt Lizzie rested her hands on her hips, lifted her head back and said, "I reckon it's going on thirty-five year."

Chapter 9

Shade and Emily had been sitting on the stream bank for over an hour, when he saw her walking up the road. She was wearing a white blouse and a gray skirt that rode just about her ankles. The brown leather satchel thrown over one shoulder was bulky and at odds with her small frame. She seemed wholly absorbed in the world around her, stopping to examine a flower or the pattern in the bark of a tree, even as Miss Tessie tagged along beside her. He could see her puzzling over something, and then as she turned to speak to Tessie, she suddenly laughed like a young girl, her hand flying to her face. It was a gesture at odds with her refined looks and distant manner. He found he was wholly unprepared for the way the joy of her girlish laughter knocked him back.

Emily begged tirelessly since her first day at school to have her teachers visit and spend the night. When at last Miss Claire and Miss Tessie agreed to come, it had sent his ma into conniptions. Already she had made an apple stack cake and a sweet potato pie. She had cleaned everything twice over. Shade had not been allowed to sit down before she thought of yet another chore for him. Instructed to kill two chickens, one to fry and the other for dumplings, he had been glad to escape the house. When he brought the chickens to her he said, "Ma, I don't know for the life of me how two little women can eat all this." The look on her face had quickly told him that his opinion on the subject was not welcomed.

Reckoning that it might be safer for both Emily and he if they found another place to spend the day, he offered to go fishing and take Emily along, promising to bring back some nice trout to add to the bounty. His ma, whose mind was on other things, had waved them out of the house without a second glance.

He had not even baited his hook in the last half hour. Watching Emily, the dappled light on her earnest little face as she cast her line, was enough to keep him content.

Claire looked up and spying him waved a greeting, seemingly not at all frightened or embarrassed that he had been watching her. She came toward him extending her hand as he rose to greet her. Before he could shake her hand she pulled it back.

"I am so sorry, Mr. Morgan," Claire said showing her hands palms up, "I am afraid I have charcoal all over my hands. I have been sketching today."

He watched as she unselfconsciously wiped her hands on the underside of her skirt hem. Looking up, a crooked smile cutting across her face, she said, "It is fortunate my skirt is gray."

The hem of her skirt was wet and bits of leaf and dirt clung to the folds. Her shoes were muddy as though she had been wading in the stream. A smudge of charcoal ran down one side of her clear face, radiant from the walk. A faint knowing smile cut across her face.

"Emily tells me you draw beautiful pictures," Shade said finally.

"In the eyes of a child," she said with a dismissive shrug.

"Don't let her fool you Mr. Morgan," Tessie said coming forward. "She is a fine artist."

"It is easy when everywhere I look nature seems to be putting on a play for my benefit," she said looking up, her eyes scanning the forest. "For this act, the trees have changed their costumes from hues of green to splendid garments of reds and golds. Nature it seems has bestowed a bounty of favors. I do so love these mountains, Mr. Morgan."

"Yes ma'am," Shade said trying to take in her words. He was accustomed to the sparse and circumscribed way his neighbors spoke and he had never heard anyone speak the way Claire did.

Suddenly, Claire saw Emily and waved to her. Emily, dropping her fishing pole, came running quickly. "And how are you today, Miss Emily?" Claire said warmly.

Emily stopped short and smiled shyly. "I'm fishing," she offered.

"And are you catching anything?"

Emily shook her head.

"Well, I am sure you will catch a big fish soon."

Emily blushed and turned her face to her shoulder.

"We are after more'n fish today," Shade said brushing Emily's curls from her face.

"Oh, and what would that be?" Claire asked.

"Well, this is Emily's favorite fishing hole. The water rushes down over those rocks and pools right by that big sycamore. Sometimes it's enough to come out here and sit a while." He did not tell her that the look of sadness he sometimes saw in his daughter's eyes left him feeling helpless. How could he tell her that Emily had started to keep her own little cemetery just up the hill from the cabin where she buried dead chicks and rabbits, birds and once an owl that she found caught in a trap. He watched as she tended the burial site gathering flowers and ferns to place on the tiny mounds, singing hymns and reciting simple Bible verses. Children were not sheltered from death in the mountains but still she seemed so young to have learned the ways so well.

Claire gave him a curious look but said nothing.

"Miss Claire, Miss Tessie come fish with me," Emily pleaded.

A look passed between Claire and Tessie.

"I would love to fish with you Emily. I haven't fished since I was a little girl about your age," Tessie said taking Emily by the hand.

When they were far enough away, Claire said, "I just wanted a moment to talk to you about Emily.

"Has she done something wrong?"

"She is a delightful young girl, Mr. Morgan. I truly appreciate you letting her attend the school."

"It's been good for her. I have been meaning to thank you for teaching her to draw. It has meant more to her than anything."

"You don't need to thank me. Emily is a born artist. She is a delight to have in my class".

"Thank you, ma'am," he said, his voice coming out raspy. "Her ma had the gift but she always had the family to look after so she never had time."

"Yes, I think how difficult it has been for me to steal time from all my duties at the school to draw. I imagine such a thing would be especially hard after a day of farm chores."

"I remember she would sometimes draw pictures for Emily," he said his voice trailing off.

"Emily seems to like it very much," Claire said. "Drawing pictures."

"I catch her now drawing in the dirt with sticks. I had to stop her from taking burnt wood from the fireplace and drawing on the sides of the house. Your hands today put me in mind of hers."

"Maybe I can get her some proper charcoals and a sketch pad. Has Emily shown you some of her drawings?"

"I don't think there is a body up and down Roaring Fork that's not seen 'em," he said chuckling. "If you could tell me what to buy, I can pick it up next time I'm in Knoxville."

"I'd be delighted," Claire said. "What I want to talk to you about is the school. I want to exhibit Emily's drawings at the Harvest Festival. I hope you will come. It will be a chance for all of the children to show what they have been learning."

"After all the teachers have done for Emily and my family, I couldn't stay away."

"Thank you, Mr. Morgan." Then catching him by surprise she said, "I admire your boots."

He looked down at the boots he had worn for the past three years as though he hardly recognized them. "They're right handy," he said, at last.

"My mother sent me a pair," she said, "but they really were not suited to hiking in the mountains."

"It can get rugged up here," he admitted. "I admire you and Miss Tessie for walking all this way for Emily." It was over two miles from the school to where they stood, most of it up hill on a rutted wagon road.

"Oh but you see, I went to Ogles store and bought another pair," she said lifting her skirt slightly with a wry grin. She was wearing the exact same boots as he.

"A wise choice, I'd say." Feeling as foolish as a school boy for the way the sight of Claire's ankle made him feel, he said, "If you are wandering around up here by yourself, you best be careful. These mountains are full of rattlesnakes and copperheads. A bite from either one could kill you."

She puffed up, obviously offended by his words. He was not sure why he had even said it, to be helpful or just to have something to say.

"If someone were with me, what might they do?" she asked.

"Most likely go for help," he went on, defending himself.

"And would that greatly improve the odds of my surviving?"

"Not by much, I reckon," he said. He batted at his face as though being pestered by gnats, which was how she made him feel. "Still if you broke a leg...."he tried again.

"I appreciate your concern, Mr. Morgan," she said, cutting him short. "I think I have a perfect right to go where I please. After all, this is nineteen twenty and women now have the right to vote."

"Stop and tell that to the next rattlesnake you meet and you'd have about as much chance as a pig in a dog race."

Suddenly a grin broke out on her face. "I see your point, Mr. Morgan."

"Folks around here get along because they have learned a thing or two about living in these mountains but you strike me as the type who likes to fish in troubled waters," he said, not unkindly.

Her eyes sparkled. "And you Mr. Morgan are a philosopher and quite a judge of character." Without warning, she leaned toward him, her voice deep and low. "The truth is I adore my fellow teachers, but if I have to sit through one more afternoon of needlework and polite conversation when all about me lay these beautiful mountains, I fear I will scream. And that, Mr. Morgan, I pray you will keep to yourself."

Startled by her words and the smell of her hair, which clung to him like a morning glory vine, he pulled away abruptly and stood nodding at her. She was the most confounding woman he had ever met. She was at once proud and touchy and at the next minute open and laughing at herself.

Claire seemed not to notice his discomfort. Taking the satchel from her shoulder, she searched through its contents and then triumphantly pulled out a camera. "Emily how would you like me to take a picture of you and Miss Tessie?"

Emily's face lighted up and she clapped her hands together.

"Move just a little over here where the light is better," Claire said.

Shade watched as Emily, on Claire's instructions, took up her pole again, baited the hook and began fishing. Claire walked about taking different pictures as she chatted with Emily and Miss Tessie. Shade could not help noticing how his daughter was soaking up the attention like a plant turning to the light.

When he glanced down, he noticed that Claire's sketchbook had slipped from her satchel. He stooped to pick it up. It was a drawing of Baskin Falls, a place he had known all of his life. It was as familiar as his own hand and he thought he could name every rock and yet when he looked at the sketch it was as if another world had opened up to him. She had captured something that was beyond his ability to name. He could not imagine how it was possible to grow up in the Smoky Mountains and not believe that God was in everything, but he did not think until now that such a thought could be reflected on a simple piece of paper. He longed to see more of his beloved mountains through the eyes of this woman.

He heard Emily laugh and he looked up to see the two of them whispering. He wondered what secrets they were sharing and he wondered if knowing Claire would change his life as much as it had already changed his daughter's.

Chapter 10

"Sun sets early in the mountains," Shade said, motioning to Emily. "Your Granny Kate will be waiting supper."

Emily jumped up immediately and ran to her pa calling back for Claire and Tessie to join them. As they walked up the wagon road, they were never far from the rush of the mountain stream. The land around them had been cleared and held the sad remains of the summer's crops.

Curious, Claire asked, "Whose land is this?"

"I own around a hundred acres," Shade answered casually. "It belonged to my pa before he died four years ago. Only about forty acres is fit to farm."

Claire looked over the rocky fields running up and down hillsides and wondered how even that were possible. "It must be a lot of work?"

He nodded. "Sarah was a better hand than me at gardening," he said simply. "I had two brothers but they died young."

Claire looked at him expecting the magnitude of his words to show on his face but his expression gave away nothing. "So that just leaves you to do the work?"

"It keeps me busy for sure. Emily and Ma help out with a lot of the work."

"I feed the chickens and gather their eggs," Emily said proudly.

"Would you let me help you do that? Claire asked. "I am learning to feed the livestock at school."

"I'll show you how. It's not hard." Emily said suddenly full of herself. "Most of the nests are in the chicken house. Some of the hens run off and make nests in the woods and you have to hunt for them. Then you have to watch for snakes."

"So, I have been told," said Claire, casting an eye to Shade.

"She can do it Pa. I'll help her," Emily said catching the look.

"I don't reckon I'll be the one that's going to try to stop her," Shade said, a grin splitting his face.

As they topped the rise, Claire was surprised to see a two-story frame house surrounded by several outbuildings. Larger than any of the cabins she had seen, it was painted white with green trim around the windows. A fence of wooden palings marked off the front yard. A split rail fence set off the chicken house, barn and smokehouse. A short, sturdy woman stood on the porch in a starched dress, her iron gray hair pinned neatly in place. She alternated between ringing her hands and fretting with her hair. The dog from Emily's drawing came out from under the porch and barked once. The woman pointed and yelled, "Dink, that'll do," and the dog slunk back under the porch.

"Ma's waiting on us," Shade said. "She's got on her best bib and tucker."

Claire gave him a confused look.

"She dressed up 'cause the teachers are coming," he explained.

"I hope she didn't go to a lot of trouble for us," Tessie said.

"Lordie, I couldn't of stopped her if I had hogtied her," Shade mumbled as he went ahead of them.

As soon as Shade introduced Claire and Tessie, the woman said, "You can call me Granny Kate. Everybody 'round here does. Now, get on into the house." She herded the women into the house like a mother hen rounding up her chicks. "I've got supper all ready."

"Let these women catch their breath after their trip," Shade said.

Granny Kate rushed ahead unmoved by his words.

The front room had a large fireplace with a wooden mantle surrounded by several straight back chairs. There was only one window in the room and a linen curtain covered it. A hand carved bedstead filled most of one side of the room. The most beautiful blue woven coverlet Claire had ever seen lay across the bed. She wondered if Granny Kate had gotten it out of some chest where she kept the best of her things just for this occasion. It made her realize suddenly that as nervous as she had been about spending the night with a mountain family, they were equally anxious about her visit. She walked to the bed and gently touched the coverlet. "Oh, Granny Kate, what a beautiful coverlet," she said. "Did you weave it?"

Granny Kate beamed. "My grandma made it back before I was married. She give it to me when I wed."

"Tessie isn't it lovely."

"It's beautiful weaving," Tessie said as though she had been doing it all her life. "You know we are going to be setting up weaving classes at the school." She talked about Aunt Lizzie and setting up the loom and how the school hoped to get some of the older women to teach weaving.

Claire looked at how all of the threads wove so beautifully in and around one another coming together to form a pattern. She thought of some woman sitting at her loom, patiently, thread after thread, creating such wonder. "What is this pattern called?" she asked.

"Why honey, that is a Rainbow by Moonlight."

"Rainbow by Moonlight, what a perfect name," she said. When she looked up they were all looking at her and she wondered what her face had revealed. "What does that name mean?"

"My grandma made that pattern and named it," Granny Kate said, pride in her voice.

"Is there truly such a thing as a rainbow made by moonlight?" Tessie asked.

"Not many people ever see one. My grandma said if you ever seen one it would haunt you for the rest of your days."

"So your grandma created this pattern after she saw one?" Claire asked.

"She spent the rest of her life trying to explain it to folks, to show them what she had seen but she never felt like she could get it right."

"Please tell us the story? What did she say?" Claire asked.

"She and Grandpa Herman hadn't been married long," Granny Kate began, as though she had told the story many times. "Caught out late one night coming home, they had to set up camp. They cut some boughs for shelter and soon dropped off to sleep. Grandma woke up sometime in the night when she heard rain on the trees. The night was unusual bright with moonlight, and the sky was dancing with shadows. For reasons she never could discover, she got up and walked to the edge of a cliff that overlooked the valley. She always said it was as if something called her to do it. When she looked out into the sky, there was a beautiful arc of color. The moonlight passing through the rain had formed a rainbow. She said she just stood there for a while as if it was a dream. Finally, she ran back to wake Grandpa Herman. When they got back it was gone."

"Do you think she wondered if she dreamed it?" Claire asked.

Granny Kate looked at her sadly. "It was real to her, no doubt about it. Later when my mama was born, she used to take her out sometimes when it was a full moon and try to find it again. She never saw another one. I think she thought folks didn't believe her."

"But you believed her," Claire said.

"I believe it is not meant for everyone to see a rainbow by moonlight. It takes a rare and special person to carry that gift."

Claire ran her fingers over the coverlet and thought about what Granny Kate had said. She thought about the spirit of a woman who could create such a magnificent coverlet woven from the deep need to express her most transformative experience. She longed to absorb that spirit through her fingertips.

"Do you know how to weave this pattern?" Tessie asked.

"My grandma never made another one. When she died, she left the draft to my mama. No matter how much my mama tried, she was never pleased with the way her efforts turned out. Finally, she give it up for good."

"Did you never want to try to weave it?" Claire asked.

"Lordie honey, I thought about it for most of my life. I just knowed I couldn't do it justice. Now, after all these years, somehow it don't seem right. The only one who might of been able to have done it justice in her day was Aunt Lydia."

"Yes, Aunt Lizzie told us she was quite the hand to weave," Tessie said. "Evelyn promised to take us to meet her soon."

"Aunt Lydia is choosey about her company," Shade spoke up.

They all looked at him as though they just realized he was in the room.

"I could take you to see her. She likes me well enough," he offered.

Granny Kate cocked her head to one side and gave Shade a puzzled look.

Claire watched as a look passed between the mother and son, then she turned aside.

Shade waited patiently for her to speak.

"Thank you, Mr. Morgan," she said. "That would be very kind of you."

"You young folks must be about starved," Granny Kate said. "Emily you show these ladies where they can wash up while I finish getting the food on the table."

Emily led Claire and Tessie outside to the back porch where a basin sat on a wooden table. A heated kettle of water sat wrapped in a tea towel next to a clean bar of soap. Tessie poured the water into the basin and washed her hands and then helped Emily to wash hers. Then she took Emily by the hand and led her back inside.

Claire was the last to finish washing on the back porch and when she came into the kitchen, she could not believe the bounty of food—fried chicken, dumplings, green beans, potatoes, and cornbread. Her stomach let out a groan of hunger and everyone laughed. She blushed crimson. "The walk up must have given me an appetite."

"It's a good thing you are hungry," Shade said. "I think Ma's cooked for the whole of Roaring Fork."

He pulled out a chair for her. She smiled a grateful smile. The table, covered with a white oil cloth, held a vase of asters in the center. Claire was touched that they had gone to so much trouble for the teachers' visit.

"Emily, will you say the blessing," Granny Kate said.

Emily, her hands steepled, bowed her head. "Dear God, thank you for this food. Thank you for my teachers, Miss Claire and Miss Tessie. Thank you for letting them come to spend the night. Thank you for Pa and Granny Kate. Watch over Mommy in Heaven. Amen."

Granny Kate began to shovel food onto their plates. Fussing about the table, she refused to sit down until she was satisfied they had enough of everything. Soon the only sound was of forks hitting plates as they concentrated on their food. Before Claire could ask for more, Granny Kate popped up, moving about the kitchen to refill glasses, offering more of everything and filling up plates again.

"This fried chicken is the best I have ever eaten," she managed to say between bites and the green beans and these stewed apples."

She watched as Tessie nodded in agreement her mouth stuffed with the delicious food.

Granny Kate beamed at them and said, "Eat up, now, they's plenty. Don't be backward none."

When everyone at the table began to put down their forks and to chew more slowly, occasionally leaning back in their seats with sighs of pleasure, Granny Kate got up and cut them each a slice of pie. "Sweet potato pie was Shade's daddy's favorite," she said shyly as she set the slices down. She poured them each a cup of coffee before sitting back down.

Claire cut off a forkful of pie and plopped it into her mouth. "Um," she said as the pleasure of the gooey custard reached her tongue. "I think sweet potato pie is going to be my favorite too."

"Mine too," Tessie chimed in.

Granny Kate blushed but the pleasure of their praise showed in her eyes.

Shade was the first to pull away. He leaned back and coupled his hands behind his head. "Mama, the richest man on earth never had a finer meal."

"Thank you son," Granny Kate said softly. As though by sign, she got up and poured him another cup of coffee.

To Claire it was such a loving gesture, a practice born of intimate knowledge and family. She had probably done the same for Shade's father at every meal of their lives until he died.

"Thank you for a wonderful meal, Mrs. Morgan," Claire said.

"Well, it's nothin' fancy," Granny Kate said modestly.

"Truly, I can't remember when I have eaten better food."

Granny Kate reached over and patted her gently on the hand a soft smile on her face. "Granny Kate," she corrected. "Call me Granny Kate."

"Granny Kate," Claire repeated.

"Claire and I will do the dishes," Tessie said.

"No, I won't hear of it," Granny Kate said.

"Oh but, we always do the dishes when we visit, don't we Tessie," Claire said. She sounded as though she had spent a hundred nights in mountain homes.

Tessie nodded.

"Well, it will give us a chance to visit," Granny Kate conceded.

"Emily, we've got chores to do," Shade said grabbing his hat from a hook by the door. "We usually do chores before supper but I reckoned Ma wouldn't wait."

Tessie washed the dishes as Claire dried. A familiar routine they had done many times together at the teacher's cottage. Granny Kate covered the leftover food with clean cloths as she told stories about what it had been like to leave her family in North Carolina to start a new life in Tennessee.

"I met Jack when he was logging in Cataloochee Cove. I was a silly little thing but I felt big enough to marry," Granny Kate said chuckling behind her hand. "I was afraid of might near everything, especially panthers. I was used to bein' around my family. I hadn't ever been away from home. When we moved off up here, our closest neighbor was two miles away. I wouldn't let Jack be gone overnight. I liked to of cried myself sick the first few months."

"How did you get over it," Tessie asked.

"We had a bad winter that first year. Snow piled up to the windows, wind howled down the mountain. Jack seen as how, I was having a hard time. He offered to take me home, back to North Carolina and my mama. Well, that done it, I couldn't of lived with the shame of him taking me home. I set my mind to making it through and when spring broke, I knowed I'd be all right."

"How old were you?" asked Claire.

"Fifteen," she said. "Poor Jack was just eighteen and having to put up with a foolish girl. He would even make me play pretties. He was a good hand to make things. One time he made me a cornstalk fiddle. There weren't much too it but I learned to play a tune or two. Then before long, I started to have a family of my own and it wasn't so lonesome. We made a good life here."

"And are you still afraid of panthers?" Claire asked.

She thought for a moment gazing off as though the answer lay in the distance. "I reckon, I'd be a fool not to be, but you can always find something to worry about if you go lookin' for it. When the boys were all little, one or the other of 'em was always getting hurt. Amos the oldest was the worst to dare the others to do some fool thing or another. Shade loved his older brother more than was good for him, so if he said jump out of the barn loft and see if he could fly, he'd try it to please Amos."

Granny Kate smiled a wistful smile.

Claire wondered at the courage that it took to talk about a dead child. She was afraid to say anything for fear of saying the wrong thing. Granny Kate seemed to have a need to talk about her children, even those lost to her, as though it somehow kept them close and alive in her mind.

"Shade was always trying to make up for being sickly as a baby, as if he thought he'd missed too much," Granny Kate went on. "Him and his brother Caleb was just a year apart and they run these hills from daylight to dark. I couldn't keep'em inside even in the dead of winter."

"Three boys must have made for a lively household,"Tessie said sweetly. "It must be different having Emily."

Granny Kate laughed. "She's a good girl, that's for sure. Shade fusses over her all the time. I try to tell him you just have to turn it over to the Lord. When you've lived as long as I have, you learn not to dwell on your fears," she said, "that steals your peace."

Claire could see where Shade had gotten his philosophical bent. Granny Kate did not talk about the tragedies that had befallen her life, the loss of her husband and sons. Most likely, Claire thought, she had set her mind to that too.

As they put away the last of the dishes, Emily threw open the kitchen door. "Miss Claire, you promised you would help me gather the eggs," she said breathless.

"Well, if I promised," Claire said smiling. Granny Kate handed her a basket filled with ground corn and leftover bread. As they headed to the chicken house, Emily explained what her duties would be.

"You throw out the food and the chickens come and eat it. Mostly they scratch for worms and bugs during the day."

Claire made a face.

"The eggs don't taste like bugs," Emily explained. "They just taste like eggs."

"Do you have a lot of chickens?"

She nodded. "Pa built a chicken house for them. He put a door in so I could go in and get the eggs. He put a little door up high with a ladder so the chickens could come and go when they want. They go in at night."

"They don't all look alike. What kind is this one?' Claire asked. She had little knowledge of chickens beyond the eggs on her breakfast plate or the leg she had for dinner.

"That is a Plymouth Rock. They are good to eat but they don't lay many eggs. You get more eggs from Rhode Island Reds."

"You know a lot about chickens," Claire said.

"Ma taught me," Emily said proudly. Then she quenched up her face in a pained expression and swallowed hard.

Claire did not correct her as she might have done at any other time but took Emily's hand and walked along.

All mountain children were taught, Claire realized, the way their parents had been, by working side by side, each season providing its own lessons. Planting, hoeing, harvesting the garden, chopping wood or carrying water, the children were an essential part of survival in the mountains.

"Emily, Granny Kate's waiting for you on the porch," Shade said walking out to meet them. "Take the eggs on in the house."

"Emily showed me all around. I didn't know a child could know so much about chickens," Claire said.

"She could be showing off a might, I reckon," he said wryly. "I'm proud of her just the same."

He shuffled his feet in the dirt as Claire studied him. "You know you are nothing like...," she hesitated, "I mean a lot of the books I read..."

"You mean I am not lazy and shiftless, or was it ignorant and a mean drunk?"

"And then there is grim and humorless," she added with a laugh.

"I've heard it all. I know what's said about mountain folk. They make fun of the way we talk, dress and live. They think we live up here in the mountains because we got no choice in the matter."

"It isn't like the people here haven't talked about the teachers and the funny way they talk or dress," Claire remarked.

Shade grinned, revealing the truth of what she said. "The truth is my home is here in the Smoky Mountains," he said simply. "I know the name of every family up every cove in these mountains. I can name every stream, bluff and mountain. I know when it's time to pick wild grapes and gather hickory nuts. I know how to hunt or fish for any living thing in these woods. I have walked every inch of my land until I could close my eyes and name you every hemlock, maple, tulip or silverbell." He stopped talking and turned his head to one side. Listening for a moment, he said, "You hear that sound?" That is the sound of a creek rushing over mountain boulders. All my life I have woke up and gone to sleep to that sound. I never want to live outside of earshot of that sound. This is my home. My people are buried here and I plan to live out my life and be buried here too."

The air was thick with his need for her to understand the pride he had in his heritage. He was such a strange mixture of gentleness and ferocity, it kept her off balance. His honesty was wild and beautiful and she found herself confessing, "I think you are fortunate to feel the way you do about this place. I envy you that. I don't remember ever feeling so at home any place I have ever been."

"My soul feels settled here."

"And my soul has always felt restless wherever I go," she admitted. It was more than she had meant to say but she could not take it back.

He stood for a long time without speaking. "I saw that in you the first day we met. I reckon you can't help it. Some folks are just born to be that way, same as I was born to plant my feet here in these hills."

The sky darkened and the night birds began to sing. In the distance, a great barred owl let out a lonesome call.

"What was that sound?" Claire asked.

"It's a hoot owl," Shade said. "Listen, it calls out eight or nine hoots and then it waits for an answer. It's calling out to other hoot owls."

Claire cocked her head and listened. The sounds of *hoo hoo to hoo, hoo hoo to hoo aw* filled the air. Then the softer echo sounded from a more distant owl. "Is that its mate?"

"The male has a deeper voice. After a while you can tell them apart."

"Why do you think they call out like that?"

Shade's tall frame was silhouetted in the fading light as he spoke, "Some folk's think that an owl's call foretells death."

"Do you believe that?"

"No," he said shaking his head. "Folks are always trying to predict what is to happen next in their lives especially if it's bad like the knowing of it could prepare them somehow."

"You don't believe in knowing the future?"

"What I believe is not even owls can foretell for sure what's to happen next. I think they call out to one another because they are like most creatures. They don't like to be alone."

"It is a haunting sound," she mused.

"It can be company after a while."

She smiled as she thought about his words.

"Emily sets a lot of store by you," he said at last.

"I think a lot of Emily," she said.

"I know she may leave here someday. It can't be helped. She has a right to her own life, to use her gifts as she sees fit even if it takes her away from here. I know a seed can't grow till it finds the right soil."

Claire had come up the mountain proud of herself, full of self-assurance that she was opening new vistas for Emily and the other children. She knew that most of the parents wanted their children to have the opportunities they had not had. Shade, she was sure, wanted that for his daughter as much as any of them. What she had never considered was the risk, the chance these parents were taking that they might lose their children to that other world outside the mountains. "Emily loves her life here," she said.

"Maybe that will always be true," he said turning his face away. "I reckon what I'm trying to say is that I think Emily needs you to grow into the woman she is to be."

His words knocked her breathless. "Shade," she said, his given name slipping from her lips.

"Promise me one thing," he said stepping close enough to her that she could feel his breath.

"Of course," she whispered. She could not imagine what it had cost this proud, reserved man to come to her asking for help.

"Whatever happens, I don't want Emily to come to look down on her home place," he pleaded, taking hold of her arms.

The powerful grip of his hands dug into her but the naked ache in his voice overshadowed the throbbing in her arms. The thought crossed her mind that she should be afraid but she was not. "I would never do anything…," she hesitated.

He gave her a pained expression. "My people have lived on one side or the other of these mountains for generations. Everything I know was passed down from my people. Their school was these mountains and they had a stern teacher," he said.

He let go of her and looked at his hands. She watched him shake his head, his brooding form silhouetted against the night, as though he could not believe what he had done. She stopped herself from reaching out.

"If you made it through your schooling," he went on, "your reward was to live here in these mountains free and beholden to no man. I think I have reason to be proud of the way they struggled and survived."

"Yes, I would but wish for that kind of courage," she said truthfully.

"It does take a different sort to put aside what the world has to offer in trade for the freedom to breath and wander at will," he said.

She could feel his eyes on her and she wondered at his ability to touch the soft places of her soul. It was as though he were asking if she could be that 'different sort' of person. Could she bear up under hardship, forsake the world she knew to have the life she longed to live? She had no answers.

"The folks that first settled in these mountains wouldn't know the place now," he said pensively. "My folks lived hardly in sight of the smoke of another chimney for most of their lives. Now, there is a world of folks living up these coves. I expect a world more to come. Big logging companies have cut all the forest away and folks that used to get by on their own have come to depend on those jobs."

"You are thinking that it will be a different kind of world for Emily."

He nodded. "Emily will need a different kind of courage."

"In fact, you have no doubt passed on a great deal of that self-reliant nature to your daughter. In time, it will serve her well, I think."

"I have always done my best for Emily," he said, "but she is going to be tested in ways I'm not prepared to help her survive. She may need to go out and make her own way in the world the way you have."

Claire was not at all sure she was making her own way in the world. She marveled that Shade could see her as confident and sure of herself.

"She will need what you have to give her," he said more firmly.

"Then, I promise to do all I can," she said. She had no understanding of what her promise meant or where it would lead her. She only knew he needed to hear it.

He nodded, seemingly reassured by her promise. "I saw your sketchbook today," he said abruptly.

His words came so unexpected they caught her off guard. "I hope you weren't disappointed. They're only sketches."

"I have been walking these mountains all my life, but today when I saw your drawings, I saw a different world I had never seen before. It was like the boulders and the trees pulled me in and showed me the life hiding inside."

Claire could not find her voice. In all her years in art class, no professor or fellow artist had ever expressed so perfectly the way she felt when she painted. Now here standing in the fading light, this man so oddly different from her had given words to her most intimate feelings. Gently, she reached out into the night air almost touching his face before she withdrew her hand. Then without speaking, they walked back to the cabin bound together by the words they had spoken in the dark.

Chapter 11

The sun was not yet up when Frannie threw back the covers and hopped out of bed. She had tossed and turned all night, excitement crawling up her spine like a bug every time she thought of the Harvest Fair. Her dress, laid out on a chair, was ironed to a crisp finish. The words to the song she had been practicing all month ran through her head. She shook Dealie awake. "Time to get up!"

Dealie popped up like a spring. She was as excited as Frannie for the coming event. Quietly they slipped on their old clothes so as not to wake Martha Jane who could be fierce in the mornings.

Frannie stoked the fire and added more wood while Dealie took the bucket and headed to the spring for water. They had used all the water the night before to bathe and wash their hair. As soon as it was light, she would let the chickens out to scratch. She wanted to make sure her chores were done so her ma would not call her back at the last minute. She was trying to keep up her schoolwork and not miss too much but her ma called on her a good deal. Sometimes she missed a day of school if her ma had extra work for her to do.

Her favorite thing about school was reading, especially since she had gotten glasses. A doctor had come from Knoxville to test the children's eyes. She had not known until then that she could not see. It was a wonder to her to have the words on the page be clear and bright. She would sit all day and read if she could, but there was a world of things to do at school. Her teachers treated her as if she could do anything and she loved them for that. When Miss Bishop, who could sing and play the piano, picked her out to sing, she thought her heart would burst with joy.

When the family finally gathered for breakfast, Frannie collected their plates to wash them almost before they had swallowed the last bite. Her food sat heavily in her stomach, having gone down in a lump.

She helped Dealie dress and together they rushed out the door. She glared back at Martha Jane who sat brushing her hair and staring into the mirror as though she had all day. "It's not my fault if you're late," Frannie said.

Martha Jane turned her back to Frannie and continued to primp. Frannie let out a sigh.

Her ma stepped between the girls and pushed Frannie and Dealie out the door. "Go on now. Your sister will be along directly."

"Ma don't forget now. Be at the schoolhouse by eleven o'clock," she yelled.

Her ma stood on the porch, fist to forehead, and watched them walk down the hill. Frannie hoped that her folks would come as they had promised, but they were shy around strangers. She had brought home a poster from school that the children had made to show what all they would be doing. It had taken her a week to talk her ma into showing her baskets and then she had fretted for days over which ones to send. There would be displays of sewing and baskets and the girls cooking class would be making dinner on the ground. The boys would be showing off their farm training and the chicken coop they had built. There was to be a play and what the teachers called 'recitations.' It was more than Frannie could hold in her head at one time.

"Dealie did you memorize your poem?" Frannie asked.

"How many times do I have to tell you. I know it by heart," Dealie said.

"Say it to me then."

"Don't go bossing me," Dealie said, throwing her head back. As they walked on down the mountain, however, without another word, she began to recite the poem perfectly.

Frannie listened even as the words to her song ran like a train on a track through her head.

By ten o'clock, the rooms were ready. The main room was filled with baskets of ferns the girls had dug. Boughs of red sumac ran across the fireplace mantel. Great bunches of goldenrod sat in front of panels covered with autumn leaves. Paper Japanese lanterns were strung from the ceiling. The blackboards were filled with writing papers and drawings.

The students, teachers and parents all gathered in the main room. Miss Bishop walked to the front and welcomed all of the parents who had come to see the program. Then she said the prayer and everyone said amen. Frannie's folks had come in late and stood in the back of the room and she listened for their voices but she could not tell if they had said amen too.

Everyone stood to have the salute to the flag. Frannie knew that her song came right after the flag salute, and the poems. Then Miss Bishop called Dealie up to recite her poem. Frannie was nervous for her, but Dealie seemed unafraid as always. Having always been a child who preferred climbing trees and doing cartwheels, Dealie was not one to care about her looks but she did have one vanity, which was her hair. Vowing to grow it long until she died, her ma had given in only if Dealie, because of her tomboy ways, would keep it braided. Today, however, Frannie had brushed it out and it hung thick and shiny around Dealie's face.

Dealie only had four short lines and Frannie said them with her under her breath, her lips moving as she recited, *the goldenrod is yellow, the corn is turning brown, the trees in apple orchards, with fruit are bending down.* When Dealie finished, she gave a quick bow and everyone laughed and applauded. Frannie applauded the loudest of anyone. She was proud of her little sister and relieved that she remembered her part.

Then Emily Morgan was called to the front to recite her poem. Frannie thought Emily looked just like an angel would look, with her blond hair and blue eyes, and she recited her poem softly, not boldly as Dealie had done. Everyone applauded, especially her pa who stood off to the side leaning against the wall.

Then Miss Bishop gave the older girls the signal by raising one hand. The girls gathered in front of the piano. Frannie's knees began to knock as she looked out over the crowd in the recitation room. She wanted to wave to her folks in the back of the room but she stopped herself. She wished they would come to the front so she could see their faces and know that they were proud of her.

Then Miss Bishop started to play and suddenly she was no longer afraid. Her voice came out strong as she sang, 'Did you ever see a lassie, a lassie,' and when they got to the part where the song went, 'go this way and that way,' the girls all swayed together their arms waving in the air. She could see people start to tap their feet and when the song was finished, they all applauded.

It was all she could do to wait until Miss Bishop had dismissed the students to run to her folks and lead them to the different rooms where the student projects were displayed. The first room she took them to was where the girls sewing class had laid out all of their work. She showed them the sewing bag she had made, along with some of the fancy work Martha Jane had done. As mad as she got at Martha Jane, she was still proud of her sister.

Then she hurried them along to the next room where the blackboard was covered with school papers and drawings. Miss Claire stood talking to Shade Morgan. They were looking at a drawing that Emily Morgan had done. Emily stood next to her pa and stared up at Miss Claire. Frannie's heart squeezed tight in her chest and she tried not to be jealous. Miss Claire was wearing a gray skirt and bright white blouse ironed crisp and her hair was done up on top of her head. Frannie thought she was the most beautiful woman she had ever seen. When she saw Frannie, she smiled and made her way over to them.

"Frannie you sang beautifully," she said sweetly.

"Thank you, ma'am," Frannie said, her stomach jumping to her throat. She had daydreamed that Miss Claire would single her out like this and now it was happening. It made her feel happy and shy at the same time.

"She don't get it from me," Mary said shaking her head. "I never got a voice for singing."

"Your daughter has a lot of talents," Claire said. "You should be very proud of her."

Her pa stood hat in hand. "We are right proud of all our girls," he said putting his hand on Frannie's shoulder. He had never been one given to praise and Frannie fought back the tears that threatened to fill her eyes.

"Why don't you show them your writing? Frannie has an excellent hand."

Frannie could not hide her smile as she led her folks to the board and explained to them how she had copied poems in her best handwriting and another paper was a story she had written about catching salamanders. They looked at her wide-eyed and nodded as she spoke. Suddenly, she felt like the parent explaining this strange unknown world to her folks. Before school, her small world had never reached beyond church and visiting neighbors. At school, she had other children and at noontime, they played new games like 'my ship comes in' and 'three-deep.' Sometimes they ran races and even the teachers would play. She loved all of her teachers and she was proud of the way they praised her work and never had to scold her. This was her world now, this world of books and learning, she thought.

Then she took her ma into a room leading her to a basket that she had made and sent along at Frannie's urging. The basket labeled with the name *Mary Riley* had a blue ribbon on it. This was Frannie's surprise. She looked from her ma to the basket and back beaming a smile.

"What's it got a ribbon on it for," her pa asked.

"It means you won for best basket," Frannie said, once again the interpreter of all things foreign.

"Lordie," her ma said. "I never won nothing in my life." Then her hand flew to her heart. "What will folks think?"

"I reckon they'll think you are a good hand to make baskets," her pa said.

Her ma's cheeks filled with color but Frannie could tell she was pleased. They stood for a while taking it all in and then they went out back to the farm displays where the boys had built a chicken coop for their shop project. Some of the boys stood by proudly explaining what they had learned. The boys were required to care for the farm animals that belonged to the school and to tend to the garden as part of their training. All around were baskets of apples and pumpkins they had grown that year.

The family strolled back to the schoolhouse where Martha Jane stood beside long tables set with all kinds of food. She was wearing her best dress, one she had made in sewing class and her hair was done up. She was talking to a boy but they quickly split up when her folks came around the corner. Frannie could not understand the way Martha Jane was always pining after some boy or another.

Martha Jane had been nervous, as were all the girls when they learned they would be cooking food for the Harvest Fair, but they had soon gotten into the spirit and cooked for two days making pies, cakes and bread. Other folks in the community had brought food and the tables were full to overflowing.

Many people were already eating sitting on the ground talking and socializing with neighbors, while children ran around playing. Frannie and her folks filled their plates and found a place to sit. Frannie realized with all of the excitement of the morning that she was starving. Deciding, with one last look at her folks, that the day was turning out just as wonderfully as she had imagined it, she launched into her food with delight.

Out in the schoolyard Dealie was with a group of children playing 'drop the handkerchief' and some of the bigger boys were playing tug of war. Miss Claire walked by taking pictures with her Kodak and took one of Frannie with her folks. She promised to show it to Frannie when she got them developed.

"The baseball game is starting out front," Miss Tessie walked by to announce.

Frannie grabbed a piece of cake as she went by the tables and they followed the crowd to the baseball field. Miss Agnes was organizing the teams, for they were not just from the school but also from the Glades, Green Brier and Sheep Pen.

The crowd cheered loudly for the home team. The game wore on into the afternoon until finally they won six to four. Frannie felt like a rag doll, she was so tired from all the fun and excitement of the day. The sun was beginning to slant in the sky as her folks gathered up the girls and they made their way up the mountain to home. Martha Jane and Dealie were fighting as to who could talk the most about what a wonderful day it had been, but for Frannie it was all beyond words. She could hardly contain it all in her small body. It had been the best day of her life.

November 5, 1920

Dear Lenora

You can imagine how thrilled I was to find your letter waiting for me when I went by the post today. I braved the terrible weather, for it has been raining here for days, because I was so in hopes of hearing from you. I could hardly wait to get back to the cottage to read it. How wonderful that the children are well. They have grown and look so big in your pictures. I hope they do not forget their Aunt Claire.

I do miss the lovely fall weather. The rain has taken the last of the radiant leaves from the trees. Mud is everywhere now. The streets are rutted and almost impassible. I am so grateful that the Pi Phi's saw fit to build boardwalks up the main street and some of the side streets or the simplest trips would be impossible in this weather. I have spent these last days cleaning my room, which was much in need of attention. How did you like the pictures I sent of my room? It is really quite plain with just my table, my blotting pad, and my writing papers. Did you notice on my dressing table, I have the boy's pictures? The mirror is really in bad shape and not too clear but I find I have little time to look at myself. Of course, I must spend much of my time scraping the mud from my shoes which is a task never finished around here. At any rate, I find confinement to my room difficult since on most days of the week you will find me walking to visit the homes of my students. On Saturdays and Sunday afternoons, it is not uncommon to walk ten to twelve miles. You would perhaps not know me for my fair skin has quite a rosy glow and I have become most robust of health. It has given me considerable confidence so much so that the other night when we were all awakened by a crashing noise outside the cottage, I ran outside without thought to my safety and in my nightgown. The other teachers had a good laugh when they discovered me trying to catch one of our milk cows that had broken through the fence. My life here is daily filled with such adventures so that I have become accustomed to what may seem odd to you my dear sister. I think perhaps that Mother would be perfectly horrified as this is not how she pictured her daughter's life. I have picked up a number of expressions such as 'yonder' and 'fixin' to do something. I said to Tessie this morning that I thought it was 'fixin' to rain again today. Truly, I think after a while I will not know how to act in the city.

Forgive me if I gave the impression in my last letter that all here is grim work and giving on my part for you see that is not the case. It is true that I am busy from morning until sometimes late into the evenings but if you could see the faces of the children, you would understand. They are so terribly grateful for the simplest of things. I admit that I grow irritable at times when they sometimes come with their lessons poorly prepared and appear at times content in their ignorance. Just the other day, I was quite put out with them and I fear I made myself clear on that point. When I returned from my noon meal, they had made right their desk, finished their lessons and for the most part appeared quite contrite. You see, they are sweet little ones after all, so likeable and generous and it is I who is in need of more patience. If only I had your dear nature.

Since I last wrote, I have visited some of the local schools. They are sad one-room log buildings furnished only with benches and one blackboard behind the teacher's desk. The schools are heated by one rusty stove to keep the children from the cold that must come readily through the chinks in the logs. The buildings have only one or two windows and are dark and cramped. The children have few textbooks and most often must furnish their own. It is a wonder to me that we do not have more students at our fine Pi Phi School. Indeed, some of our students walk past schools near their homes to come here. Still many of the parents cling to the old schools because they want their children close by and they fear change.

I hope that the next time I write it will be by the glow of electric lights. Miss Bishop has promised a Delco generator for the school by Christmas, which could provide lights for the cottages and a number of homes in the community. Everyday here, we see improvements and it is most gratifying. Overall, the people here have been so much more accepting of me than I have of them. I have only begun to look beyond the external differences to the fine and likeable people who live in these mountains. They have in them fundamental qualities of perseverance and courage that allowed them to build a life in a mountain wilderness. We are bringing them new wants and new thoughts. It will be the young people who will bring about change here. To be a part of that brings me both joy and a grave sense of responsibility. I am beginning to find my way here, my dear Lenora. Please wish me well. Know that I think of you and the boys often.

Your loving sister
Claire

Chapter 12

It was the kind of drab chill November morning that ordinarily made Claire want to pull the covers over her head and think of spring. This morning however, she had sprung out of bed, excitement making her limbs twitch. Despite the damp mist, Claire was warm from searching out Lady, one of two horses that belonged to the school. She found the horse standing contentedly out by the baseball field and led her back. Phyllis Higinbotham, the new school nurse, had already saddled Dan, the other horse, and tied on her medical bags.

"Here let me help you," Phyllis said. "I am getting to be an old hand with these two."

Claire held Lady's reins as Phyllis saddled the horse. They led the horses down the lane and out to the main road. They shook the mud from their boots and mounted their rides. In the month Phyllis had been at the school, she had made over a dozen trips up the mountains to treat the sick. Today they would ride far up into Sugarlands, a community named for an abundance of sugar maples, to check on a young boy suffering from pneumonia. Phyllis would advise the family about treatment and report back to the doctor who was coming from Knoxville to Gatlinburg the next day to do examinations at the school. If the boy were better, the doctor would not have to make the arduous trip up the mountain.

Claire, who had never made the six-mile journey up to the most isolated parts of the community, begged to go along. Phyllis warned, the journey would not be an easy one. The road was nothing more than a narrow path and so soon after a rain could be knee deep in mud. She had done some riding but never under such difficult conditions. Still, she was not to be discouraged.

With some effort, she finally coaxed Lady into motion. Dan balked as Phyllis tried to mount him as though he was aware of the hardships the day might bring. Sitting astride Dan, who was stout and long legged, Phyllis looked small in her dark wool suit and gray felt hat, but she confidently took the lead. "I hope to be there before noon," she said.

Noon was still several hours away, Claire noted. In the short time Phyllis Higinbotham had been the school nurse, Claire had come to admire the woman's calm nature and tireless dedication. "Have you visited this family before?"

"No, I haven't but the doctor was there two weeks ago. The boy was quite ill. I am hoping he will be much improved."

"How will we find our way?"

"I have found I must rely solely on the good will of the people," she said cheerfully. "There are no maps so I must stop and ask for directions wherever I go."

Before long, they came to a familiar farmhouse. Phyllis called out a greeting to Mrs. Wheeler who was standing by her fence.

"Good morning, Miss Phyllis," the woman called back. "Good morning, Miss Claire. I missed you at Sunday dinner."

"You know I hate to miss your wonderful cooking Mrs. Wheeler but I had papers to grade," Claire said. "I'll be sure to come next week." It was not altogether a lie, for Claire had graded papers that evening but first she had gone back to the cottage packed her sketchbook, and gone out into the mountains to spend the day. Quite by accident, she had run into Shade Morgan and they had talked for a while. They were both shy and uncomfortable at first to find they were alone together again. As they talked, she had secretly sketched his portrait. She was not especially skilled at drawing people but when she showed him, he seemed both flustered and pleased. She had not given it to him as she might have to someone else but instead had held on to it. Since then she had taken it out at times and studied his face tracing the sharp angles with her finger, pondering the brooding look in his eyes.

"Mrs. Wheeler, the doctor will be at the school tomorrow to check up on the children," Phyllis said. "I wouldn't want your children to miss out."

"They'll be there, Miss Phyllis," Mrs. Wheeler assured.

Claire realized that the sight of Phyllis riding old Dan was already a familiar one in the community. As they rode on, Claire said,

"You seem to have made some progress in getting to know people in the community."

"It takes a long time to win peoples confidence," she said. "Right now, they don't quite know what to make of me. I am a nurse so I can do some treatments, but for others I must rely on the doctor. I fear they see me as neither fish nor fowl. It is my responsibility to win their trust."

"Did you realize when you took this position how difficult it would be?"

"I was a nurse in the war in western France. I saw many dark and terrible things. I was sorely tested but I returned with an even greater sense of duty to those who are suffering," she said patiently. "So even though it may be difficult, I do not believe it is impossible."

"What is it you hope to do here?" Claire asked genuinely curious.

"I want to open a clinic," Phyllis said in her straightforward manner. You know, children here die every year from diphtheria when a simple inoculation could save them. Mother's get no care before their babies are born and newborns and children get no care often until it is too late. With a clinic, I could provide inoculations against a host of infectious diseases, first aid for the many cuts, scrapes and broken bones and much needed advice on nutrition and personal hygiene."

"Do you think all of that is possible?"

"That and more, I hope," she said confidently. "It is so important. In time with enough medical supplies, the visiting doctors could do routine operations such as tonsillectomies and the dentist could pull teeth."

They came to a downed tree covering their path. Phyllis expertly wangled Dan around the obstacle and up the embankment. Not to be outdone Claire cajoled the hesitant Lady around the tree, breathing a sigh of relief when they were finally clear. Phyllis had not asked her why she wanted to come along on this journey and for that, Claire was glad. She was not sure she could explain. Ever since she had come to the mountains, she had wondered how it was possible to understand another culture, to be fully accepted and accepting. When Shade had extracted his promise from her, she had challenged herself once again to find the secret.

As Claire and Phyllis rode on, they forded three streams and detoured around numerous more deadfalls before stopping at last at a cabin to ask directions. A man in a faded blue shirt, overalls and a stained felt hat sat in a straight-backed chair on the porch. Phyllis called out a hello.

"Howdy," called back the man.

They dismounted and walked to the porch where the man sat idly. One side of his face was grossly distended. Without warning, he shot a stream of tobacco from between his lips. Claire watched with fascination as it arced and landed in the dirt a good two feet off the side of the porch

"We're looking for the Levi Wilson place," Phyllis said.

"You're near there. It's about a mile on up. Take off to the right when you see a big hollered out chestnut tree. You shouldn't have no trouble findin' it from there.'

"I thank you," Phyllis said.

"You are welcome to a drink of spring water," the man offered.

Claire looked at the bucket sitting on the porch, a gourd for a dipper, and then she looked back at the man whose mouth was stained with streaks of tobacco. Surprisingly, Phyllis took the dipper up to her lips and drank without hesitation. Claire followed her lead glancing at the gourd briefly to look for tobacco stains.

"I am glad the weather has held today after all the rain," Phyllis said.

"You most likely wouldn't be making this trip in the rain," the man said.

Phyllis agreed. They chatted on about the weather, how it could turn quickly in the mountains and how it was best to be prepared. Phyllis talked as though they were in no hurry at all.

Claire noticed the man's arm wrapped in a grimy rag was seeping blood. Drops were beginning to collect on the porch and yet Phyllis did not mention it. She talked on unhurriedly about the news she had picked up along the way in her visits.

Finally, as they made to leave, Phyllis said in passing, "I see you've hurt your arm."

He looked at the bloody rag and back to Phyllis as though it had slipped his mind. "Fell on my dang axe this morning. I was fixin' to get some wood cut up. My woman carries on like a dang fool if I don't keep a sight of wood in."

"I could take a look at it. I'm Miss Phyllis; I'm a nurse with the Settlement School and this is Miss Claire, she is a teacher."

"Folks around here call me Uncle Balis," he said cordially. "I've heard tell of you. Are you going up to see about Levi's boy?"

"That's right," Phyllis said. "Doctor Milo asked me to look in on him."

At the mention of the doctor, Uncle Balis eyes widened. Phyllis had told Claire that the doctor, being a man, was more readily trusted.

"I reckon it would be all right if you want to take a look," he said, as he eyed the women.

Claire fetched the medical bag and watched as Phyllis untied the rag and revealed the wound. Any squeamishness she felt was overcome by Phyllis' practiced manner. The axe had sliced through his forearm leaving a vicious red gash. It was no doubt painful but Uncle Balis bore it without so much as a grimace.

"What did you put on this, Uncle Balis?" Phyllis asked.

"It's a poultice of sulfur and alum. I put that on to stop the bleeding and keep it from poisoning."

Phyllis merely nodded, her face a mask. As she worked cleaning and disinfecting the wound, she continued to chat with Uncle Balis telling him the news from Gatlinburg and throwing in, along the way, instructions on the need to keep his wound clean. "I'll be back in a week and change the dressing," she said when she finished. "Do you have anybody here to send for me if it gets worse?"

"My woman's gone to Elkmont to visit with her sister. She should be back in a day or two. I reckon she is going to be a might upset with me though."

"Well, you can't help an accident," Phyllis said, "besides it should be looking better by then."

"That's the thing," he said shaking his head. "Last spring I was bit by a copperhead. Lost the tip of my little finger," he said holding up the mangled digit on his right hand.

"You were lucky it was not worse," Claire said. She felt something of an expert having been cautioned repeatedly about snakes since her arrival.

"Yes'em young lady, if it had been a rattlesnake, I'd most likely be dead."

They waited as Uncle Balis stroked his chin as though pondering the meaning of it all. Then he said, "Last winter a year ago, I was cutting down a tree and it fell on me."

Claire felt obliged to ask, "Were you badly hurt?"

"Broke my leg was all. My friend Joe Russell, I've knowed him all my life, he's as good a man as can be found in these parts, he pulled me out from under that tree. He said if I hadn't fell back into a hole it would have killed me."

"So you are worried your wife will be upset to learn you have had another accident," Phyllis said trying to catch the meaning.

"Last time I got hurt my wife said, "Balis it looks like I'm never going to get shed of you."

The women looked at each other, surprise showing on their faces. "You think she will be upset that you were not killed this time," Claire asked incredulous.

Uncle Balis sat quietly for a long minute puzzling over his words. Then he looked up solemnly and said, "The way I explained it to her, I am using everything the good Lord give me to work with and if he don't want to take me, that's his business."

Claire seeing the gleam in the old man's eye realized she had been completely taken in by the story. She laughed aloud. She was just beginning to catch on to mountain humor, the unhurried storytelling, the poking of fun at oneself and the spinning of life's tragedies into a smile. "Perhaps, you could promise to try harder," Claire said, with only a hint of a smile.

Uncle Balis looked at her for a brief moment and then let out a loud guffaw. He slapped his knee and shook his head chuckling. "I'll be sure to tell her that. I'll try harder," he repeated. "I like you little gal. You be sure to come back up and see me."

"I'll do that Uncle Balis," she said.

Uncle Balis rose without a word and went inside. He came back with his good arm clutched to his chest and slowly held out his thick weathered palm full of chestnuts to Phyllis. "For your payment," he said.

"Thank you, Uncle Balis," Phyllis said. Scooping the chestnuts into her hand, she put them into her pocket.

Uncle Balis sat back down on his porch and watched as the women mounted their horses and rode on up the mountain. Claire could see him still nodding and smiling to himself. She wondered if he would be sitting there patiently waiting for someone else to come by so he could tell his story again.

The trail was rocky but dry and the day was slowly warming. They decided to stop at a clearing to rest and eat the meager meal they had brought along. Claire stretched her limbs and checked around a nearby boulder for snakes before sitting down out of the shadows where the air was not as chilled. Several chipmunks upset by their arrival ran off chattering their protest. Only one ran back to glare at them and then with a flick of its tail disappeared over the side of a log. Phyllis laid out their dinner of boiled eggs and apples. They eagerly ate their well earned dinner, dividing Uncle Balis' chestnuts between them.

The leaves of autumn, which had been bright and rich with color, lay in layers around them, the magnificent reds and golds now faded to hues of brown and tan. The mountains once so brilliant with color rose up through the mist in gossamer shades of purple and indigo. The sun broke suddenly through the clouds triumphantly declaring its power as it sent out beams of light on the peaks and valleys below.

Claire sketched the scene in her mind. She had saved one last chestnut and she put it in her pocket thinking to eat it later on the ride back. Lying back on the rock, she looked up through the trees to the sky and felt her head spin as the clouds moved overhead and the earth seemed to shift beneath her. She wanted to hold on to the smell of the musty leaves and the blue gray of the sky forever.

Before applying to teach at the Settlement school, she had been offered a position as a clerk in a Chicago office. It occurred to her that she could be sitting in an office filing papers and taking dictation. Instead of having her lunch under an open sky, she could be eating in a greasy diner if she could afford it on her eighteen dollar a week salary. She could be spending her evenings in a room-and-board hotel for women, washing out her hosiery in a basin to be worn again the next day.

A sudden rustling in the woods brought her bolt upright. "What was that," she whispered. The crunching of leaves and snapping of twigs grew louder before it moved away growing more faint. "Do you think it could be a bear?"

Phyllis sat calm and unruffled by the sound. "It is late in the season for a bear." she said confidently. "Besides I think we are the only ones foolish enough to be on this trail today."

Claire laughed heartily and felt the ache in her sore and bruised body. The thought amused her, that her mother had been against her going to Chicago for fear it was too dangerous and unseemly for a young woman alone. Instead, here she was riding a horse up a rocky trail and wondering if the sound she heard could be a bear.

It had shocked her to learn soon after coming to the school that her application had almost been rejected because it was thought she might not be constitutionally suited for such difficult work done in such a Spartan place. Indeed, she would not have been the first to flee from the harshness of teaching in the Great Smoky Mountains and the school had learned to choose its candidates wisely.

She felt a certain grace in having been chosen and now she could not imagine a more unpardonable sin than not being fully awake to the joy of it. Holding her arms up to the sky, she threw back her head and smiled. When she came to herself, Phyllis was staring at her. She gave her a languid smile. Phyllis, who appeared so undaunted by the ride and so serious in her work, gave her a telling look that said she too was aware of the adventure.

After three frustrating hours, they topped the hill and came to a clearing where there stood a one room log cabin with a falling down fence surrounding a bare and muddy yard. Pigs and chickens alike scattered as they rode up. It was the most unkempt place Claire had ever seen.

"The higher up the more hardscrabble the life," Phyllis said laconically as she dismounted and tied Dan to a post.

Claire followed her lead and without hesitation they made their way to the ragged porch propped precariously on stones. A man sat on the porch idly rocking.

"Howdy," the man said as though he saw strangers regularly.

"Mr. Levi Wilson?" Phyllis questioned.

"That'd be me," the man nodded.

"Howdy, Mr. Wilson, I am Miss Phyllis the school nurse. I have come to see about your boy Luther."

"Doc said you'd be here. My woman has been lookin' for you."

A ragged barefoot boy flung open the door and sent a chicken squawking from beneath the porch. He led them inside the tiny cramped cabin rank with the smell of wood smoke and cooking. The room was filled with beds and the walls were covered with old newspapers. A table sat cluttered with dirty dishes and pots. There was no room to move and the air was so thick and heavy Claire could feel it on her skin. She dared not look around but cast a glance here and there. One window in the cabin was dirty and let in scant light. The other window boarded up from the outside was missing its panes of glass.

Five small children stood around like shadows all knees and elbows in their thin clothes. Their innocent eyes, big and full of curiosity, followed every move the women made.

An old woman sat next to the fireplace spitting tobacco into a scant smoky fire. Her head bobbed as she rocked and she hummed softly to herself. She seemed not to notice the women.

On the other side of the fireplace was a double bed. A woman humped up on the end of the bed gently patted a pile of stained threadbare covers. Her face was as drained of color and weary as the tiny face that poked out from the ragged quilt.

"Mrs. Wilson, I am Phyllis the nurse and this is Miss Claire."

"Call me Arlie," the woman said her voice raspy. Getting up from the bed, she picked nervously at her tattered apron. "We have been lookin' for ya to come."

"We came as soon as we could," Phyllis said. "The rain kept us away."

"You didn't have no trouble gettin' here?" Arlie asked.

"No trouble," Phyllis said cordially. "Uncle Balis gave us directions."

Arlie nodded.

The children gathered around and began to all talk at once and Levi Wilson soon joined them. The woman by the fireplace, who had not been introduced, strained her head toward them to catch the conversation. Occasionally, she called out when she could not hear what was said and Arlie would repeat it to her. They were eager to hear the news from Gatlinburg and were full of questions.

Although they had made the long trip to see the child, Phyllis socialized as though she had all day, unhurriedly answering their questions before she finally asked about her patient. As much as her gift lay in her training as a nurse, it was surpassed even more by her genuine kindness and her ability to gain the trust of her patients.

Claire took the children aside and gave them each a piece of hard candy she carried in her pocket. They ate it greedily; licking their lips long after it was gone. Then she taught them a rhyming game while Phyllis examined the boy. The children were dirty, their hair matted and uncombed but their eyes sparkled with delight at their own cleverness as they took turns reciting. In the dim light of the cabin, amidst the worst grinning poverty Claire had yet seen in the mountains, she recalled Shades words to her when she had praised Emily's artistic gift. He had simply said, "God did not stop handing out his gifts when he got to the mountains."

When Phyllis found her patient to be much improved, the family begged them to stay for supper and spend the night saying 'we don't get many visitors'. Phyllis graciously declined saying she had other folks waiting for her back at the school who needed nursing.

Claire gathered the children on the front porch and took their picture. Looking through the lens of the camera, they looked small and far away. She felt the need to do something for them but she had nothing to offer, having given away the last of the candy. Then the children hugged the women all around and waved their goodbyes. Abby the smallest among them jumped off the porch and followed them, stopping when she got to the fence to call a haunting good-bye.

Claire looked back overwhelmed by the longing in the girl's eyes. What mysteries lay behind that longing, she wondered. Could this little girl's hopes and dreams be so different from what Claire had felt as a child? Was she not learning that in the heart of every child a tiny seed of dreams lay like an acorn looking for fertile ground?

She rode her horse back to where the child stood. Taking something from her pocket, she leaned down. The girl held up her tiny hand and in it, Claire placed the last chestnut.

Chapter 13

It was nearing dusk by the time the women rode up the main street of Gatlinburg, their horse's hoofs making sucking sounds in the roads muddy ruts. Intending only to bathe and fall into bed, they were greeted by Tessie running down the steps calling their names. Wearily, they led the horses to the shed, unsaddled their mounts and gave them a bit of hay.

"I thought you would never get back," Tessie said.

"Tessie, we had the most amazing adventure," Claire said. "The trail was simply horrid, if it could be called a trail."

"You must tell me all about it later," Tessie said breathless. "Doctor Milo has come early from Knoxville and he has brought another doctor with him."

"Two doctors," Phyllis said. "That is wonderful news. We will be able to examine twice as many children tomorrow."

"Yes, they are waiting at the hotel to take supper with us. You must get cleaned up right away."

Claire and Phyllis looked at each other, their clothes covered in mud and laughed. As tired as they were from their journey, they hurriedly washed their face and hands, changed clothes, and headed out to the Mountain View Hotel.

Half-a-dozen boarders joined the teachers at two long tables at the hotel dining room. Dr. Milo, an older man who had been coming to the mountains to work for years, introduced his new associate, "This is Dr. Henry Wyatt. He has recently graduated from the Medical School at Syracuse University and has come to join me in my practice."

As the introductions went around the table, Claire could hardly concentrate she felt so tired and nearly faint with hunger. She looked at the tables laid out with fried chicken, beans, corn, baked apples and hot biscuits and almost groaned aloud.

Evelyn Bishop and Phyllis sat down across from Dr. Milo and began immediately discussing their plans for the next day. "I am hopeful that the inoculations and examinations that we will do tomorrow at the school might someday be done on a regular basis in a permanent clinic." Phyllis explained.

"Your dedication is most admirable, Miss Higinbotham," said Dr. Wyatt.

"Thank you Dr. Wyatt but I am simply doing the task at hand."

"With great vision and energy," Dr. Milo added.

Phyllis would have none of their praise. "In my short time here, I have seen whole families suffering from pellagra born of a poor diet of endless starches. Typhoid is a constant threat from the crowded living conditions. The mothers and their babies get no care at all. Hookworm and trachoma plague the children."

"Yes, Dr. Milo had explained as much to me," Dr. Wyatt said, braving the assault.

"Then perhaps, I might persuade you to set up office hours once a month in Gatlinburg, Dr. Wyatt."

"Now, Phyllis," Dr. Milo said intervening, "please give the man time to eat his supper before you start twisting his arm. You will find him much more pliable on a full stomach."

They all laughed and finally, when Claire thought she could not endure her hunger much longer, Evelyn announced that they should eat while the food was still hot. Claire and Tessie were seated across from Dr. Wyatt. Two of the men sharing the table were boarding at the hotel and they began to discuss the fishing trip they had planned into the mountains the next day. Dr. Wyatt listened politely, nodding occasionally.

The doctor was dressed in a dark double-breasted suit, his blond hair well groomed and stylish, his soft hands scrubbed clean. Claire studied his clear blue eyes, the sensual turn of his jaw and the way he tilted his head as the men talked. She thought him wholly unsuited for the work he had come to do, then quickly felt ashamed realizing how others must have viewed her in a similar fashion.

"We are looking forward to catching brook trout," said the older man who had introduced himself as William. "I understand they are native to this area but that rainbow trout have been added to the streams in recent years."

"That sounds most enjoyable," Dr. Wyatt said. "I look forward to trying my hand at fishing some day."

"We have hired a guide to take us into the mountains for a few days of hiking and camping," the other man, whose name was Joe, added.

"A sensible idea," Dr. Wyatt said politely.

"Mr. Huff has arranged it all. Our wives will be joining us at weeks end to go horseback riding in the mountains," Joe said. "They are not so much for camping."

Claire thought about what Shade had said about strangers coming to roam the land he called home. These men, she thought, would go home and tell their friends about their trip. Next year they would be back and others would join them.

She watched as a tall, slim man walked to their table and pulled out a chair.

"Good evening, I am Jim Thompson," he said by way of introduction. "Just in from Knoxville."

"Please won't you join us Mr. Thompson," Evelyn said. "Are you up here to take photographs?"

"Yes, ma'am," he said sitting down. "I'll be up by daylight to head out."

"Mr. Thompson is a professional photographer," Evelyn explained.

"And you have come to photograph the mountains," Claire said.

"Yes, I come regularly. I've been up here prowling around these mountains for over five years and I've not covered them by half."

"What is it you hope to capture Mr. Thompson?" Dr. Wyatt asked.

"Why, the beauty of these mountains," he said, astonishment in his voice. "I take photographs because words fail me, although my friends say I never quit babbling about the beauty of this place. Every time I blaze a new trail up here, I never fail to see something that could take a man's breath away."

"I envy you the adventure, Mr. Thompson. I too have found these mountains to be breathtaking," Claire found herself saying. She felt suddenly shy in the saying of it, as though she had given away a secret about herself.

"You are not alone," Mr. Thompson said kindly. "Have you been to the top of Mount LeConte yet?"

"No, I am afraid I have not yet had that opportunity."

"Oh, you shouldn't leave the Smoky Mountains until you have seen the sun rise and set on the mountaintop," he said enthusiastically.

"Then I shall make a point of it, Mr. Thompson," Claire said.

"There's been talk of trying to preserve this land, you know. Turn these mountains into a national forest or even a national park," he said.

"What an intriguing idea," Claire said, pondering the thought. She wondered what such a thing would mean to the people who called the Great Smoky Mountains home.

"Do you think that might happen?" Dr. Wyatt asked.

"Well, I'd like to see it happen, but until it does, I plan on capturing it with my camera."

Claire thought of the simple sketches she had done and wondered again how anyone could capture the beauty of what she saw around her. Dr. Wyatt turned suddenly and smiled at her as though he had been reading her mind. She held his gaze and smiled back but she drew the veil over herself using her reserve to put some distance between them. The doctor turned aside but not before she caught the puzzled look in his eye.

Dr. Wyatt lifted the platter of fried chicken and offered it graciously to Tessie who blushed crimson and took a small piece.

Claire, whose ravenous appetite was usually outpaced only by Tessie's, glared at her. Then she took the platter and put two pieces on her plate. Taking something from each bowl as it was passed, she continued to fill her plate, eating and eating until the moment came when she felt full enough to sit back and catch her breath. She had been vaguely aware of the conversations going on around her but it had been a distant drone in her ear. Tessie nudged her bringing her back from her reverie. She looked up from her plate to realize the doctor was speaking to her.

"I understand you attended Wellesley, Miss Blackburn. You must be quite exceptional," he said.

For a moment, she was too affronted to reply. "Truly, Dr. Wyatt, I assure you I am not," she said.

Dr. Wyatt found himself floundering, his discomfort showing in the tightness of his shoulders. "I merely meant that Wellesley is a fine school with very stringent requirements," he said with a conciliatory shrug.

"I am sure if more women had the opportunity they might prove themselves more than capable."

"You are undoubtedly right Miss Blackburn. Perhaps, now that women have the right to vote, you will throw out the cads who have kept women from their rightful place in this world."

"You mock me, Dr. Wyatt?"

He studied her like a man who wished he might leave the room and re-enter by another door. He smiled at her good-naturedly as he scanned her face looking for leniency. "Indeed, I would never," he said humbly. "My sister Victoria has been a tireless suffragette."

"In fact it would be my great delight to use my vote against those who have opposed women," she said trying to be offhand and airy. She felt contrite that she had reacted so unpleasantly to the doctor.

"Miss Tessie was telling me about the wonderful things being done here at the school," he tried again.

"Yes, I am afraid I can't take much credit as I have only been here a short time," Claire said, "but I am finding my time here most rewarding."

"She tells me also that you are an artist."

"Tessie has spent far too much time talking about me, I see," she said. "It is she who has done wonders with the children."

"Being so close to Boston, you must have visited the Art Museum there," he said undeterred.

"Yes, I did on occasion go to Boston," she said politely. "It is a lovely city." She had spent hours in the Fine Arts Museum wandering the rooms, lost in the beauty. As her friends had chattered endlessly, excited to be in the city, she had studied the architecture and the scenes that unfolded around her on the streets.

"I was in Boston recently to visit a friend who was a fellow classmate at the university. We saw a wonderful performance of the *Merchant of Venice*. My friend is a great fan of the theater."

"Tessie loves the theater, don't you," Claire said trying to draw the conversation away from her. She was uncomfortable with the doctor's attentions and she felt bad for Tessie who was so obviously smitten.

"Then you both must come to Knoxville," he said not waiting for Tessie's reply. "I am sure I can find suitable entertainment. In fact, I know just the thing," he said excitedly. "You must come next month for the grand opening of the Riviera Theater on Gay Street. They will have live Wurlitzer music and it should be quite an event."

Tessie looked at Claire pleadingly.

"It's true I haven't had the opportunity to visit Knoxville," Claire said.

"Then be my guest," he said.

"That is very kind of you Dr. Wyatt," Tessie said answering for them both.

"Then I shall make the arrangements," he said. "I am living with my sister, Victoria, and her husband in a lovely house on Luttrell Street until I can arrange for a place of my own. It is quite adequate and I believe you would be most comfortable during your stay. My sister would see that you were properly chaperoned."

"Your sister would have no objections?" Claire asked.

"I think you two would have much in common," the doctor said with a wry grin. "Her husband spends a great deal of his time teaching at the university. She would welcome the company. You can catch the street car up town and visit the shops and perhaps have a bite at one of the cafes."

"That sounds delightful," Tessie said. Her green eyes sparkled iridescent with excitement.

"I would welcome the company too, of course," he said graciously. "I am afraid I have been so busy I haven't had time to get to know many people in Knoxville."

They talked on about the theater, the arts and the books they had read and Claire realized how much she had missed such conversations.

"What made you decide to set up practice in Knoxville, Dr. Wyatt?" Tessie asked at last.

"I think perhaps I read too much *Robinson Crusoe* and the *Leatherstocking Tales* as a child," he said. "I am afraid they made a conventional life seem too boring."

Claire laughed despite herself. "Surely, that can not be your only reason," she said. She found herself relaxing and thinking she had judged the doctor too quickly as was so often her way. After all, he had been most gracious, entertaining them all night with stories and world events and until questioned saying little of his own life.

"My sister had some influence on my decision," he said. He looked at Claire pointedly as though to say indeed you misjudged me. "My sister and her husband spent time in China as missionaries," he went on looking back to Tessie. "It was a year filled with hardship and suffering. What she bemoaned the most however was that there was great sickness that she felt helpless to do anything. When she visited the hospitals there was very little care being given and all she could do was bring a moment of kindness."

"Your sister sounds like a lovely person," Tessie said.

"She impressed upon me that compassion without true service has little meaning. When Dr. Milo contacted me about his efforts here in the mountains, I felt drawn to that work," he said. "I hoped this would be a place where I might be of service."

"From what Phyllis has told us, you should have quite the opportunity tomorrow," Claire said.

"Last year they tell me there was an outbreak of diphtheria," Phyllis said joining the conversation. "Mothers had to stand by helplessly and watch their children suffer when there is a vaccine available."

"I understand your distress Miss Higinbotham," the doctor said kindly. "If one has ever seen a case of diphtheria, the thick gray covering in the back of the throat, the difficulty breathing, it can be most unpleasant."

"I have seen much worse things, Doctor Wyatt. My distress comes from the fact that it is so unnecessary. That is why I am so delighted that you are here to help."

"Then I look forward to tomorrow," he said.

"Then we had best be getting our rest," Phyllis announced unceremoniously.

As they made their way out of the hotel, Doctor Wyatt offered to walk them back to their cottage but Phyllis would not hear of it, saying the doctors needed their rest and that the women would be perfectly fine. The disappointment showed on Tessie's face and Claire could not wait to tease her.

"You like him," she said as soon as they were alone. They sat on the stairs leading up to their rooms as they had many times chatting about their day before retiring for the night.

"No, I don't," Tessie said.

"Yes, you do. That's why you didn't eat your supper."

"You like him too," Tessie countered.

She gave a laugh of mild exasperation. The doctor had found her attractive, there was no doubt about that, but she had done everything possible to deflect his interest away from her. "He was very nice and quite the gentleman," she said, "but I am not interested in him as a suitor."

"I don't think there is much danger, the way you treated him."

"Whatever do you mean? Was I unkind?" Claire said shocked by the accusation.

"You seemed offended by his every word," Tessie said.

She examined her reaction to Doctor Wyatt and realized it was something she had done instinctively to every man she had met since turning sixteen. The armor she cloaked herself in was worthy of a medieval knight. Hundreds of interlocking habits were painstakingly woven together to form her shield against an early marriage. Like the knights of old, her armor could be cumbersome and kept her at a distance.

"You are right, Tessie. I fear I was a bit abrupt," she said. "I suppose I was just tired from the long day."

"Are you truly not interested in him," Tessie said.

Claire looked at the longing in Tessie's eyes. "Truly," she said emphatically.

Tessie hugged her as though that settled the matter. "Oh thank you Claire," she said.

"Whatever are you thanking me for Tessie?"

"Well, I just know you could have anyone you choose and that Dr. Wyatt would never look at me if he could have you."

"Don't be silly Tessie. Any man would be fortunate to have such a wonderful woman in his life."

"Do you think so Claire?"

"Believe me when I say, you would not want a fool who could not see that."

"Claire you are the dearest friend."

"And you Tessie."

"I am sorry I said you were unkind to Dr. Wyatt."

Claire laughed. "You are forgiven."

"I suppose we had better go to bed if we are to get up early," Tessie whispered dreamily.

"I think I shall just sit here a moment more," Claire said. "I think I am almost too tired to sleep."

"Go to bed before you get too cold," Tessie said gently.

"Yes mother," Claire joked.

When she was alone in the dark, moonlight streaming through the window, it came to her that she had never put on her armor for Shade. Could it be because she had never considered him an appropriate suitor? He was after all older than her by several years and a recent widower.

She had caught Shade making sidelong glances at her but there had never been anything untoward in his looks. She thought her presence simply sent him into confusion as though he did not know what to make of her. She was as much an interloper in his life as the tourist who had come to fish the mountain streams. No, his interest in her revolved around his daughter and she was not willing to construe his actions as anything more. Even if sometimes, the words he said to her echoed in her thoughts and came back to her at odd times of the day.

Still it surprised her the way she had hoarded her thoughts of him. She had never written of him to her sister, describing him in letters the way she had talked of other mountain people. She had not shared her thoughts of him with Tessie and giggled over them as she had done about Doctor Wyatt. She had kept her thoughts of him to herself.

Struggling up the stairs, she undressed and fell heavily into bed. Watching the moonbeams play upon her quilt, she thought of the mountains outside drawing near and cradling her gently. After a time, she let go and fell into a dreamless sleep.

Chapter 14

The schoolchildren had been instructed for weeks to take word of the clinic home to their parents. Phyllis had spoken in the local churches letting them know what was to take place, spending a great deal of time breaking down their fear of new ways, and convincing the stoic mountaineers to accept the help that was offered. Still everyone had been nervous that morning, unsure if the community would come out to support the clinic.

As it turned out, their fears had been unfounded and from the moment the doors opened, it had been a busy day, with only a short break for a noon meal that they had eaten quickly in one of the classrooms. Many of the schoolchildren came alone but just as many of the parents came bringing along younger children. Evelyn stood at the door greeting people and directing them to Claire who wrote down names and whatever health information she could glean from them. The work was slow and complicated, for Claire did not want to appear to pry, and wanted the families to feel welcome and at ease. Many of the children had never seen a doctor and they were especially unsure about getting a shot.

Frannie sat next to Claire taking on the job as her assistant, getting her freshly sharpened pencils and drinks of water when needed. She had simply shown up that morning, her cotton dress pressed and her face scrubbed clean, eager to be a part of the clinic. Her eyes were bright behind her new glasses and her brow furrowed with the seriousness of her work as she straightened papers and put the desk in order.

"Frannie you are such a help," Claire said. "Perhaps you will be a nurse someday."

"No ma'am," Frannie said decisively. "I am going to be a teacher like you and Miss Tessie."

"Why Frannie that is wonderful," Claire said. She could not resist the child's naturally earnest nature. Frannie was indeed meant to be a teacher, Claire thought. She was an industrious worker, always helping the younger ones with their lessons, staying behind to clean the blackboards or sweep out the classroom.

The clinic was set up in the center room of the school. Dr. Milo and Agnes were handling the boys as they received their examinations. Dr. Wyatt and Tessie were handling the girls and the babies. A screen had been put up between them to provide some privacy for the girls. After their examinations, Nurse Phyllis was giving inoculations for diphtheria and smallpox.

That morning at the teachers cottage while they had been getting ready, Tessie had volunteered to be Dr. Wyatt's assistant. Claire had laughed and then felt ashamed, apologizing when tears welled up in her friend's eyes.

"You just caught me on a particularly homesick day," Tessie said, by way of explanation.

"Well of course you are homesick," Claire said consoling her. "You have been away from home a long time."

"My younger sister is getting married," she confided at last.

"Is that not good news," Claire inquired.

"I should be the one to marry first," Tessie insisted.

Claire, never having been in love, could not fathom the suddenness and depth of her friend's infatuation with Dr. Wyatt. But she understood that her sister's sudden engagement had upset the proper order of things.

There had been little time for socializing since the clinic opened. Dr. Wyatt had removed his suit coat and rolled up his sleeves as soon as they arrived. A lock of his blond hair had fallen onto his forehead giving him a boyish look as he focused on each case with surprising interest.

A number of young mothers had brought in babies already and Claire had been impressed with Dr. Wyatt's care and concern. He talked to the mothers regarding proper nutrition for both themselves and their babies. Gently, he brought up the need for cleanliness for the babies health and their own.

Outside the weather was cool but crowds of folks gathered using any excuse to socialize. Some brought their children from several miles for the opportunity to have them examined by a doctor. At one point, during a rush, even Claire had taken a turn at dressing small cuts and scrapes, the children giving themselves over willingly to her attention. At times, she winced in empathy as she disinfected the wounds but the children's pain seemed dulled by their curiosity.

As the afternoon wore on the crowds began to thin. The doctors were planning to be done by three o'clock so they could make the journey back to Knoxville before dark. Claire had heard Phyllis remark earlier that she had inoculated eighty children so far that day. As successful as the day had been so far, they were all growing weary.

At two o'clock when the door opened, Claire looked up to see Shade and Emily. Evelyn greeted them graciously and they stood talking. Claire realized that she felt inordinately happy to see Shade. She had not seen him since running into him on the mountain. For reasons that escaped her, she was eager to tell him about her ride on horseback up to Sugarlands. Her need to show him that she was getting out into the community and meeting people, that she was making an effort to understand his world, made her feel like a silly schoolgirl. Still she was delighted when he finished talking to Evelyn and headed her way.

Emily came bouncing up to the desk her blue eyes alight, her cheeks still rosy from the cold. "Miss Claire, guess what I did today," she said.

"Hello Emily," Claire said smiling. "It's good to see you."

"Did you guess?"

"Well, let me think," Claire said, chin in hand. "Did you go fishing?"

Emily shook her head.

"Did you play a game?"

Again, Emily shook her head.

Claire looked to Shade for help.

"That's enough Emily. Tell Miss Claire what you did today."

"Me and Pa went to Pigeon Forge in a wagon," Emily said proudly.

"I had to take a load of tan bark," Shade said by way of explanation. "I had a notion to be back before now. Are we too late?"

"You are just in time. The doctors are still here but they will be leaving soon. Let me just ask you a few questions about Emily." Claire wrote down the information Shade gave her. When they finished, he seemed hesitant to leave.

"Ma said she will be expecting you up again for supper soon," he said.

"That's very nice of her. Tell her I am sorry that Tessie and I have not had a chance to get back. We had a lovely time."

"I'll tell her," he said still hesitating.

"I suppose Emily should go ahead. The doctor will be waiting," she said.

"I wanted to tell you," he said, shifting his weight from one foot to the other. "I talked to Aunt Lydia. She said to bring you up anytime."

"Why Shade, that's wonderful of you," Claire said. "I look forward to it."

"You'll like Aunt Lydia," he said, more confidently. "She's a character."

"I have heard so many stories about her. I can't wait to see if they are true," she said chuckling.

Emily looked at them, impatience showing on her face.

"Are you ready to see the doctor Emily?" Claire asked.

"I need to ask you something," she said.

"All right," Claire said.

"Does it hurt to get a shot?" Emily said with an uncharacteristic straightforwardness.

Claire thought Emily sounded like Granny Kate questioning her about a piece of mischief. Struck by how the girl had blossomed since starting school, she tried not to let the smile show on her face. "Why Emily, you are one of the bravest young girls, I know. Didn't I see you bait your own hook when you were fishing?"

"That's easy," Emily said.

"I could never do that," Claire said.

Emily's eyes grew big as she thought it over. "Really?"

"Yes, really."

Emily looked doubtful. "Have you ever had a shot?"

"Oh yes, I have had many shots."

As Emily stood pondering the notion, Levi Wilson came in the door with his wife and family in tow. For an instance, Claire feared that the young boy they had gone to see had died of pneumonia. She held her breathe as Mrs. Wilson herded the children toward the desk.

"Mrs. Wilson, how nice to see you. How is your son?" "He's some better," she said flatly. "My ma is staying with him."

"I am so glad to hear it."

I brung you my younguns to have the doctor take a look at 'em."

"I am so glad you did, Mrs. Wilson," Claire said sincerely.

"I buried two younguns already," she said without expression. "I've growed afeared of losin' these little ones too. I believe you are good women and mean right by folks. If I can do somethin' to help these ones, I want to do it."

Claire was touched by the woman's courage and the love of a mother. "Let me write down the children's names and the doctor will see them."

"I don't want no needles," Levi Wilson said rushing the desk. "That's against Gods way."

Mrs. Wilson cowered for a moment and then regained her voice. "Levi we come all this way to have the younguns took care of."

Claire was unsure what to do. She did not want to step between a husband and wife.

"Levi why don't you come outside with me," Shade said. "We need to talk." He took the man by the shoulder and led him outside. "Emily," he called back, you do as Miss Claire says."

Emily looked at Claire and then at the scraggly band of Wilson children. She studied Abby still barefoot in November. Her bones stuck through her thin dress like wire and a tremble shook her body.

Suddenly, Emily rolled up her dress sleeve and stuck her arm out to Claire.

"I'm ready for my shot, Miss Claire."

"Why thank you Emily. The doctor will be glad for your help."

She walked with Emily to Dr. Wyatt's station. As she looked back, she could see Abby rolling up her sleeve exposing her birdlike arm in imitation of Emily. She gave Emily's shoulder a grateful squeeze. Emily looked up, her lips pressed bravely together, and then she took Tessie's hand.

When Claire had taken care of all the children, she returned to find Mrs. Wilson leaning against the wall. "You look pale," she said.

"A bit tired, I reckon," she said.

Claire suspected the woman might be pregnant again but said nothing. She brought a chair and then instructed Frannie to get a cup of coffee for Mrs. Wilson.

"Levi's not a bad man," Mrs. Wilson explained.

"Why, of course not," Claire said.

"My folks thought I had gone crazy when I married him and they said as much," she said without humor. "Truth is he's not above workin' me to death but it's not more than I've knowed all my life. I've worked like a grown man since I was big enough to lift an axe or a hoe. I want somethin' better for my younguns."

"You know the school is planning to teach weaving classes soon. If you are interested there might be a way you could sell what you make to earn enough money to send the children to school."

"I recollect my Granny Elma at the loom," she said.

"Then you might like to weave," Claire said cheerfully.

"I aim to learn," she said the decision having been made. "I am right tired of farming."

"As soon as I know more, I'll come up and tell you all about it."

Mrs. Wilson sat with her hands in her lap. The skin of her hands was as dark and wrinkled as tree bark, the knuckles red and swollen. Still she nodded her head determinedly.

After the last of patients left and the Wilson clan had been sent on their way, the doctors and teachers stood on the school steps recounting the day's victories.

"I think you can be most pleased by the turnout today, Miss Higinbotham," Dr. Milo said.

"I still hope to have the entire community vaccinated for typhoid before spring, Dr. Milo," Phyllis said.

"Not one to rest on your laurels, I see," he said good-naturedly.

"I hope to see you again too, Dr. Wyatt," Phyllis said.

"I saw a number of cases of malnutrition among the babies. I think that is something that must be attended to," Dr. Wyatt said.

Phyllis nodded as though this was a revelation to her but Claire could see that she was pleased to have engaged the doctor's interest.

Shade came bounding up the steps.

"I want to thank you Mr. Morgan," Claire said. "I was at a loss as to what to do with Mr. Wilson."

"Levi's a good man," said Shade.

"Oh forgive me," Claire said. "Let me introduce you to Dr. Milo and Dr. Wyatt."

The men shook hands.

"Andy Huff mentioned your name," Dr. Wyatt said. "You've worked as a guide on occasion."

"I help him out now and again, when he needs me," Shade said.

"He tells me you are an expert on these mountains. I wonder if you might take me fishing sometime."

"I'd be happy to do it."

"I warn you, I've not had a lot of experience fishing. I've spent the last few years with my head in a medical textbook."

"I reckon the fish won't know that," Shade said with a grin.

Claire snickered, then coughed, and cleared her throat when she realized she was the only one. Dr. Wyatt gave her a concerned look, which she waved away.

"Yes well, it might be spring before I get the opportunity," Dr. Wyatt went on.

"I ain't aiming on going no place," Shade said.

"I am afraid we don't have time to tarry if we are to make it home before dark," Dr. Milo said.

"Of course, we can make our plans another time," Dr. Wyatt said.

Shade nodded.

"Tessie it was a delight working with you today," Dr. Wyatt said graciously.

Tessie turned a lovely shade of pink.

"And Claire, I'm looking forward to the two of you visiting Knoxville. I regret that I did not have time to see your paintings. Perhaps, I will have that opportunity at another time."

"Thank you, Doctor Wyatt."

"Please call me Henry. I will let you know about the theater arrangements."

"That would be delightful," she said graciously. She felt inexplicably uncomfortable discussing her visit in front of Shade. At the same time, she felt resentful for feeling she needed to explain.

Evelyn walked the doctors to their automobile. Claire, urged along by Tessie, walked down the steps to see the men off. Evelyn had brought along her camera. She had been taking pictures of the clinic all day. Herding them all together in front of the car, she took a picture. The women stood in the middle with the doctors on each end like bookends.

Evelyn urged them in closer and yet closer.

Claire gave a little start when she felt Dr. Wyatt's shoulder bump against her.

He blinked vaguely but said nothing by way of apology.

Then Claire offered to take a picture with Evelyn in the group. By the time they finished the air was growing cold and Claire rubbed her arms to warm them. "It's getting chilly," she remarked.

The doctors nodded and took that as a sign that they were at last free to go. The women watched until the car was out of sight before they turned to go. It had been a long but gratifying day. Claire was exhausted and eager to have it over. Tomorrow they would fall quickly back into their routines but for now, her mind was on a hot bath.

She wanted to remind Shade of his offer to take her to see Aunt Lydia and plan a day for their visit. When she looked back to the school steps where she expected to see Shade and Emily still standing, Claire realized they were gone. They had slipped away without saying good-bye.

Chapter 15

Henry Wyatt was waiting hat in hand, as the train pulled into the railway depot. Claire and Tessie watched as he searched the passenger cars for their faces. Setting off early that morning, they had been relieved that the weather had held. Tingling with excitement over their visit to Knoxville and laughing like schoolgirls, they watched as the miles fell away and so did all the responsibility of the past months.

Stepping down from the train, they took a moment to brush the wrinkles from their skirts. They waved to the doctor, who spotting them, raised his hand in greeting.

Looking genuinely pleased, he ran to greet them. He suddenly stopped short.

"Good day ladies," he said politely. "I hope you had a pleasant trip."

The rather shy, nervous man who stood before Claire seemed a sharp contrast to the confident doctor she had observed at the clinic. "Thank you, Dr. Wyatt, we had a fine trip," Claire said, "and how kind of you to meet us at the train."

"Please…call me Henry," he said stammering, "and I wouldn't hear of allowing you to find your own way."

"So good to see you again Henry," Tessie said shyly. "We have so looked forward to this visit."

"As have I, Miss Tessie," he said.

Tessie beamed.

Glancing at Claire, he smiled. Then recovering himself he said, "Please come this way." He motioned with his hand. "Dr. Milo was kind enough to loan me his automobile."

They climbed into the car, Claire careful to place Tessie up front next to the doctor. They waited while, at Henry's instructions, the porter carefully loaded their luggage. Then they set off in high spirits with Henry chatting amiably and pointing out the sights.

"My sister has planned a little gathering in your honor tonight," Henry said.

"Oh, I hope she hasn't gone to too much trouble," Tessie said genuinely.

"Not at all, just some friends from the university," he said dismissively. "I assure you, Victoria is quite looking forward to your visit. She could do with a bit of female companionship."

They pulled up to a large Victorian home painted a muddy brown and trimmed in burnt yellow. A broad porch ran across the front and as they came up the steps, a woman with silky blond hair and fair skin, who looked strikingly like Henry, greeted them at the door.

"Victoria our guests have arrived," Henry said jovially. "May I present Miss Tessie Morgan and Miss Claire Blackburn."

"Welcome to our home," Victoria said with a gentle smile.

Victoria hugged Tessie. "Tessie, Henry tells me you have a wonderful way with the children."

Tessie hugged her back like a lost friend returned home at last.

Then Victoria turned to Claire and embraced her. Claire gently returned the hug. Victoria was thin and her frame felt gossamer beneath her dress. It reminded Claire of how sturdy she had become over the past months of long walks and hard work.

"And Claire, I understand you are the artist," Victoria went on.

"Henry is being quite kind," Claire said. "And I can see where he gets it. You are most gracious to have us in your home."

"I have been so looking forward to your visit," Victoria said. "Henry has talked so much about his trip to the mountains and all the fine work the school is doing. I can't wait to hear more."

"Tessie and I would be delighted to tell you all about it," Claire said.

"For now, I am sure you would like a moment to rest. Please let me show you to your room while Henry brings in your things," she said.

As Victoria led them down the hall and up the stairs, Claire looked about the house. After the simplicity of the teachers' cottage, the rooms seemed crowded with furniture and bric-a-brac. The overheated air felt thick and heavy on her face.

"After you freshen up, would you join us for a cup of tea?" Victoria asked. "Dinner will not be for a few hours. Did you have anything to eat on the train?"

"Aunt Lizzie packed a small basket for us," Tessie said. "I have two apples left. Almost everyone in the mountains has an orchard and the apples are quite good if you would like to try them. I mean for you to have the basket as a gift when Henry, I mean Dr. Wyatt, fetches it from the car. The mother of some of our students made it and it is lovely."

"Tessie you are the dearest," Victoria said. "I shall keep the apples all to myself and eat them as I sit alone on my porch. It will be my little secret."

"Then I wish I had brought you a basketful," Tessie confessed.

Victoria smiled and patted Tessie's hand. "I was unaware you had relatives in Gatlinburg," she said.

Claire and Tessie looked at each other.

"Aunt Lizzie isn't related," Claire said. "She takes care of us all at the school. Everyone calls her Aunt Lizzie."

"Of course," Victoria said. She opened the door to a room at the end of the upstairs hall. "This will be your room. I hope you do not mind sharing. I haven't gotten around to furnishing all of the rooms yet."

"It's beautiful," Tessie exclaimed.

Victoria beamed. "Do you like it? I was not sure. I am not quite the hand at putting such things together. My husband's parents gave us most of our furniture. "

"It's perfectly charming," Claire said. The room was very different from the rest of the house. Done in pale rose wallpaper, with a soft pink coverlet, the room was light, airy, and altogether pleasant.

"Thank you, Claire. If you need anything, please just call. Henry will bring your things up any moment. I'll just go make us some tea."

Victoria made as if to leave. At the door, she paused. "Claire, Henry tells me he asked that you bring your portfolio."

"Yes, he was kind enough to express an interest in my work."

"I wonder if I might see your paintings. Could you bring them along to tea?"

"I would be delighted."

"Then I shall see you both shortly," said Victoria, closing the door as she slipped out.

Tessie threw herself across the bed. "Isn't this a lovely room? I always wanted a room like this growing up."

"It appears to be the only room in the house that looks like Victoria."

"Isn't she the nicest person," Tessie said.

"There is something in her face, don't you think, a slight sadness around the eyes that strikes me as lonely."

"Well, they haven't lived in Knoxville very long. Perhaps, she has yet to make a true friend. At least, she has Henry and now she has us," Tessie said cheerfully.

"It makes me appreciate the friendships I have formed at the school, the closeness I feel for you and the other teachers," Claire said. Suddenly she was keenly aware of her good fortune.

Tessie's face broke into a smile at Claire's confession.

Claire took off her shoes and the women sat cross-legged on the bed talking and laughing like the old friends they had become. They heard a light rap on the door. Claire went to open it. Their luggage sat in the hall. Henry had left it without a word.

They quickly put on their shoes, straightened their hair, brushed the wrinkles from their clothes, and went down to the parlor to join Henry and Victoria for tea. Claire reluctantly took along her paintings. Some of them were from her college years and they had faced the criticisms of her professors but a number of them were new. She was especially unsure of the ones that she had done of the Great Smoky Mountains.

"Do come join us," Henry said, jumping up as the women entered the room. He took Claire's portfolio and placed it on the buffet.

Claire and Tessie sat down just as Victoria brought in the tea. She put the tray on the butler table.

"Please let me help," Tessie said springing up.

They had hardly been served their tea when Victoria said, "Claire, I can't wait any longer. Won't you show us your paintings?"

"I hope you will not be disappointed," Claire said, honestly.

"Henry has told me all about them," Victoria said.

"But Henry has not seen my work," Claire protested.

"Tessie has championed your art. I trust her judgment," Henry said.

Claire gave Tessie, who seemed quite pleased with herself, a look of amazement. Even Tessie had seen only a few of her paintings and only after a considerable amount of pleading. Reluctantly, she opened her portfolio to reveal her canvases. She started with her oldest works.

"Why they are perfectly lovely," Victoria said.

"You paint in oil," Henry said, "was that a personal choice."

"You mean because oils are seen as a masculine choice," she answered.

"Yes," he said simply.

"It was a choice I was forced to make because of the general prejudice against women artists combined with the notion of watercolors as feminine. I thought if I were to be taken seriously, I would have to choose a serious medium."

Henry merely nodded and continued to go through each canvas studying each with a painstaking eye. Victoria stood next to him, her eyes catching his occasionally, but she said nothing. Claire thought she should be used to such scrutiny after all the years at school but she felt overly warm and lightheaded. Finally, they turned over the last of her old works to reveal the watercolors she had done of the Great Smoky Mountains.

Victoria took in a sharp breath. "Claire this is exquisite," she exclaimed.

"Truly remarkable," Henry murmured as he turned over another painting.

"Why did you never show these to me?" Tessie asked.

"Hardly more than working sketches," Claire protested, but she could not keep her pulse from racing at the words of praise.

"They are so delicate and subtle, so imbued with emotion," Victoria said. "Watercolor is the perfect medium for such illusive beauty. That's why you chose it, I assume?"

"Yes," was all Claire could say. Secretly, she delighted to have her vision confirmed. She remembered how she had almost been overwhelmed by the raw beauty of what she saw, inspired and yet timid in the face of what nature had provided. She had poured herself passionately into her paintings of the Great Smoky Mountains but always felt her talents fell short of the beauty before her. "You are indeed kind in your comments," she added at last.

"You must listen to Victoria," Henry insisted. "She has long been an admirer of art and she is not one given to false praise."

"I have no talent of my own but I can appreciate it in others," Victoria said. "This is what you were meant to do. Your watercolors convey your deep emotional response to the landscape. They have an authenticity and honesty not present in your earlier work. Do you agree Henry?"

"I do indeed," Henry said, smiling.

"Would you care if I showed these to some of my friends in New York?" Victoria asked.

Henry gave his sister a look of pure gratitude.

Claire's heart fell. She wanted Victoria's interest in her work to be genuine. She had no desire to take advantage of Henry's need to advance his affection for her. At the same time, she was particularly taken by Victoria's enthusiasm and how she seemed transformed by her discovery. "I am overcome by your generosity," Claire said genuinely, "but I could not ask it of you."

"You need not ask," Victoria said with a warm smile, "it would be my delight."

They barely had time to dress for dinner, Victoria having rushed off in a panic when she realized the time. After tea, Victoria had accompanied the women back to their room where they sat on the bed talking for some time. Victoria confessed that before her marriage she had dreamed of being a museum curator preserving works of art and arranging exhibitions. When Claire questioned her further, she said it had only been a childhood dream. Before she left, she confessed that their guests for the evening were all friends of her husband, Joseph, and that she found them somewhat stodgy and boring. Victoria admitted that she was finding her role as professor's wife profoundly less fulfilling than the time she had spent as a missionary. Her confessions brought on a guilty apology and then a round of laughter from them all as Victoria swore them never to divulge her secret.

Tessie stood before the mirror in a gray and pink stripped dress that set off her complexion perfectly. The soft fabric clung to her ample breast and the low-slung waist softened her hips, creating a stunning effect. Her hair, pulled up into soft curls, fell gracefully around her face. Still, she stood fidgeting with each lock.

"You look perfectly lovely," Claire said. "Henry will be beside himself."

Tessie blushed. "Claire you mustn't tease."

"Tessie, what am I to do with you," Claire said with obvious frustration.

Claire had quickly pulled on a simple navy silk hobble-skirted dress that came just above her ankles. She had not worn it since college. At her request, her mother had sent it to her for this occasion. Brushing out her hair, she tied it atop her head in an elegant twist. With a brief look in the mirror, she declared herself ready.

Tessie, holding her stomach and looking at her as though she might faint, let out a low moan of distress.

"What ever is the matter," Claire asked. "Are you ill?"

"You look so beautiful," Tessie said tearfully. "How can I ever hope to…?

"Oh no, I won't have it," Claire declared. "I've told you before that I'm not interested in the good doctor."

Tessie smiled nervously. "I've seen how he looks at you."

"Look as he might, it will do him no good."

"I see how he laughs at your humor or sits rapt at your conversation. How he looked at your paintings today. I could never be that interesting."

"Tessie, I am genuinely grateful to Henry for his interest in my work. Beyond that, I have done nothing to encourage him. I have done everything I could to avoid his attentions. You did in fact point that out after our dinner at the Mountain View Hotel. What more would you have me do?" Claire demanded.

Tessie looked at her befuddled. "I don't know," she said woefully, "I only know, he doesn't notice me," she said, tears welling up.

Claire put her hands on her hips and stamped her foot. "Tessie, you put me in mind of Martha Jane Riley 'foolish over a boy.' Stop pining around, we are here for a holiday and if you ruin it for us, I'll just be... well, I'll be upset."

Tessie looked stunned and then sniffled like an injured child. Tears began to leak from between her closed eyelids and her clenched mouth turned down at the corners.

Regretting her outburst, Claire took a handkerchief from her bag and dabbed at Tessie's swollen eyes. Then she hugged her. "I am sorry Tessie I didn't mean any of that. It is going to be all right. Victoria loves you already. That should stand you in good stead with Henry shouldn't it?"

Tessie nodded her head. She took the handkerchief, blew her nose, and gave a little congested cough.

"Now, promise you will go and have a good time. You have spent far too much time worried about Henry and you have forgotten all about how we are going shopping tomorrow and then to a picture show."

"All right," Tessie said. "I suppose I did get a little too worked up. But you must promise me something."

"Anything," Claire said.

"Promise me..." Tessie said, hesitating.

"What is it Tessie?"

"Promise you won't be quite so prickly with Henry or the other guest tonight," she blurted out.

"First you accuse me of being interested in the doctor and now you say I am prickly," Claire said throwing her hand into the air. "I am not being prickly. I merely like to state my opinion. I do not understand why it is not possible for a woman in nineteen-twenty to speak her mind. We are not living in the Dark Ages."

"I do so admire your passion and you are far more gifted than I at expressing yourself," Tessie said. "I know that I am not sophisticated enough to have quite your confidence in my opinions." She hesitated and looked away.

"Why do I feel there is more you wish to say," Claire said.

"Must you take everything so seriously?" Tessie said pleadingly. "Must you carry every argument to its furthermost conclusion to make your point?"

Claire started to counter Tessie and then she caught herself. She laughed aloud. "Yes, you might have a point," Claire said with a wry grin. "I do tend to believe that if only people could see the world through my eyes it would be a better place."

Tessie blinked repeatedly. "I didn't mean that Claire, truly I didn't. It's just that you sometimes act like people mean you ill when they do not. "

"Don't worry, Tessie. This is not the first time I have had my somewhat volatile personality pointed out to me but never so sweetly." Taking Tessie's chin in hand, she forced her to look her in the eyes. "I promise I won't be prickly if you will promise not to be all moony-eyed over Dr. Wyatt."

"Was I as obvious as that?" Tessie asked horrified.

Claire gave her a look.

"I promise," Tessie said contritely. "And I promise you can speak your mind all the way back to Gatlinburg."

"Oh I fully intend to do just that," Claire said. "But for now, let us see if we can't get you engaged to Dr. Wyatt before the evening is done."

"Claire you are the dearest friend," Tessie said blushing.

Taking her by the arm, Claire said sweetly, "Come along now, we have a party to attend."

Chapter 16

The men had been discussing prohibition for the past half-hour. Victoria's husband, Professor Joseph Chitwood, whose physical bulkiness was a match for his plodding speech, believed it was a necessity to bring sobriety to the masses that were in all respects unable to save themselves from their own excesses. Professor Widmer, an associate at the university agreed wholeheartedly, congratulating Chitwood on his wise and studied opinion. Mrs. Widmer, a member of the Women's Christian Temperance Union, in words barely above a whisper, voiced her gratitude for the families saved. Clasping her hands together piously, she spoke of the horrors wroth on innocent children by the many fathers carried away by the evils of alcohol.

It made Claire wish that she had paid more attention to the stories she had heard of the mountain people making their own alcohol. She wished that she had tasted moonshine so that she might have a scandalous story to tell. Then remembering her promise to Tessie, she politely kept her thoughts to herself.

The dining room was a dreadful red and dripped with drapes and scarves. The heavy ornate mahogany table was set with fine china upon which Victoria had served a miserably overcooked roast. Claire ate it with delight, thinking of the fun that had distracted the women as the roast met its fate.

At Victoria's request Claire sat next to Henry and across from Tessie. Seated next to Tessie was an assistant instructor to Professor Chitwood by the name of Daniel Parker. It worried Claire that his invitation had no doubt been issued to even out the table and provide an escort for Tessie. Looking somewhat ill at ease in his job, he had added little to the conversation.

"Miss Blackburn won't you and Miss Morgan please tell us more about your experiences at the Settlement school?" Daniel Parker inquired timidly.

His question, Claire thought, sounded as though he had been practicing it for sometime in his mind, hoping for his opportunity. "Tessie has been there almost two years," she said smiling at her friend.

"Really," Victoria said. "You must find it most rewarding."

"The children are so eager to learn and so grateful for each experience we bring to them," Tessie said her face glowing.

"Yes, Henry was most taken with his experience," Joseph said smugly.

"And what about you, Miss Blackburn? Have you found your time in the mountains to be rewarding?" Mrs. Widmer asked.

"Rewarding indeed," Claire said guarding her words. "I receive a great deal more than I give." She was not eager to share her experience with this group and not just because of her promise to Tessie but because it had come to mean too much to her. At times, the thought that she had done so little left her feeling profoundly sad. She had taught the children a few songs, read them stories and given them a glimpse into her world. For this, the children had given her their boundless enthusiasm and unguarded affection.

"I too found that my...our time in China," Victoria said hesitantly, "to be equally rewarding. It is true what you say, that I received far more than I had to give."

"Yes, well, it was our Christian duty," Joseph said with a wave of his hand, "Victoria's idea actually. As for myself, I find it strange that young women of your backgrounds would submit themselves to such discomfort and hardship. Do you not find it somewhat demanding on your constitution?"

Before Claire could answer, Henry spoke up.

"The day I went to the mountains, Claire had ridden all day on horseback up into the mountains where she assisted Nurse Higinbotham on her rounds," he said looking quite pleased.

Henry's defense of her had a kind of possessiveness that she resented. "Yes, Tessie and I find we are quiet capable of meeting the demands, don't we?" she said without looking for confirmation. "In fact, we have grown considerably stronger in our constitutions."

"But don't you think that Settlement schools are something of a waste of resources?" Professor Widmer countered.

"If by resources you mean the intellect and talents of women, I could not disagree more. Women have a valuable contribution to make to society, Professor Widmer. I think we proved that during the war. I happen to believe that women are uniquely suited to solve the many ills of this world."

"Perhaps," Professor Widmer mused, "but in this case would it not be more productive to bring mountain people to the cities? After all, this kind of pioneer existence might have been necessary to settle the country but it seems outdated. According to the United States census I think you will find that most people in America now live in cites."

Claire bit her tongue.

Tessie gave her a pained expression.

With a gentle nod, she acknowledged her plea.

"It has been the philosophy and intent of the Pi Beta Phi Settlement School from its inception to help the mountain people remain in their homes," Claire explained politely. "It is the purpose of the school to help enrich the lives of the mountain people not to disrupt them."

"Surely, you must realize that faced with the opportunity most mountain people would not continue to choose desperate lives of hardship, isolation and poverty," Professor Widmer went on.

"I realize no such thing, Professor Widmer," Claire said, her voice rising.

She could feel Tessie's kick under the table.

"I admit that I had a similar belief when I first came to the mountains," she said unable to stop herself. "I believed that mountain people were there because they were trapped by their own poverty and ignorance. I have since come to see that although some are poor and some are ignorant they are neither impoverished nor stupid. Many have very rich lives with the support of close families, they have the knowledge of generations passed down to them, and they have the natural beauty of the mountains that surrounds them."

"You and my Victoria have a great deal in common," Joseph said. "You both have romantic notions about life."

Victoria gave her husband a pained expression and then looked away.

"I do not think that a life of ones own choosing is a romantic notion," Claire said passionately.

Victoria's eyes grew wide and she gave Claire a satisfied smile. It made Claire wish she had the courage and conviction equal to her argument.

"Then what would you call a romantic notion, Miss Blackburn?" the professor challenged.

"I would call an evening at the theatre a romantic notion," Henry interjected, looking at Claire.

They all laughed as though he had made a great joke.

Tessie looked relieved.

Claire gave her a look of apology. She had surprised even herself in her defense of mountain life. She knew that deep in the ridges of the Great Smoky Mountains lay whole communities where people scratched out a living on worn out rocky soil. They lived out their lives in tiny crowded log cabins never attending a day of school or seeing a doctor. That was one kind of poverty, but she knew there was another kind of poverty, one of spirit that came from working in the cotton mills fourteen hours a day and going home to a small, crowded room in the city. Reminded of something Shade had said to her, "I've never had to starve or beg and when I wake up in the morning nobody tells me what I'm to do with my day," she realized that she was just beginning to understand why people would endure hardship to cling to a place they called home.

Underneath the table, Henry reached for Claire's hand and gave her a besotted look. Claire almost sighed aloud. He would not be the first man to mistake her need for independent thought as a wanton nature she did not possess. He would not be the first man to indulge her like a spoiled child but only because he mistook her outspokenness for lavish flirtation.

She felt censored by Henry's efforts to cut short her retort. Helpless to do anything without causing a scene she allowed his hand to rest on hers.

Henry went on to describe the gala opening planned the next evening for the new Rivera Theatre on Gay Street. "The theatre has a Wurlitzer organ and seats over one thousand people. It is being hailed as the shrine of the silent movie."

"It sounds delightful," Tessie said.

Claire gently slipped her hand from Henry's and reached for her water glass. "Will you be accompanying us Mr. Parker?" she asked.

Daniel Parker looked shocked to be included in the conversation and nonplussed for having asked the question that had precipitated such spirited discourse. He merely stared for some time and then recovering briefly, he said, "Dr. Henry was kind enough to invite me."

"Well, it will be wonderful to have you along," Claire said pointedly.

"I am a great fan of the movies," he added. "And of course, the company will be delightful."

"Yes, the movie is a DeMille entitled "Conrad in Search of his Youth," Henry said, searching her face like a child eager to please.

Even though Claire felt trapped between Henry's obvious affection for her and her loyalty to Tessie there was very little she could do about it at the moment. She would find a way to make her feelings clear to him before the holiday was over. He had after all, been perfectly kind and generous to her in planning such a delightful holiday, she had no desire to hurt his feelings. As for now, she was determined not to let it spoil her holiday.

The group soon found themselves caught up in a lively discussion of film, the men defending film as the new art while the women favored literature as true art and feared for its demise. Despite her promise, Claire found herself arguing forcefully for the many benefits to society that had come from great writing. Surely, even Tessie, she thought, could not begrudge her spirited opinions on reading. Still she was relieved when Victoria said she had a marvelous new game they had brought back from China called Mah Jong and she was desperate to teach it to them.

Later, when they fell into bed after midnight, Tessie and Claire agreed it had been a delightful evening. Tessie chatted excitedly going over the whole of the evening in detail until Claire thought they might be up all night. Soon, however, she heard Tessie's breathing even out to a gentle rhythm.

Claire found herself still awake, and thoughts of those first weeks she had spent in the mountains floated through her mind. How difficult it had been adjusting to the strangeness of her new world and feeling out of place with both the teachers and the mountain people. Here in this staid and refined home in Knoxville was a familiar place—one she could slip back into with ease. It occurred to her, as it had so many times before, that she could direct her life down a simpler path and it would all be so easy. Henry would eagerly accept her attention, she could settle down to a life of domesticity, and watercolors by the lake on Sunday afternoon as her husband read his medical journals. Her mother for once could be pleased with her and could talk to her friends about the privileged life her daughter was living. But she knew instinctively that she could not abide it. The thought took the air out of her and left her suffocating under its weight. She was not sure when it had come to her that in accepting such a life she would lose the better part of herself. All of her life it seemed.

The distant cry of a train whistle filled her dreams as she drifted off. It sounded just like the barred owl she had heard on Shade's farm up Roaring Fork. That night, the sound had been unfamiliar and frightening. Now it seemed to speak to her, calling her back to the mountains. Smiling to herself, she let the darkness take her there.

Chapter 17

The trolley dropped them off at the four hundred block of South Gay Street. The street was already alive with well-dressed shoppers. Automobiles competing with the trolleys crowded the street filling the air with a din of discordant sounds.

The day was chilly and Claire, Tessie and Victoria pulled their coats about them as they headed off. Claire was excited about buying gifts for her nephews for Christmas. Lenora had written that the boys were disappointed that she would not be coming home for the holidays. The school was planning a party for the children. The Pi Phi's were collecting toys and dolls from all over for the event. Claire was reluctant to miss the only Christmas she might share with the students.

They found a bookstore where they browsed reading aloud to one another from each new find. Finally, Claire bought a copy of *Hound of the Baskervilles* by A. Conan Doyle which she planned to read later to the children if she could get Evelyn to approve. If by chance, Evelyn found it wholly unsuitable, she added a copy of *Rebecca of Sunnybrook Farm* by Kate Wiggins to her purchases. Victoria bought the latest Zane Grey as a surprise for her brother. Tessie found a copy of *Little Kingdom Come* by Fox and tears welled up in her eyes at the memory of her mother reading it to the family when they were young.

At the stationers, Claire bought a sketchbook, some pencils and more ink and stationery for her letters home. For Evelyn and Agnes, she bought bookmarks and secretly for Tessie a new diary. Tessie wrote in her diary everyday and kept scrapbooks with pictures of all her students. Claire started out with grand hopes of keeping a diary when she had first arrived at the school but that dream had given way to days too filled with activities.

Victoria then took them to Millers Department store, which was filled with so many beautiful things, that Claire and Tessie did not know where to begin. They tried on new hats and scarves checking each selection out in the mirror. Claire found a chicory blue scarf, which she loved immediately and beyond reason. When she wrapped it around her neck and turned to show it off, Tessie and Victoria gasped, crying out that she "simply must have it." She had thought to save most of her money for gifts, but in the end, she could not deny herself this small indulgence.

Going on Tessie's advice, for Aunt Lizzie she bought some hose. For her nephews she bought Lincoln Logs and an Erector set. It was a big expense but she imagined their surprised faces when they opened the packages and she could not resist. She hoped it would make up for her not being there.

Tired from their morning of shopping but in high spirits, they walked up the street to the drugstore. They ordered root beers and sat watching the people as they hurried on their way.

"This has been such fun, Victoria," Tessie said.

"Yes, you must let us return the favor by visiting us in Gatlinburg," Claire said.

"Henry has asked me if I would like to come along to his next clinic," she confessed. "He is most eager to return but he tells me the roads may be impassable until spring."

"Yes, the roads can be quite horrid," said Tessie, with obvious disappointment.

"But spring is not so far away," Victoria said cheerfully.

"Then promise you will come in the spring."

"I have been thinking about…that is Henry has encouraged me to get my training to be a nurse," Victoria said tentatively.

"Do you think you would find that a fulfilling life?" Claire asked.

"Henry seems to feel I am bright enough but of course he was always the brilliant one," Victoria said. "He is already establishing quite a practice here. When Dr. Milo retires he will take over his entire office."

Claire felt as though it was her mother selling her on a beau. "You should do what you want," Claire declared.

"Yes, that is what Henry tells me. Henry is most taken with your independence," Victoria said. "He is trying to encourage me to be more like you."

Claire felt stricken by Victoria's word. She looked at Tessie who did not look up from her drink. "I am not as independent as all that. I have learned so much from the other teachers at the school. Tessie who has such a tender way with people has taught me not to let my natural reserve keep me from doing what is most needed."

Tessie smiled her thanks.

"Then I admire you both," Victoria said.

"We are the three most wonderful people in the world," Claire said raising her glass in toast.

Victoria and Tessie raised their glasses laughing just as Henry walked through the door.

"I see I need not have worried about the three of you," he said.

"Henry we have had the loveliest of times," Victoria said, a radiant smile lighting up her face.

"I have come to offer you ladies a ride home," Henry said bowing graciously.

"Oh, you shouldn't have bothered," said Claire. "We can take the trolley."

"But I want to tour you about the city first," he said. "Did you know the university has quite an extensive art program?"

Claire felt ensnared in a web that Henry and Victoria had woven long before she had arrived.

As they began to load into the automobile, Victoria suddenly held back. "Oh dear, I forgot I must go by Market Square and get a few things for a late supper," Victoria said. "Tessie won't you go with me. It is just up the street. We can meet these two back at the house."

Tessie looked surprised. She searched Victoria's face for the meaning of her words. Before she could respond, Claire jumped from the car. "I will be happy to accompany you Victoria," she said with a winning smile. "Tessie you go along and tell me all about it when you get back."

Tessie got reluctantly into the car looking curiously at Claire who waved gaily to them as they drove off.

"You are the little devil," Victoria said.

Claire turned to see Victoria shaking her head.

"You know Henry is quite besotted with you," she said. "And we had it all arranged for the two of you to have some time together."

"I am sorry to spoil your plan," Claire said, "but if Henry truly values my independence as you say, he must allow me to practice it."

"I know dear," Victoria said with a sigh, "but I was so looking forward to having you as my sister-in-law."

"Then Joseph would surely take you back to China to be rid of my influence."

Victoria laughed and gave Claire a hug. "Perhaps we might still be friends."

"Of course," Claire said. "How could it be otherwise?"

"It's Henry I am concerned about," Victoria said. "He is really quite a shy man. I have never seen him so captivated by any woman."

"Henry is a dear man and he's been so kind. If I had any desire to marry he would be an excellent choice, but I do not. Henry might indeed find me challenging, might I say, but he would discover soon enough that I am not the best choice for what he truly desires. I feel that Henry is eager to marry and have a family of his own. Have I judged him wrongly?"

"On the contrary, I think you are correct in your assumptions. He has spoken often of his desire for a large family."

"Since it is my intention that I shall never marry, would Henry not do well to turn his attentions to one more suited to his desires?

"Tessie you mean?" Victoria said with a knowing smile.

"She would not have me tell it," Claire said.

"You have revealed nothing that I had not discerned," Victoria said kindly.

"Perhaps in time, Henry will judge me more kindly knowing that I have made my intentions clear early."

"Henry would never judge you as anything other than what you are, a dear and wonderful person," Victoria said.

"Will he be so very disappointed then?"

"Don't worry, dear," Victoria said kindly. "I shall have a word with him and sort things out."

"I would be most grateful," Claire said.

"Affairs of the heart cannot be dictated, of that I am most sure" Victoria said. "I cannot fault Henry for being entranced by you but he listens to my advice."

"I do hope that you will still be my friend, Victoria. You and Henry have been so kind, I would feel dreadful if I lost the two of you."

"You can never lose a true friend," Victoria said, putting her arm through Claire's. "And I am always a true friend."

They turned their backs to the chill December wind and headed up the street together.

Chapter 18

It had been a wonderful holiday, but Claire was eager to get back to Gatlinburg. Stowing their packages carefully in the rack above the seat, they dropped exhausted into their seats.

"Wasn't it all such a dream," Tessie sweetly said.

"The theater was beautiful and the music delightful," Claire said, stifling a yawn. She had been pleased to find Henry both cordial and gracious at the theater. Victoria, who seemed so unhappy in her own marriage, had been willing enough to bow out as matchmaker and have a word with her brother. Much to her relief, he had chosen deliberately to seat himself next to Tessie.

She could hardly complain that she had spent the evening next to the insipid Mr. Parker who had all the endearing qualities of a puppy. It had come to her later that in rejecting Henry, she had once again shut out a possibility for her future without any direction of her own. Her time at the school was growing shorter and yet she still was unsure of what her future held. A sense of having tinkered with the delicate balance of fate swept over her.

She was genuinely touched when Victoria had reassured her that she was still interested in showing her paintings and demanded to keep them. They had hugged warmly with Victoria promising to write. Even Henry had given her a quick embrace before they had stepped onto the train.

"I am tired," Tessie said dreamily, "but I don't want to sleep for fear I will forget something that happened before I have time to write it in my diary."

"I hardly think that will happen, Tessie," Claire said wearily. "You have talked of nothing else all morning."

Tessie merely giggled.

She had come back from her solo auto tour with Henry with her cheeks rosy bubbling with excitement over having seen the town. They had even been by Henry's medical office and stopped at a diner for coffee and apple pie. Henry had given Claire a smug look, which she had accepted as her due, allowing him this small indulgence to smooth over his wounded feelings.

As the train chugged its way out of Knoxville, Claire leaned her head back against the seat and looked out the window soothed by the rhythmic swaying of the passenger car. The sky was grey, the clouds hanging low and heavy. The seasons came with such comforting predictability, she thought, and winter would not hold off much longer. This would be her first winter in the mountains but before her year was over, she would have a memory of every season.

"Claire," Tessie whispered softly.

"I'm awake," Claire said, turning her head and reluctantly opening her eyes. "You don't have to whisper."

"I need to tell you something," Tessie said, her voice carrying a slight edge.

Looking at Tessie's scrunched up face and pained expression, Claire could only wonder at the confession she was about to hear. "If it is about forgetting to put a coin in the basket for the lady's room attendant, I did it for you," Claire said.

Tessie gave her a puzzled look. "What…?"

"Forget it dear," Claire said. "I was just teasing you."

"Oh," Tessie muttered to herself.

"Tell me then. What is it you have on your conscience? I want to know," said Claire, sitting upright.

Tessie moved away from her and slumped down in her seat.

"Come along, it can't be all that bad," Claire coaxed.

"I don't know how it happened really," Tessie said putting her fist to her lips.

Claire reached over, took her friends hand, and held it between her own. "We only have a few hours to Sevierville. Won't you please tell me so we can get some rest?"

"Henry asked me to write to him," she said, the words tumbling out of her mouth.

Claire snorted a laugh through her nose. Of all the words she expected to hear, she could never have predicted such a confession. "He asked you to write to him!"

Tessie looked stricken. "I told him I would. Are you upset with me?"

"No, I'm just a little surprised. What exactly went on between the two of you on your little tour of the city?"

"It was all very respectable," Tessie said defensively.

"I didn't mean that. It's just that you were only gone for two hours and now he wants you to write to him."

"Bless you for letting me go riding with Henry," Tessie said. "I know he meant to go with you, but once we were alone, we just talked the whole time and I think he truly likes me."

"I knew he would, Tessie. How could he help it? I think that it is perfectly wonderful that he wants you to write," Claire said.

"Do you mean it, Claire," Tessie begged. "You don't think that I am being foolish."

"Yes, I mean it. I think Henry is a fortunate man indeed," Claire said sincerely.

"Thank you Claire," Tessie said, letting out a loud sigh as though she had been holding her breath.

They both settled back into their seats lost in their own thoughts. Soon Tessie was asleep, her head lulling gently back and forth. Claire, suddenly wide-awake, could only watch the scenery pass by. It both puzzled and amused her, that nothing to do with people ever went the way she thought it would. She hoped that Henry was sincere in his affection for the tenderhearted Tessie. She knew that her friend was already laying out her life as straight and true as the tracks on which the train ran. Tessie knew as surely as she knew her own name how her life was to be.

Just as surely, Claire knew that her own life would never run true. As delighted as she was with Victoria's interest in her paintings, she was not convinced that anything would come of it. However, she was returning to the mountains with even greater conviction that no matter how ragged the pattern of her life might appear to others it would be her own. Dozing dreamily, she repeated the thought again and again to the rhythm of the train until at last it soothed away her doubts.

When she opened her eyes, she thought she might be dreaming. Snowflakes fell from the sky like errant spider webs let loose from their moorings. Shaking Tessie awake, she cried out with delight, "Look, Tessie."

They pressed their faces to the window and watched as snowflakes danced magically past them fluttering to the ground like white moths. Claire felt a fever of impatience wanting to race ahead to the mountains to see what wonders the snow had wrought.

"Mr. Huff is supposed to pick us up in his automobile," Tessie exclaimed.

"Oh dear, he may not be able to make it," Claire said, shaking her head.

"What are we to do?"

"Perhaps, we could stay with Evelyn's parents in Sevierville. When we get to the station, we can find someone to take us there."

"What about school?"

"Try not to worry, Tessie. I'm sure Evelyn will understand," Claire said, as they pulled into the depot.

The first thing she saw was Shade Morgan atop a jolt wagon, his hat and coat covered with snow. Jumping down, he brushed himself off and sauntered toward the depot.

"Andy sent me to look after the two of you," Shade said by way of greeting as the women stepped down from the train. "We best hurry, this snows likely to follow us back to the mountains."

He looked down into Claire's upturned face and she felt foolishly grateful. "I am so happy to see you Shade," she said. "We were worried about getting home." Her voice hung on the word home, catching her by surprise.

He grinned at her. "No need to worry," he said calmly. "I'll get you home safe. That's why I brought my mule, Molly. We've made this trip dozens of times in all kinds of weather taking goods to Market Square in Knoxville."

Claire thought of how she and Victoria had only the day before strolled through the huge market filled with goods and crowded with people. The noise and clutter had fascinated Claire. She pictured the tall self-possessed Shade wandering among the crowded stalls as he made deals with the vendors.

The women watched as Shade removed the tarp from the wagon seat and helped them up. He handed them wool blankets to throw over their laps and loaded their things into the wagon carefully covering them with a tarp.

The snow continued to fall as they headed out. It was beginning to cover the ground and cling to the trees. Claire wedged between Shade and Tessie felt like a small child peering into a snow globe.

"First snowfall was always the time of year my brothers and me would set rabbit traps," Shade said glancing up at the sky. "I always looked forward to winter for that reason."

Claire was surprised to hear Shade mention his brothers. She looked at him enthralled by the gleam in his dark eyes. "How do you trap a rabbit?" she asked.

"We'd make us up some simple traps. You take a hollow log. Black gum is the best because it hollows out with age," he said earnestly. Then you close up one end, put you a triggered door on the other end and bait it. Then you wait."

Claire loved that Shades voice held all the nerve shattering, pent-up suspense of a young boy held back by waiting. Furthermore, the way he talked, it was as though he fully expected her to go out and build a trap as soon as she got back to the school.

"What did you use for bait," Tessie asked.

"I learned to use a slice of apple 'cause it don't rot so fast and we always had plenty," Shade said. "One time my brothers snuck into Ma's cabbages she had put by and baited their traps with cabbage leaves. She found out about it and that was the last time."

"Did she whip them?" Tessie asked. She sounded concerned about the possible suffering of two boys now long gone.

"She didn't have to whip'em. A look was always enough from Ma," Shade said with a wry grin.

"How long did you have to wait to catch a rabbit?" Claire asked.

"Well, that's the hard part for a young boy you know, that waiting," he said chuckling. "I could hardly wait for first light and many a morning I'd get up before daylight and go out into the cold to check my traps."

"And did you usually catch a rabbit?" Claire asked.

"Most times, I'd catch one or two. We lived on rabbit meat through the winter. One time I went out to check my traps and reached in to find a possum. That thing 'bout tore me up. That's when I learned better than to put my hand into a trap without looking. After that, I'd give my trap a big shake before I opened the door."

"Did you eat the possum?" Claire asked.

"If I had took it home, my ma would have cooked it, but me and that possum parted ways before I could get a hold of him. I never was fond of possum."

Claire laughed picturing Shade as a young boy wrestling an angry possum. As they rode toward Gatlinburg, Shade continued to regale them with stories of his youth in the mountains.

As they rode along, Claire felt warm under her blanket, sitting next to Shade. He had dropped his treading-gently way with her it seemed, or maybe it was she who had changed. Whatever it was, she hardly noticed the jostling of the wagon on the road that had seemed so rough on her first ride into the mountains.

Still by the time they pulled up in front of the teachers' cottage she rejoiced at being home. Suddenly she felt cold, wet and aware of every tooth in her head.

"Won't you come in for something hot to drink and a bite to eat," Claire said as Shade unloaded their packages.

"That's kind of you to offer but I'm still yet to see Andy Huff before I head home. Emily will be looking for me. She was upset with me for not letting her go today."

"Then you'll say hello to Emily and Granny Kate for us," Tessie called as she headed up the steps arms loaded. "Thank you again for picking us up at the station and bringing us home."

"Proud to do it," Shade said with a tip of his hat.

"Yes thank you Shade," Claire said collecting her bundles.

He made to help her with them and they collided. Claire went slipping about in the snow before she finally fell on her backside sending packages flying.

"Are you all right," Shade asked bending over her.

"I'm fine," she said breathless. When she looked up at him, snowflakes fell on her face.

He lifted her up, plucked a flake from her eyelash, and held it out to her in the palm of his hand. She looked at the delicate flake cupped in his calloused hand and her breath caught in her throat. She watched in wonder as it melted.

Shade closed his palm around the place where the snowflake had been and then he looked up studying the sky. "Tomorrow looks to be another fine day," he declared. "I'll be by to take you to Aunt Lydia's like I promised. Best wear your boots."

Surprised but pleased that he remembered his promise to take her to meet Aunt Lydia, she followed his eyes as he watched the snow falling heavier now. His sharp nose and carved cheekbones seemed to soften as the snow covered his hat and coat. She imagined him as he had been as a young boy waking early to check his traps, eager to be on an adventure.

"I think tomorrow should be a perfect day indeed," she said.

Chapter 19

He liked the way she stood, head and shoulders back, feet set apart, hands on her hips. He had never met anyone like her and yet she reminded him of someone. It was a feeling that lingered as Claire lifted her head, dark eyes searching and breathed in the cold winter air.

"You wore your boots," Shade said coming to greet her.

"You seem surprised I can take instruction," she said.

He did not know how eyes so deep and dark could catch so much light. He could see the mischief dancing a jig in them. "I reckon I can handle a few surprises," he said

She laughed a throaty laugh.

The day was clean and crisp. The snow had left in the night but it was deep enough to leave a track as they walked up the road along the Little Pigeon River past Ogles Store.

"I hope you don't mind walking in the snow," he said by way of conversation.

"It's beautiful. The ground and trees all covered with snow look like a fairyland," she said. "I hope that I might never come to take such beauty for granted. I'm glad to be back in the mountains in time to see the first snow fall."

"It's good …that you got back," he said haltingly. He wanted to say that it was good to have her back. He had not asked her about her trip to Knoxville and he would not ask her now. Something in him wanted to hold off knowing. He would not have her know of his growing feelings for her for he would not put that burden on her. It was enough to be walking up the road with her by his side.

Far up on the mountains, the evergreens cloaked in their new winter garments glistened. "Somehow looking up at the peaks all covered with snow, their haunting beauty seems so distant and untouchable," Claire mused.

He felt the same thing looking into her face. Before he could betray his thoughts he said, "If you're ever up there in a snowstorm, it's stillness like no other. Then a wind comes up and the pines begin to moan. It's as mournful a sound as you are likely to ever hear and you'd swear they were trying to talk."

"What do you think they are trying to say," she said.

"It's a puzzlement," he confessed. "I just know I feel better after I've been out in the woods for a while and heard that sound."

They walked on in the winter sun. The snow was imprinted with the tiny tracks of birds, squirrels, chipmunks, and shrews. "Looks like something's been digging by this tree root," Shade said pointing. "Maybe a shrew has a den in there."

"What tireless little workers," Claire said delighted.

They strolled on alone except for the world of creatures going about their lives as usual.

"You'll like Aunt Lydia," Shade said at last. "She's a character."

"How long have you known Aunt Lydia?" Claire asked.

"All my life," he answered. "Most everybody around here has called on Aunt Lydia for sickness or to birth their babies. She's eighty years old now and knows everybody in these parts and all their kin dead and alive."

"Does she have anyone to help her?"

"She says she is slowing down and she can't do what she used to do. The last time I was up to visit she'd been out gathering apples. She had a couple of bushels setting on the porch."

"Well isn't it good she can still do things for herself?" she asked.

"The thing is, I swear if I didn't know better, I'd say she had skinned right up that apple tree to get'em."

"Did you ask her?"

"I did," he said. "I had to get my courage up to do it. Aunt Lydia can be touchy if you say anything about her getting old."

"What was her answer?"

"She wouldn't say whether she had or hadn't been climbing trees. What she said was, "all the low hanging fruit has already been picked." Then she give me a look that told me I'd best mind my own business."

"Something I would love to have seen," she said chuckling. "I mean I would love to have seen her climbing trees and I would love to have seen the look she gave you."

Shade chuckled remembering it. "She's a better hand to make do than most," he said simply. "When she was younger she raised her own crops, took her own corn to mill, made or bartered for just about everything they ever needed."

"How did she do all of that by herself?"

"She had to make her own way."

"Aunt Lizzie said she raised her own sheep for wool, sheared it and made it into coverlets," Claire said with awe in her voice. "Sheep to wool, she called it."

"Weren't nobody to do it for her and nobody to tell her she couldn't."

He could see the words settling over her.

"I see what you mean," she said with a shake of her head.

They turned off through the remains of a cornfield where a few stalks stood like weary sentinels. Down at the bottom of a small rise and at the base of a hill stood a tiny cabin.

"Old timers call this Holly Butt Mountain," Shade said with a crooked grin. "Aunt Lydia don't much approve of that since she is a good Christian woman. She renamed it Holy Branch. It's to her way of thinking that these mountains was made by the hand of God and that was not to be taken in lightly."

"I tend to agree with her."

"They say she can quote the Bible from cover to cover."

Claire gave him a doubtful look.

"I've never set with her long enough to prove it," he said with a shrug, "but then I'm not one to doubt Aunt Lydia."

Before Shade could knock, the door of the one room cabin flew open. A tiny little woman with brown eyes and scraggly white hair came out the door like a whirlwind.

"Go in and make yourselves to home," she said energetically. "I'll be in directly," she said.

The door was low and Shade had to stoop to get inside. The ceiling was only an inch above his head. The room was dark with only two tiny windows long ago dimmed by dirt and soot. As his eyes adjusted to the dark, he could see that the cabin was just as he remembered it. It was filled from top to bottom and corner to corner. Dried plants of all description hung from the ceiling and a table near the wall was covered with an assortment of household things. Only near the fireplace was there space cleared out for a few chairs.

Aunt Lydia came back inside with sticks of wood in her arms and added them to the fireplace, which was already ablaze with a roaring fire. Pots and pans hung on the mantel as it was her only place to cook.

Aunt Lydia pointed to the straight back chairs that ringed the fireplace and motioned to Shade and Claire to sit down. She then joined them picking up two rectangular paddles she had been working on when they arrived. Working with practiced efficient motions, she drew the top paddle over the bottom one repeatedly.

"Aunt Lydia this is Miss Claire. I told you about her."

"You're one of the teachers at the Settlement School," Aunt Lydia remarked.

"Yes ma'am," Claire said graciously.

"You're doing some fine work. That school has been a help to many a youngun around here."

"Thank you, Aunt Lydia. That is kind of you to say."

"You don't let them schoolchildren get the better of you, do you? Some of them bigger boys can be a handful."

"It was a struggle at first," Claire said lightheartedly.

Aunt Lydia nodded. "You make them younguns mind."

"I'll give it my best try, Aunt Lydia."

"That's all you can do, I reckon," Aunt Lydia agreed. "I always tried to make my own younguns mind."

"It must have been difficult raising your children all alone without your husband to help?"

"It was hard and it was a pleasure. When they was little was the best time in the world. It is easier to have children on the toes than on the heart. Back when my children was on my toes was the best of it. When they are on the toes it's easier; when they are on the heart it's worse."

"I think your children are fortunate to have such a mother," Claire said wistfully. A flush came to her cheeks and she changed the subject, "What are you doing with those paddles?"

Aunt Lydia looked at her hands and then at Claire. "This here is cards," she said. "I'm carding wool. Carding is breaking up the wool so it can be spun into thread."

"May I try it?" she asked.

Aunt Lydia handed her the cards. "Just pull the top one over the bottom with a steady hand," she said demonstrating with her hands. "Draw it across towards you. Use a good bit of pressure."

Claire worked diligently pulling the card across three times as instructed, her face pinched in concentration. "I'm afraid I'm not very good," she said pulling the paddles open to show her work.

"No shame in not knowing how. Everybody starts somewhere," Aunt Lydia said matter-of-factly. "It's been ages since I've carded wool myself but it comes back to you. Them young teachers come up here and put me in mind of it again. She took Claire's hands and showed her how to apply just the right pressure.

"Now you got it," Aunt Lydia said when the work met her approval. "Now push it backwards," she said demonstrating the motion.

Claire followed Aunt Lydia's lead. The wool transferred to the top card and formed a roll.

"Do that two more times and it'll be ready to spin," Aunt Lydia said confidently.

Claire continued her work and then waited until Aunt Lydia gave her approval. She gave Shade a self-satisfied grin when Aunt Lydia placed the roll with the others ready to be spun into thread.

He was struck by her delight in learning something new. "You're a natural all right," Shade said poking fun.

She gave him a look through the slits of her eyes, her lips pressed firmly together.

"I like it when folks admit they don't know something better than when they act like they know everything," Aunt Lydia said glaring at Shade.

Shade chuckled softly under his breath.

"Aunt Lydia, do you like to card and spin," Claire asked.

"It's a comforting kind of work," she allowed. "It takes patience and faith and I've got plenty of both. You know what the Bible says about patience and faith?"

"No, Aunt Lydia, I'm afraid I don't," Claire confessed, "but Shade tells me you know the Bible very well."

"The Bible calls patience and faith, the fruit of the Spirit," Aunt Lydia said without pausing. "There is strife in everything, you see. Folks act as if they should be above strife. Many a time when life gets tough, folks act like God broke a promise to them. The truth is God never said they wouldn't be hard times." She clasped her hands together to add power to her words. "I've seen a heap of ups and downs and had a world of trouble the whole world through, and I hope I get to a better place some day. But the trials of this world must be borne with patience. This world is only a stopping place."

Shade watched as Claire leaned in closer to the old woman. Her head was cocked to one side as she took in every word. He wondered what answers she was seeking from this solemn faced woman who still had a twinkle in her eye and a whisper of mystery in her words.

"You take an apple tree," Aunt Lydia mused. "It tries every season to produce apples but sometimes there's no rain or a late frost comes and kills the blossoms. That tree just keeps trying season after season until it makes a good crop of apples. The way I see it folks are no better. They don't have no more right than an apple tree to expect to go through life without some hard times. And in time, the fruit of them hard times is patience and faith."

Claire leaned back hard in her chair and rocked on the balls of her feet as though pinned there by force of Aunt Lydia's words. The firelight danced in her black eyes as they searched the flames.

Shade could see that she was weighing her own 'patience and faith' and like most folks found them wanting. Unlike Claire, he had heard Aunt Lydia's speech before. He stepped in to save her. "I am afraid it is in most folk's nature to expect a great deal more from their hardships," he said. "I've been as guilty as most, I reckon."

Aunt Lydia nodded. "I expect so," she said simply.

They sat quietly for a long time each lost in their own thoughts. Shade got up and put another log on the fire.

'Course, I like to make baskets too," Aunt Lydia said lightly as though they had just been discussing the weather.

Claire looked at Shade searching his face bemused by the sudden turn of the conversation. Then she turned back to the old woman. "Tell me about your baskets," she said.

"I've made lots of baskets. I reckon I like to fool with my hands."

As Aunt Lydia explained to Claire about the difference in using white oak splits or willow in her baskets, Shade realized that in all his life he had never seen a woman sit idle without some busy work in her hands. Until Claire had asked the question, he had never thought to ask if there was any pleasure in it.

"Aunt Lydia, show Miss Claire a jar of your ooze," Shade said.

"I've got a new batch just made," Aunt Lydia said.

She rose slowly from her chair and went to the table.

"She makes her own medicine from plants and bark," Shade whispered. "It's sure to cure you if the taste don't kill you."

Returning with a jar of brown liquid, Aunt Lydia said, "There's everything in these mountains a body needs to get by."

Aunt Lydia held out the jar. Claire took it gingerly in her hands.

"Take a sip," she said.

It was a command not a request.

Shade watched as Claire took the bottle to her lips and drank the brown liquid. He waited for her to spit it out and go sputtering around the room as he had so often done as a child. Instead, she gave a tiny grimace as the ooze when down and then she gave him a wicked smile.

"Shade drunk a plenty of this when he was a youngun," Aunt Lydia said. "It appears to have done you some good. You growed up big and strong."

"Brought out my ornery streak," he teased, giving Claire a look.

Aunt Lydia would have none of it. "Don't you go trying to fool nobody Shade Morgan for you are as good a man as runs in these parts."

Claire looked at him as though she had a word or two to say on the matter but then she cut herself off.

"That cured me of dropsy last winter when folks didn't think I would live," Aunt Lydia said. "I'll tell you how to make it. You might need it."

Claire handed the jar to Shade and leaned forward to listen attentively her chin in her hand.

"Get you some star root. Shade can get it for you from the glades. He knows where. Bile it up with some sourwood."

"How much of each?" Claire asked.

"Why as much as you can hold in your hand," she said.

Claire nodded, her face solemn.

Shade admired the way she listened in earnest as though she might go home and stir up a batch that very evening. Aunt Lydia went on for some time instructing Claire to the last detail until she felt satisfied.

"When you've done all that," she said leaning back in her chair, "add just a pinch of anvil dust."

"Anvil dust," Claire questioned.

"Don't you know what anvil dust is?"

Claire gave a puzzled look.

"Why it's the dust from around a blacksmith's anvil."

"Of course, anvil dust," Claire said with a nod.

"Now do it the way I told you and it'll make as fine a medicine as any doctor could give you."

"Thank you Aunt Lydia," Claire said. "I will try to remember everything you told me."

At last when Aunt Lydia grew quiet and Shade could see that she was tired, he caught Claire's eye. "I think we had best go."

"Oh, yes," Claire said. "I have lessons to prepare for tomorrow."

As they walked to the door, Shade said, "I'll bring Emily to see you soon."

"I'll be looking for you."

"I enjoyed my visit Aunt Lydia," Claire said.

"You come back any time. I'm most always here."

At the door, Claire hesitated. "Shade tells me you live here alone. Doesn't living here alone bother you sometimes?"

"I get visitors right regular and I've got good neighbors. I try to do good by everybody. I try to treat everybody just like I'd have them treat me. The more you can do that, the more it will come back to you. Besides, this is just my home. I've spent my happiest days here."

"In all your years of living here were you never afraid?"

Aunt Lydia looked at them quizzically and rubbed her chin. "I never seen but one 'fraid in my life," she said pausing in thought, "and that was one night when I seen something black out in the yard. I went out to it and give it a hard kick and it was my little black kettle."

Claire burst into a hearty laugh and rushed to give Aunt Lydia a hug. "I had a wonderful visit. Thank you for having me."

"You are welcome any time young lady," Aunt Lydia said.

As soon as the door closed, Claire turned to him, crossed her arms and stood poker straight. "Aunt Lydia is not really choosy about her visitors is she?" she said.

"What do you mean?" he asked surprised by her question.

"You said she was choosy about her visitors but that you would be happy to bring me to see her. It seems, however, that by her own admission she has lots of visitors."

She said it with a smile but he felt her search his face looking for something against which she needed to guard herself. Here was a woman not given easily to trust. He had walked a fine line with her. "Well, I thought you might be more at ease if I come along," he said as honestly as he could.

She conceded the point with a nod.

"I enjoy visiting Aunt Lydia too," he added feeling like a foolish boy. She had a way of making a man question everything he had every believed about himself, he thought.

She uncrossed her arms and relaxed her shoulders.

Shade resisted showing his relief. "I reckon you can make your next visit on your own," he said teasingly.

"Oh Shade, I am sorry. You must find me a most difficult person."

"You can keep a man wondering what's coming, I reckon," Shade said, his brow furrowed.

"Please forgive me," she pleaded, looking up into his face. "I do thank you for bringing me."

"Happy to do it," he said. Unable to hold her gaze without wanting to say more, he looked away. He stomped his boots in the snow to shake off the cold along with his unspoken words. "We best head back," he said simply.

As they walked off, bundling themselves against the chill wind, Claire stopped and looked back at the cabin. Her eyes had a faraway look.

"Did you forget something?" he asked.

"I was just thinking," she whispered hoarsely.

He waited for her to go on.

"When I talk to women like Aunt Lydia and the other women in the homes that I have visited I begin to wonder that as difficult as their lives may seem, if they don't have a certain freedom born of hardship. I wonder if some of the women who followed their husbands over the mountains to settle here did so because they knew that no one would question what they were capable of doing. They did what they had to do because they were needed and it kept their families alive."

"Claire," he said and then hesitated. He had thought of her often but he was unaccustomed to speaking her given name. "I think Aunt Lydia would be the first one to say her life ain't been easy."

She sighed heavily. "But she was never turned back by the thought. Somehow she knew she was a match for the task."

"Maybe she knew but most likely she couldn't be sure. Life has a way of bringing out in folks what is in their nature."

"She is a strong woman made stronger by the many tests she has endured," she mused.

He could almost feel the jumble of her thoughts. Searching for the right words he said, "You don't have to accept what people want to put on you no matter where you live. You just make your own way."

Her eyes widened and surprise showed on her face. "You see more courage in me than I possess."

"No, I don't," he said honestly. "Believe me Claire, I am a simple man. I mostly live my life as it comes to me but you act like a panther that's been cornered by a pack of hunting dogs."

"Well, my mountain philosopher, I don't know if I should be flattered or hurt? she said, smiling.

He did not smile back at her but instead asked, "What is it that brought you here to the Smoky Mountains, Claire?"

"You think I was chased into the hills?" she said, with a toss of her head.

He refused to let her make light of his words. "You're searching for something and now for some reason you think you've found it here in an old woman's hard life and a tiny cabin."

Tears welled up in her eyes. He had not meant to be so hard on her. He had not even realized he had pushed her so far. Before he could voice his regret, she turned away and headed back down the trail.

He followed her. They did not speak for a long time.

Finally, without turning Claire said, "I came here to teach because I was afraid to live the life I had dreamed about for so long."

She did not stop but continued walking down the trail. He let her go at her own pace.

"I wanted to go to New York or Paris and open my own art studio," she went on after a while. "I wanted to make my own way as an artist but I lacked the courage so I came here."

She stopped finally and turned to face him, her face a mask of pain.

"I have never told anyone that before."

"And just what was it made you think you might die from the telling of it?"

She gasped. Then unexpectedly she laughed.

It was what he could never get over about her. The way her face flashed like a thunderstorm when she was offended. Then just as quickly came a dazzling smile like the sun from behind a cloud.

"I feel just like a fire fly caught in a jar," she said, her voice taking on a mountain twang.

"Now who's the mountain philosopher?" he quipped.

"It's just that I feel that I have disappointed so many people," she said once again taking a serious tone. "I gave myself this year to find my way, now with the time slipping away, I am still unsure as to what I might do. Furthermore, I hoped my time here might at least be of some use. I have received so much from the children and the people here. In turn, my contribution has been so little."

"You know when we first met and you went to Sunday dinner at the Wheelers, I watched the way you held yourself, standing back away from folks. Now, I see how good you are with Aunt Lydia. I see how you have accepted the folks here and how they have come to accept you."

He could see the doubt in her eyes.

"And you mean the world to Emily," he pressed on. "You've changed her life for the better and I know she's not the only one. There's no way the children would say you've been a disappointment."

"Thank you, Shade. You are more than kind to tell me these things."

"I only say it because it's true."

"I have come to feel safe and comfortable here in ways I never felt before."

He kicked the snow with the toe of his boot, his mind fumbling to form the words he wondered if he dared speak. "You know, I don't know much about art but I have seen some of your drawings. It appears to me that you could take a lifetime and never run out of things to paint in these mountains."

She studied his face and he thought she could read in his eyes the selfishness of his words, the hidden meaning behind them. He had never spoken this way to any woman, not even Sarah, and it left him feeling raw as if he had taken a tumble down a rocky riverbank.

"I have come to love these mountains," she said wistfully. "I feel that I have...some people believe," she hesitated, "that I have done my best work here."

He waited not wanting to break the spell of the moment. "It appears to me like you set your feet on a different path just by coming here. That was a brave thing to do. You set out not knowing what was ahead. That is all anybody can do. I know you don't see it that way because you are always measuring yourself by other folk's yardsticks. The way I see it you expect an awful lot from yourself."

"It is just that I do feel held up to other people's measurements," she said, her voice raspy with frustration. "Furthermore, I am unsure what my own measurements for my life should be."

"Be patient to what is in your heart," he said. "In time it will tell you."

"You think I could use a little of Aunt Lydia's patience and faith," she said.

"Sometimes that's the only answer to what life offers up," he said gently.

"I was just thinking that if I had a cabin like Aunt Lydia's to call my own, I could come back to the mountains whenever I wanted. Just knowing there is a place here for me...." her voice trailed off.

She looked at him and her eyes were alive with excitement. He could see the pulse beating in her throat. She had not taken his meaning as an invitation to stay. She was telling him that one day soon, she would be leaving and it was a thought that he found hard to accept. Nevertheless, she had given him the possibility that she might come back if even for a short time.

He was not a man whose dreams ran too far ahead of a hope honed by experience, so his feelings for Claire had come upon him as unexpected as a grass fire out of control. He had tamped down every spark only to find thoughts of her leapt to mind when he was least prepared. Aware of the foolishness of his feelings, he had put it down to loneliness, to missing his wife. That he could be thinking of someone so different from Sarah and so unlikely was a mystery.

He did not know how a heart so full of suffering could find room for the simple joy that rushed through his veins when he looked at Claire as she stood in the sunshine and shadows of a cold winter day. She had come to the mountains in search of something but he was sure it could not be him. Still the thing he had on his side was that he was a patient man. Aunt Lydia would be proud for he could give an apple tree a run for its money when it came to patience, he thought.

They had reached the main road. The sun was beginning to drop in the sky. The sharp cold bit at Shade's face. "Are you getting cold," he asked. Her cheeks were rosy and he thought he saw a shiver course through her small frame. Still she shook her head.

"It's not far now," he said.

"I've had a lovely day, Shade. Thank you for that."

As he stood looking down at Claire's upturned face, he knew that he would find a way in time to give her the cabin she wanted. It was a growing feeling in him that he would do everything in his power for her. Everything short of telling Claire Blackburn how he felt. He would not put that burden on her. Her decision to stay in the mountains would be one of her own choosing. Some questions, he knew, could only be answered by patience and faith.

Chapter 20

Frannie thought she was too old for a doll but even as the teachers handed out the Christmas gifts from under the tree, she hoped for one. Her hand shook as she held the beautifully wrapped box in her hand. She wanted to be careful but in her excitement the paper ripped. Looking up, she saw that all of the other girls were trying to be careful too. The boys tore into their gifts with a reckless joy. Every girl got a doll with real clothes. The boys got games, knives or harmonicas.

The first thing Frannie realized when she lifted the lid of the box was that her doll was more beautiful than anything she had ever seen. Her ma had made her rag dolls and cornhusk dolls but she had never had a store-bought one. The doll had blond curls and long dark lashes. Her mouth was open slightly showing four pearl white teeth. Her pink and beige cotton dress had little buttons down the front. She had painted on socks and one-strap shoes. When Frannie picked her up she opened her blue eyes. Frannie felt like the doll knew her. Jennie was the name she would call her. She had been practicing it for weeks as she dreamed about having a real doll of her very own. It would be Jennie because that was a friendly and cheerful name. That was the name of a best friend. She would weave Jennie a small basket and fill it with bluets in the spring and they would sit by the stream as Frannie read books aloud.

The school had been preparing for Christmas over the last few weeks. Miss Tessie and Miss Claire had been up to visit and they had gone out into the woods to collect holly. Frannie's pa had come along to shoot mistletoe from the tops of trees. At first, her teachers had been afraid of the gun putting their hands over their ears at the loud sound. Then Miss Claire had asked to try her hand at shooting the mistletoe. Her pa was patient in teaching her to shoot, in ways he never was with Frannie, but she did not care, for she was having such

179

a good time. Miss Claire missed the mistletoe by a country mile and they all had laughed.

Her ma had given the teachers each a dainty little basket just like the one they had made over at their last visit. Miss Tessie said she would put it on her dressing table as soon as she got back and she swore it was perfect to hold her hairpins. Miss Claire, who smelled of soap and fresh air, had given Frannie a hug as she left.

As the time grew near for the Christmas party, the children fairly twitched with excitement. Even Frannie had trouble sitting still in her seat. They had learned Christmas carols and the girls especially delighted in singing them at every playtime. She had even taught the carols to her ma so they could sing them together as they made baskets. Her ma had been shy about singing at first, her hand flying to her mouth when the sound had come out too loud and free but now she enjoyed the way their voices sounded together. Frannie thought sometimes, when they sat by the fire just the two of them their voices blending in song, that she might die of happiness.

Last year was the first time that Frannie had gone along with the older children on Christmas Eve to serenade the neighbors, as was the tradition. They did not just sing Christmas carols or songs they had learned at home. They carried cowbells and pans with sticks with which to make noise and wake everyone in the house. The fun part was trying to sneak up on the house without making a sound so as not to be caught. They would wait until long after dark, some of the older boys and girls waiting until midnight before going out with as many as fifteen or twenty others. Sometimes grown ups would come along to look out for the children, and the men would carry guns to fire off when they got to the house. If the folks in the house heard the singers coming, they would run out and yell or fire off a gun into the sky. Then either way they would invite the children in for something good to eat and drink. She had explained all of this to Miss Tessie and Miss Claire one day and they acted as if it would be the most fun thing to do. This year she hoped that some of her teachers would come along with the group.

Last week the teachers had put up a tree in the assembly room and each class made decorations. The younger students made paper chains from the pages of old Sears Catalogs while Frannie's class strung popcorn together. Some of the Pi Phi friends, as the teachers always called them, sent along other store bought decorations. Just seeing the beautiful tree was a gift in itself, Frannie thought.

Word leaked out from Ogles store that boxes had been arriving from the Pi Phi's from all over, some from as far away as Boston and Detroit. Frannie located the names of the cities on the map that Miss Agnes had on the wall in her classroom.

She tried to picture the beautiful women in their fine clothes packing gifts to send to children just like her. Their hearts must be full of love if they could care about children they had never met and who were not even kin. Did they try to picture what she looked like, she wondered. Did they know she had brown hair and that she was ten years old? Did they know she loved to read and to sing?

She wanted to tell them that she was good and did all of her schoolwork so they would know that she was deserving of their kindness. If she could write to them, she would tell them how she was the first to hold up her hand when the teacher asked for help to clean the blackboard or to sharpen pencils.

Suddenly, the door opened and into the room burst Santa Claus. The children all squealed with delight. Frannie knew that Santa was really Earl Wilson who helped at the school teaching the boys farming but she was thrilled at the sight all the same. She took the stick of peppermint candy he offered her and ate it with delight, as did all of the students.

Her knowing about Santa was her sister Martha Jane's fault. Miss Bishop had cut out the pattern pieces from red cloth and asked Martha Jane to make the costume. She had been working on it for weeks. Miss Bishop told Martha Jane to keep it a secret, but she had been too full of herself and told Frannie. Sworn to secrecy by Martha Jane left Frannie humped up with the frustration of it—she was one who could keep a secret. If Dealie found out the secret, she thought, she would blab it up and down Baskin Creek before the day was out.

For weeks, Frannie had been making her ma a hemstitched handkerchief working on it everyday in sewing class. Never the hand at needlework that Martha Jane was, she was proud when she finally finished the lace-trimmed hanky. The boys in manual training class made toys for all the little ones and Martha Jane helped her paint one for Dealie. She had even gotten a hold of enough cloth from her ma to make a set of pillowcases for Martha Jane's hope chest. Martha Jane put everything she made into her hope chest for the day she would get married. And she had even managed to get a pouch of tobacco for her pa from the egg money she saved.

Frannie had never had a Christmas tree at her house. They only had the wool socks her ma knitted hanging from the fireplace mantel. Each year they got an orange, hard candy, and a brazil nut in the toe of their socks. Her ma would make gingerbread, filling the house with the most wonderful smell. She always baked a penny in it and if you got the piece with the coin, it was yours to keep. Her pa would go rabbit hunting for most of the day while her ma cooked chicken and dumplings. It was always a good day. Even Martha Jane was cheerful and left off pestering her. This year, she thought, how fine it would be to have a Christmas tree and she was determined to talk to her pa about it. Frannie pictured the two of them going together into the woods and finding the prettiest tree and then decorating it with popcorn strings and cookies her ma had baked. Her pa was not in favor of such foolishness, she knew. The few times her pa had told stories of his growing up there was never any mention of foolishness. His pa had gotten him up before daylight from the time he was five years old to help with chores. "It did not matter if it was raining or there was snow knee deep, he could always find something for us boys to do," her pa would say. She knew that he had never been allowed to go to school. He could never be spared, his pa claimed. She knew that he could barely write more than his own name and could not read more than a word or two. Maybe that was why, that in the time she had been going to school, he had come around to favor more of what the teachers were doing and to look more kindly on their ways. He enjoyed hearing her read aloud by the fire at night. He took pride that she had learned forty new songs without forgetting a word. If he could see his way clear to allow her a tree, she thought, it would be the best Christmas morning ever.

When Santa Claus waved goodbye, he told all the children to be good and they promised him they would. Caught up in the moment, Frannie found herself feverishly waving and telling Santa that she too would be good. As she looked around at her classmates, their angelic faces looking up, she wondered how many of them could keep such a promise even until Christmas morning.

Miss Evelyn stood up and quieted the rowdy crowd of students. She thanked all of the parents, who stood around the walls, for coming to the party. Then she opened the Bible and read the story of baby Jesus as everyone listened in hushed silence. When she finished, Frannie's class stood up and sang "Away in a Manger," just as they had practiced it. The song always made Frannie want to cry at the thought of the baby Jesus sleeping in a stable with cows and donkeys. Of course, she did not cry because she had learned to hold her tears, after the day Miss Tessie read the story of the *Little Match Seller* by Hans Christian Anderson and she bawled like a baby. It shamed her until she looked around to see half the class with tears running down their faces. Even some of the boys had squeezed their eyes tight together to force the tears back.

Miss Claire stood up to read the poem *Twas the Night before Christmas*. She wore a straight black and white plaid skirt that stopped just above her ankles. Her white blouse had a full collar that spread out over her long black sweater. Hardly anyone had seen a sweater before the teachers came to Gatlinburg. It caused such a stir among the women that soon the teachers were buying wool and teaching the women to knit sweaters. A tiny kerchief stood out of the pocket forming a small triangle on the front of the sweater just above Miss Claire's heart. The lace from her shirtsleeves trimmed the bottom of her sweater. Frannie did not believe a more beautiful sight existed anywhere in the world. The other students murmured amongst themselves and some even let out little sounds of oohs and ahs.

Frannie could hardly hear the words of the poem as Miss Claire read them. Even the light from the window seemed to make a halo around her. Secretly Frannie pictured herself one day standing up in front of the school as a teacher and having the students see her as they saw Miss Claire.

There was one secret Frannie was having trouble keeping. Martha Jane was courting Theo Campbell behind her folk's backs. Frannie caught her sister with the Campbell boy out behind the schoolhouse holding hands. She plain laughed out loud at the sight of them. Then she had gotten mad and stomped her foot. "Why don't you just marry some old boy if you want to hoe corn the rest of your life," she had shouted. Looking at her as if she had gone plumb crazy, Martha Jane had thrown her hands to her hips and tossed her head making Frannie want to march herself right home and tell her ma. When she turned to go, Martha Jane had come running and begged her not to do it and then sworn her to secrecy. It only served to set up a festering anger in Frannie. For the life of her, she could not figure out why Martha Jane was so determined to give up her chance to go to school. For one thing, she had heard the teachers' remark more than once that Martha Jane was one of the best hands to sew in the entire school. They held her work up to all the other students as an example. Why that meant nothing to Martha Jane was beyond her. Frannie lapped up every word of praise from her teachers like a bear after a honeycomb and craved more. For another thing, her ma was going to have another baby. She had already been feeling sick at times and Frannie had to do more of the work around the house. If Martha Jane left to marry, it would mean more of the chores would fall on Frannie. If Martha Jane married and they stayed on living with her folks, it would mean she might soon have a baby of her own and that would mean more work. At the heart of it, Frannie was afraid of anything that might keep her from going to school. Her life had taken a wonderful turn when she started going to the Settlement school. It had opened new worlds to her. Mostly it had opened up her heart to the hope that someday she might be a teacher. Once you opened your heart to the possibility of something it let in all kinds of worries along with it. Sometimes she felt like she was running with an egg balanced on a spoon, trying to get to the finish line before she dropped it and splattered her dreams all over.

January 4, 1921

Dear Victoria

You cannot know how desperate I was to receive a letter. Absolutely nothing has happened here for weeks. Tessie, finding herself too dreadfully homesick to bear it, made a last minute escape for the holidays. The weather being so foul, and a number of the teachers having left days earlier, she had to beg amongst the men to find someone to take her to the train. When she was about to give up hope, Mr. Wilson, who instructs the boys in shop, gallantly stepped forward and borrowed a wagon. I am sure it was a most harrowing trip this time of year.

The excitement of the Christmas Party having passed and finding myself mostly alone at the cottage, I have spent the last dreary days staring from my window at the gray skies. I thought that I might relish the time alone, as my days here are filled with such endless activity with the teachers, the students and all of the visiting of neighbors but it seems I have become accustomed to it and now languish without it.

Just as I was about to lapse into the most horrid self-pity your letter arrived. Imagine my infinite joy when I opened your letter to find a check and for such a considerable sum as to take my breath. To learn that you sold any of my paintings comes as a delightful surprise. To know that the watercolors of Baskin Falls and the one of the view of Sugarlands Mountain found a patron in New York is most heartening.

At your request, I will send more paintings in the coming weeks, my energy having been restored by this most marvelous of turns. I have been working from a number of my earlier sketches since you and Henry expressed such praise of my watercolors of the mountains. It appears your judgment was excellent. Please thank Henry for sending my work to the Boston Gallery. I will be most excited to hear from them.

I am indebted to you both for your many kindnesses. I look forward to spring when I hope you might visit.

Sincerely,
Claire Blackburn

Chapter 21

A knock at the door of the teachers' cottage brought Claire back from her reverie. Sitting by the fireplace, she had remained lost in thought even as the book she held slipped from her hands and fell onto her lap. The rapping on the door had forced her back abruptly leaving her unsure of where her mind had wandered. She could not imagine who could be out on a cold January day.

Opening the door, she could not contain her surprise at seeing Shade and Emily.

"Emily how lovely it is to see you. Shade, what are you two doing out on this chilly day?"

"Granny Kate sent us to fetch you," Emily said with self-importance.

"Is that right," Claire said. She looked to Shade for confirmation. He nodded.

"Is everything all right?"

"Granny Kate said there was no need for you to sit humped up here by yourself and that you best come spend the night with us," Emily said.

Claire laughed. She was genuinely touched that Granny Kate had thought of her and that she had cared enough to "fetch her."

"In that case, I suppose I should change my shoes and come along. We wouldn't want to disobey Granny Kate now would we?"

Emily shook her head solemnly.

"Come in out of the cold while I get ready."

She left them standing by the fire while she packed her sketchpad, a book and a few clothes, and toiletries putting it all in her satchel. Throwing on a jacket and her black felt hat, she tossed her new chicory blue scarf about her neck and hurried down the stairs. As she entered the parlor, Shade and Emily looked up. Emily let out a gasp. Claire's hand went to her throat. Then she felt about her head to see if perhaps her hat was askew.

"I think Emily likes your scarf," Shade said.

"You look pretty, Miss Claire," Emily agreed.

"Thank you Emily," Claire said.

Shade took her satchel and tossed it across his shoulder as they walked out. He bent down and pulled Emily's coat tight against her, lifting her collar to meet her cap.

"Emily why don't you wear my scarf," Claire said. Unwrapping it from her neck, she tied it around the girl's frail frame. "It looks so beautiful with your blue eyes."

Emily's eyes widened and she looked at her pa for approval. He smiled and gave her a wink. As they walked up the trail, Claire could see her touching the scarf, petting it and talking to it as thought it were alive.

The weather was crisp and cool but the sun was trying to break through the scattered clouds. Claire took in a deep breath. "I needed to get out. I don't know what has come over me of late that I haven't been able to turn my hand to anything productive." She could not begin to explain how perplexing her recent lethargy had left her. Having promised Victoria to send more of her work, she had been unable to as much as pick up a brush. Having defended her work against great odds at times, it was as though this propitious change in her life had left her paralyzed with fear.

"Sometimes it's good to rest," Shade said. "It's like letting a plot of ground lay fallow. It seems like a waste but some good always comes of it in time."

All the guilt she had felt at this greatest of sins, wasting time, suddenly vanished. She thought what a remarkably simple thought it was to just let things go for a while, to let whatever good to come of it come. "Perhaps you are right," she said.

Just a mile up the trail, they veered off onto a steep footpath. Claire looked at Shade for an explanation but he said nothing and walked on ahead.

"This is an old sled road," he said at last.

The narrow road, damp and carpeted with leaves, was rutted and worn deep by years of use. Claire wondered at the lives that had passed by this way. "Where are we going?" she asked unable to contain her curiosity. "Is this a shortcut?"

Emily giggled. "It's a surprise."

"Oh, a surprise," Claire said, searching Shade's face. When she could read nothing in his expression, and he said nothing, she relaxed enjoying the walk. Winter had cleared away the thick forest and opened up a new world. She took in a deep breath of the blend of spicy wood smoke from distant houses and the decay of the leaves beneath her feet. The forest, which seemed to be sleeping, was really preparing for the coming spring, she thought. Suddenly the day seemed so full of promise. Despite the chill of a passing cloud, a kind of peace came over her, a sense of all things working together for good.

On a steep slope above an old field, Shade bent down pointing to a deer track cut deep in the damp soil. "The deer cross over here to get to the spring," he said.

"There is a spring nearby?" she asked.

"Through there," he said pointing.

They crossed a hollow, shaded by rhododendron, and burst into a clearing. Claire looked up to see a tumbled down cabin and a rock lined spring just a hundred feet from where they stood. "This is an old home place. Someone used to live here," she said in amazement.

"The log cabin is near gone. Rotted away with time," Shade said with a wave of his hand. "A few apple trees remain but the forest is taking back the old fields. No one has tended to them in years."

One side of the front porch had fallen down. A hole the size of a bucket had opened in the roof. The chimney appeared to have separated from the wall and threatened to fall away. The forest was creeping up on the old home site and rhododendron crowded out the open spaces. The farm was surrendering itself back to nature. Still to Claire somehow it seemed like a fairyland secreted from the world. "What a beautiful place," she sighed. "It looks so deserted now. Why would anyone abandon it?"

"It's mostly hills and ravines. What good land there is has been farmed out," Shade said matter-of-factly."

"Who owns this land?" she asked.

"Uncle Hiram used to own it. Thirty years ago he built him a nice place across the knoll."

"Thirty years?"

"In my memory, no one has lived here."

His answer told her that he was at least thirty years old. It surprised her that she had been so curious to know. "Who owns it now?" she asked.

Looking a bit self-conscious he answered, "Its mine now."

"You own it?" she questioned, unable to keep the surprise from her voice.

"I traded it for a bit of work, it not being much good for farming."

"If it isn't good for farming why would you want it then?"

He frowned, and a look of uncertainty came over his face.

Emily began jumping up and down throwing her thin arms out. "That's the surprise," she said with a wide grin. "Tell her pa, tell her the surprise!"

"Well it's not worth much for growing nothing," Shade said, unwilling to be hurried.

His hair, as coarse and thick as a horse's mane, was sticking up on one side where he had carelessly pulled off his hat. Claire had a sudden impulse to reach her hand out and smooth it for him, but resisted. "Yes, you mentioned that."

"The way I see it though, if a body didn't plan on farming, it would make a right nice spot for a small cabin," he said suddenly, the heat rising in his face.

"Shade," she whispered nearly overcome by his words. Her hands flew to her face. "I can't believe it."

"Are you surprised?" Emily asked.

Grabbing Emily by the hands, she danced the two of them around gleefully. When they stopped, she said, "Emily, this was the best surprise."

"Pa said you would like it," she said proudly.

Remembering Shade, she turned to thank him. "Your pa was right Emily, I do like it."

"It might not look like much…," he said apologetically.

She held up her hand to stop him. "It's the most beautiful place, I have ever seen," she said, tears welling up.

"I am glad you're pleased," he said looking away into the distance.

"I have a little money," she said, thinking of the check she had just received from Victoria and the hope of more to come. "I can pay you a little along."

"You don't owe me nothing," he said. "It can just be yours for as long as you want." He stood unassumingly, holding his hat and looking out over the land. His eyes grazed the treetops and he shifted his weight from one foot to another. "It will take time to make something of this place again."

She wanted to tell him that this was the finest thing anyone had ever done for her. She wanted to throw her arms around him, lean into his strong shoulder and weep with relief that someone understood this need in her. When she looked at him, she could not summon the courage.

"Why would you do this for me?" she asked. It had come out more mean-tempered and suspicious than she had intended. She had simply meant to imply that it was a gift far beyond what was her right to expect.

He looked with a pained expression. He put his hand to his forehead as though shielding his eyes from a bright light. "I thought it was something you wanted," he said simply.

Of course, she thought, Shade was a man bound by duty and purpose. Had she not confessed to him her deepest desire for a cabin of her own? This was a man, after all, whose bloodline ran back to Scotland. His code of duty and fidelity was like the marrow in his bones. He was a man who felt compelled to do what fell to him to do.

"Truly, it will be my sanctuary," she said sincerely.

He smiled seemingly satisfied by her response.

"It may take me some time to save money for the cabin," she said laughing.

He laughed in turn. "I reckon this place will be here when you are ready. You can come here whenever you want. It will be yours to use from this day on."

"Do you think the cabin can be repaired?" she asked as she walked closer. She looked it over trying to take it all in at once.

"I've checked it over," he said excitedly. "First thing I'd do is patch the roof and board up the windows to keep the weather out. Then I'd prop up the chimney so you can have a fire. I can fix the porch easy enough. That'll make the place cozy enough for a while."

"Shade you've given such thought to this place."

"Well, I'm a carpenter you know," he said modestly.

"One among your many talents, I am learning."

He said nothing and stood looking uncomfortable with her praise.

"I could never really repay your generosity," she said earnestly. "And I'm afraid my words could never express my gratitude, Shade."

"I was hoping to trade a bit of work for some of it."

She laughed at his unexpected request. Wondering what she could ever do for Shade Morgan, she looked at him puzzled. "I am not much hand to farm and my carpentry skills are shameful I fear."

"Well, I reckon that's all right. I had something else in mind anyhow. I thought you might paint me a painting. That is something for Emily and me," he said solemnly.

"Why Shade, I would be honored," she said sincerely. "What would you have me do? Please just name it."

"Emily and me talked it over didn't we," he said glancing at his daughter. "We reckoned the right thing would come to you in time," he said.

She nodded unwilling to speak for fear her words would catch in her throat. "May I walk around the place?" she asked at last.

"There's a long, fairly level spot over here," he said suddenly animated. "I was thinking that in time you might want to build a house."

He paused and waited for her to speak.

Her mind whirled but she could not find the words. When she did not speak he went on.

"Something a little more comfortable."

She nodded.

"It is still close enough to the spring but it faces the morning sun. I thought you might like that."

She could not believe he had given so much thought to how the cabin was to face. "Shade this is a perfect spot," she said.

"Well, Emily said you talked in class about how important the light was when you paint and how you liked the morning light."

"Emily you should get a star on the blackboard for listening so keenly to your teacher."

"Shouldn't Pa get a star too?" Emily asked.

Claire saw the color rise in splotches up Shade's neck. "Indeed he should Emily," she said.

They both laughed.

He reached for her hand. "Let me show you the boundaries to your property."

Without hesitation, she took it. They walked about the place as Shade told her the history of the many lives lived out in this secluded spot. Much of it passed down from Uncle Hiram and some of it remembered from other kinfolk. She let him talk feeling in his words his tribute to an older and tougher generation and their connection to the land, which was now in essence hers to carry on.

"It seems so far away from everything, but I am sure I shall never feel alone here," she said.

"It seems out of the way now but one day soon it won't seem so set off by itself. You are still close to Gatlinburg, and I suspect in time, town will find its way closer to you."

"What a sad thought," she said pensively. "What makes you say such?"

"The road in to Gatlinburg is getting better," he said.

Claire could not help but laugh.

"It may not seem like it, I'll admit," he said agreeably, "but there's been talk of building it on over the mountain. They's even been talk of turning the Smoky Mountains into a national park. Some powerful folks have picked up that thread and they're not likely to let go of it."

"I have heard that from others," she said. She thought of the night at the Mountain View Inn when the photographer Jim Thompson had said the very same thing. "What would you do Shade if you had to give up your land?"

"Nowadays, a man don't need to look too far ahead to see change coming," he said with a shrug. "Ma won't live forever. Emily will be grown and married. That don't leave a man much to hang on to."

"Surely, you will marry again?" she asked.

He looked away the silence drawing out between them.

"I am so sorry Shade. I should not have said that. It truly is not my business."

"It's just that it don't seem likely," he said with a shrug. "That, I reckon, is a change that's hard to see coming."

"Yes, I'm sure you are right," she agreed.

To Claire's disappointment, the sun began to slant in the sky and the air took on a deepening chill. She thought of Emily so thin and frail. "I have had a lovely time but perhaps we should go before it gets much later," she suggested.

They walked on up to Shade's place in the fading light. Granny Kate met them at the door and rushed them in by the fire scolding Shade for keeping them out so late. He handed Claire her satchel and retreated outside to his chores as Granny Kate, refusing help, set the table for supper.

Shade came in with an armload of wood bringing the cold in on his clothes. "Sky's clearing up," he remarked. "It's going to be a cold one." He added wood to the fire and by the time they had eaten their soup beans and corn pone, the room was warm and inviting.

"Emily would you like me to read you a story?" Claire said as they gathered by the fireplace.

"Yes ma'am," Emily said politely.

"I brought along a book. Would you get my satchel for me please?"

Emily struggled with both hands to bring the oversized satchel to Claire. The blue scarf, which she had not been allowed to wear during supper for fear it would be soiled, was once again around her neck.

Claire pulled out a copy of *Alice in Wonderland*, and then put the bag down by her chair. She motioned to Emily to sit in her lap and then scooped her up in one quick motion.

Granny Kate pulled her darning from a basket by her rocker and began to mend a pair of socks. If she had thought it strange that her son had just that day made a deal for a piece of land with a young teacher he hardly knew from the Pi Beta Phi School, she said nothing about it to Claire. Shade too behaved as though the completely dizzying day was nothing out of the ordinary. He leaned back rocking on the legs of his chair, content in his idleness.

As Claire opened the book and began to read aloud, Emily leaned back against her and softly sighed. It seemed a lifetime ago that Claire had come to the mountains and yet it had only been a few months. When she had first ventured up the mountain to Shade Morgan's house, she had felt guarded and ill at ease. Now, as she sat reading, firelight reflecting the familiar faces around her, she felt very much at home as if folded into the arms of this family.

Chapter 22

Claire awoke to someone pounding on the front door. It came to her slowly where she had spent the night. Emily who had begged to sleep with her still dozed. She could hear voices in the front room. Quickly dressing, she slipped out and padded softly to the kitchen. The table was set, but breakfast had been pushed to the back of the stove. When she looked through to the front room, Shade stood talking to a young man. His face was solemn as he took in the man's words. Granny Kate stood nearby wringing her hands and nodding her head.

"We will be along directly," Shade said as the young man turned to go.

The young man hurried down the front steps with a wave.

"He's going on up to tell the neighbors," Shade said to his mother as he shut the door.

"What is it?" Claire asked. "Is something wrong?"

Shade turned to her and she could see it in his face. "Dealie Riley is dead," he announced flatly.

She let out a gasp as though someone had knocked the wind out of her. "I don't understand," she whispered. "What happened?"

Granny Kate rushed to her and took her by the hands. "Oh honey, she got burned up in a fire, is what Rupert was just telling us. Poor thing."

"A fire," Claire said disbelieving.

"She was bad to back up to the fireplace to get warm, her ma said," Granny Kate said by way of explanation. "It was just Dealie and her ma at home. The cow had got out and her ma had gone out to put it up. Dealie come out on fire, a screaming. Her ma burned herself near to death trying to put it out."

"How terrible," Claire said. She thought of Dealie, so self-assured and full of life reciting her poem at the Christmas party.

Now all of that had been stilled by a terrible accident. "Mary must be beside herself."

Granny Kate let go of her hands and her shoulders sagged. "The death of a child is not something a mother should have to bear. She's most likely blaming herself."

Claire knew that Granny Kate must have been thinking of her own sons.

"They want Ma to come help lay her out," Shade said.

Claire had heard that the neighbor women always came to prepare the body when someone passed away. "I know that will be so difficult for you Granny Kate. I am sorry that it must fall to you," Claire said sincerely.

"It's nothing Mary wouldn't do for me," Granny Kate said simply.

"I'll take you down when you are ready, Ma," Shade said.

"I've got breakfast ready, "Granny Kate said. "I'll get Emily up and dressed. You two go ahead and eat while it's hot."

Claire followed Shade into the kitchen. She poured them both a cup of coffee and then fixed Shade a plate. She sat holding her cup, unable to drink, while Shade moved the food around on his plate before laying his fork down.

Emily came into the room, rubbing her eyes. Shade reached out and pulled her into his lap. Granny Kate came back carrying a length of soft blue fabric in her arms. She met Shades eyes and he nodded.

"Emily, why don't you stay here with me for a while," Claire said, "just the two of us. Would you like that?"

"Granny Kate told me what happened to Dealie," Emily said softly.

"Yes, it's very sad," Claire said.

"I'll be back to get you directly Emily," Shade said. "You stay here with Miss Claire until I come for you." Shade slipped Emily from his arms and into a chair at the table. "Eat your breakfast and do your chores. I won't be long." Slowly he put on his coat as though he was in no hurry to do the chore that lay ahead. "Thank you," he mouthed.

"We will be fine," Claire assured him.

She poured Emily a glass of milk. "After you eat, why don't we comb your hair and I will braid it for you. Would you like that?" Claire asked.

Emily nodded, her cheeks full of milk.

"Then afterward, we can read some more of *Alice in Wonderland*," Claire offered.

"Dealie is in heaven now isn't she?" Emily said suddenly.

Claire was unprepared for the question. "I have no doubt she is Emily," she said.

"Granny Kate says she is in a better place," Emily quizzed.

"I am sure Granny Kate is right," Claire said.

"But why would she want to go some place without her ma and pa and Frannie and Martha Jane?"

"You are wondering how any place could be better than being with your family?" Claire asked. She realized that Emily had been thinking of her mother. She had probably been told the same thing when her mother died.

Emily nodded, tears welling up in her eyes.

"I don't think people die because they want to go to a better place or because they want to leave their families. I think they want more than anything to be with their families especially their little girls," Claire said, "but if someone must go away, isn't it good to know they are in a wonderful new place. And that if they can't be with us, they are looking down on all the people they loved and looking after them."

"Do you think my mama is looking down on me?"

"Yes, I do, and I think she would be very pleased at what a wonderful little girl you are growing up to be."

"That's what my pa says," Emily said.

Claire turned her back and busied herself cleaning up the kitchen. Slowly she let out her breath. Tested by an eight year old on a subject with which she was completely unfamiliar, she felt utterly drained. One thing she was becoming sure of, Emily was more than blond hair and sky blue eyes. She was much like Claire, a girl who had more questions for the world than the world had answers.

Later after Emily fell asleep in her arms as they sat reading, Claire heard someone outside. She quickly put Emily to bed and went out to find Shade in the barn. He had a broad piece of chestnut wood which he was fashioning into a small casket.

He looked up, his eyes full of pain.

"Emily fell asleep," she said.

"It's just as well," he said going on with his work.

"I didn't know you did this," she said.

"It falls to me sometimes," he said without looking up. "They's times it's good just to put your hands to some work."

Claire saw the length of fabric that Granny Kate had given Shade lying on the table next to Shade's tools. She picked it up.

"It's to line the casket," Shade said. "You can help me when the time comes."

She swallowed the lump that rose up in her throat. She resisted the urge to fling the fabric down.

"Ma usually does it. I wouldn't ask but I just thought you'd be a better hand at it than me," he said apologetically. "My big hands can be clumsy at times."

"Of course," she said. It was all she could manage.

Claire stood watching as Shade patiently planed the wood, feeling it with his hands until it was perfectly smooth. It was the most loving gesture she had ever seen. His shoulders were taut and his face bore the look of intense concentration. She wondered if he was thinking of his own wife and child so recently gone. Had he made their casket too? Where did a man find that kind of courage? She thought about how quickly the joy of yesterday, the hope of ones life could vanish and be replaced by such tragedy as it had for Shade and now for Mary Riley.

"How is the family?" she asked, not knowing what else to say.

He looked at her but made no reply. A shadow crossed his face.

"Mary must be grieving wildly…" she said, her voice trailing off.

"She wants you to come down."

"Me?"

"She asked for you. She said Dealie was especially fond of you."

Claire was surprised to hear it. It filled her with guilt that she had only been aware of the young girl because of her bold and rambunctious nature. It had not occurred to her that Dealie was watching her. "Oh, Shade, I don't know if I should go."

"She wants you there," Shade said as though that settled the matter. "She wants you to read from the Bible for her."

Claire felt her insides turn over. She had never wanted to shrink from doing something so much in her life. Her mind rehearsed a dozen ways she might escape the ordeal. She took a deep breath planning to offer Shade one of them when she found herself saying, "I'll be ready to go when you are."

The suffering in the room was palpable. This was like the panther that came screaming in the night, Claire thought as panic rose in her heart. She did not know how she could handle such emotion. The small cabin was filled with people who had turned out to bring food and to sit with the family. Shade took Claire by the elbow and eased her into the room. Emily clung to Shade's leg.

Mary sat by the fire. A woman sitting next to Mary got up to make room. When Mary looked up to see Claire, she let out a keening wail. "Lord have pity on me," she cried. "Lord have pity on me."

Mary's eyebrows had been burned away and her hands were a mass of blisters, but she was not asking for relief from the pain of her burns. She was asking for relief from the crushing pain in her heart. Claire knew she had to put her own distress behind her and do whatever she could for this mother in such pain. She rushed forward and gently put her arms around Mary. "I am so sorry Mary," she said.

"Did you see her?" Mary asked.

"No," Claire said looking puzzled.

Mary pointed to the bed.

Claire realized that the small form on the bed was Dealie. She stifled a gasp.

"We laid her out in that pretty little dress she wore at Christmas," Mary said proudly. "Blue was always her favorite color. She wanted to wear it everyday but I wouldn't let her."

Claire could hear the regret in her voice.

"You remember how she looked up there reciting her poem," Mary went on. "She was so proud of the way she never made a mistake."

"She was a smart girl, Mary," Claire said honestly. "All the teachers thought so highly of her." She thought of all the hopes and dreams Mary had for all her girls and how hard she had fought for their education.

"Go look at her, Miss Claire. Granny Kate put a bonnet on her to hide her head. You'd never know she was burned. Dealie always was such a fool for her hair," Mary said wistfully. "She wouldn't hear of having it cut."

In Claire's family, death had always been more hidden. Even when her grandfather died, her mother had grieved quietly, distantly. She had been allowed to turn away. Now she felt her inner resilience quicken as she summoned her courage and walked to the bedside. The form on the bed was horribly burned, hardly resembling the young girl she had known. Swallowing the bile that rose in her throat, she returned to Mary.

"Didn't I tell you she was still beautiful," Mary said.

"Yes, Mary, she is still beautiful," Claire said, sitting down by Mary.

"She thought the world of you, Miss Claire. Sometimes just a word or two from you and she'd come home a braggin' about it for days. She thought if somebody as pretty and smart as you could pay her some mind, she must be special."

The armor that Claire wore to protect herself broke open and fell from her shoulders. The pain seared her heart. Tears welled up in her eyes and threatened to spill over. She blinked them back and said, "She was a very special little girl, Mary."

"I just left her for a minute," Mary said. Her words were the sad lament of a mother who had not been able to protect her child.

"It was not your fault, Mary. It was an accident."

"If I told her once, I must have told her a hundred times not to back up to that fireplace," Mary went on.

"Yes," was all Claire could say.

"Al and the other girls had gone to take some fresh milk and butter down to the Smith's. They don't have a milk cow. You know we bought a milk cow with the money I made from baskets," Mary said looking up with a crooked smile.

Claire realized that Mary had been over every detail of what had happened in her mind. She had probably told the story many times so far, but Claire listened hoping somehow that it would ease Mary's pain. Her voice mingled with the soft talking, the crying and the occasional laughter around them.

"Dealie had a little bit of a cold so I made her stay here with me. She begged me to go," Mary said.

"You did what you thought was best. You could not have known," Claire said. Her words felt like a feeble salve against the guilt and suffering in Mary's eyes.

"I looked out to see Daisy out of the barn. Dealie named our new cow the same as our old cow Daisy because she said it was too good a name not to use again," Mary said, smiling wistfully. "She was always clever that way."

"All the teachers thought so," Claire agreed.

"Somehow Daisy must of got out of her stall," Mary said with a bewildered look.

Claire wondered whose job it had been to latch the stall. Who would this moment be going over in their minds, asking if only they had checked the latch? She thought of Frannie so diligent, so duty bound and prayed it was not her.

"I just went out for a minute. Then I seen Dealie come running. Her head was on fire. I think she must'of been backing up to the fire and stumbled. Do you think that's what happened?"

Mary looked at Claire seeking an answer.

"Most likely that is the way it happened, Mary."

"I tried to put out the fire," Mary said, holding her hands up palm out.

"You did everything you could do," Claire said.

Mary nodded but her eyes told a different story.

"I'd be pleased if you would read the twenty-third Psalm to me," Mary said. "It's always been a comfort to me. There's a Bible on the mantel there."

Claire got up to retrieve the Bible. Al Riley stood in the doorway leading to the kitchen looking like a broken man. "I am so sorry," she said feeling the feebleness of her words echo in her ears.

"Yes, ma'am, we're grateful to you," he said his voice raspy. "Mary was hoping…"

"I'll stay as long as she needs me," Claire said.

Al nodded.

Shade slipped up behind Al and put his hand on his shoulder. Claire could hear Granny Kate in the kitchen urging folks to eat. All around her the threads of the community were coming together to bind up the wounds of this family.

She sat back down next to Mary, opened the book and started to read. She was aware of the shuffling of feet, people whispering as they came and went about the cabin but she tried to lose herself in the reading.

Frannie came in and sat at her mother's feet. When Claire finished reading, Frannie began to sing softly, *In the sweet by and by, We shall meet on that beautiful shore.* Tears fell on her cheeks as she sang and her voice trembled.

Martha Jane came to stand beside Frannie and joined her in song. Their mother closed her eyes and began to rock gently in her chair.

Frannie's voice grew stronger and others in the room joined in the song, *There's a land that is fairer than day, And by faith we can see it afar.*

The day moved into afternoon. Silence came and went. No one bothered to hide the rawness of the open wound that was their suffering. In time, Claire too put down the burden of pretending and cried, letting the tears fall unchecked onto her lap. As night drew near, they sat suspended in time, held up by grief and love.

January 28, 1921

Dear Lenora

 I am writing this letter by electric light as we now have a generator for the cottage. After so many months of squinting to write my letters by lamplight, it is a delightful improvement. One has the urge to stay up all night reading, writing and making use of all the hours that seemed added to the day by this simple device.

 I was delighted to hear the good news that you are expecting a baby in summer. I cannot believe that I am to be an auntie three times over. I know you have your heart set on a girl this time. Can I expect her to be my namesake as we are sure to adore one another on sight? I expect to be home by her birth.

 I was utterly done in by the boy's notes thanking me for their presents. I could just see you standing over them forcing them to say nice things the way Mother used to do to us. Remember the horrid gifts Aunt Mimi used to send to us for our birthdays and how we rolled with laughter as we wrote how we simply adored the rose talc or the hideous hats which were no doubt her children's castoffs. What wicked little girls we were. So don't be too hard on the boys. I have put their notes on my bureau to cheer me. I do miss them terribly.

 Yesterday one of the boys in shop came running yelling excitedly. We thought something terrible must have happened but we were alarmed unduly. It seems the boys had made a sled in class and they wanted the teachers to try it out. The

children could not be contained after talk of the sled spread
through the school and we had to turn them all out to watch.
At first I was uncertain but after watching the boys go down
the hill behind the school a number of times, I decided to try it.
Are you surprised at your sister's boldness? I must admit to
a bit of trouble directing the sled and I did take a tumble at the
bottom but it was worth it. The children found it a grand sight
to see their teacher tossed about and covered in snow.

I am most grateful for the money the church collected for
the school. You must have been quite persuasive. Did you show
them the pictures I sent along of the students? Do they not
look like perfect angels? You may be surprised to learn that
many of the older students have gone on to do advance work
at Carson Newman, Berea and Murphy Colleges. All reports
are that they are among the best of scholars. It would be most
delightful to see some of my students attend college some day.

Our enrollment reached one-hundred and twenty-seven
this year. The school has already purchased sixty-seven
additional acres of land with the future in mind. An auditorium
is desired by the community and is most needed by the school.
Also an outdoor gymnasium would be most useful for the boys.

Nurse Higinbotham wants to have a full medical clinic
by fall and she is a woman of considerable determination. She
has persuaded doctors from Knoxville and Sevierville to make
regular visits to Gatlinburg.

We have added a weaving instructor to the staff. Already
three of the women have had their own looms made and are
working at home. Baskets are coming in as never before and
the attic is stuffed with them. Some of the women have already
sold their goods to the hotel guests. There is talk of starting a
craft shop to sell all the wonderful things the mountain people
are making. We are all excited by such glorious possibilities.

My dear friend Tessie has told me that she plans to stay on another year to teach. Her parents are most pleased by this decision, she tells me. You will be surprised to hear your baby sister say that she is quite humbled by the dedication of all of the teachers here. I know that we are touching the lives of these young students and it weights heavily upon me that I might be worthy of such responsibility.

You can't know how much I miss you. Give the boys a hug from Aunt Claire.

Your loving sister
Claire

Chapter 23

Spring had not quite burst through, but there were signs all about that the starkness of winter would soon give way to the expectancy of a new season. The mountain streams had broken free of the icy hands that held them bound and now roared and tumbled riotously. The lengthening days urged the still bare trees to unfurl their protective buds and fill the forest with green leaves. The fickle winds of March had picked up a new message and it whispered of the mysteries still hidden in the days ahead.

As Claire headed up to the cabin, her satchel thrown over her shoulder, she felt lighthearted. She awoke that morning with a sense of well-being—an unfamiliar feeling in the weeks past and she felt as though she had to become acquainted with it all over again. Breathing in the gentle air, she felt her spirits lift as though heeding the distant robins call to "cheer-up."

In the weeks that followed Dealie's death, the mountains stood frozen. Every mountaintop, every ravine, every cliff was covered with snow as though sifted by some heavenly baker. The rushing water of the waterfalls stopped and hung suspended in place. The world was hushed in reverent silence.

There were no fields to be plowed, no crops to tend. It was as though nature was saying "nothing to be done, nothing to be done." Nature was making a way for them to grieve through the winter. Soon enough spring would come and life would demand to go on.

Claire had felt trembly and tender for days after Dealie's death. She had experienced both the beauty and brevity of life and it had left her shaken to her soul. She had poured herself back into her classes keeping the children busy at every turn. All of the teachers, recently back from the holiday, had been doubly shocked by the loss. They had taken special care to fill their student's days so that no one might dwell unduly on what had happened.

Frannie, not one given to frivolity, had come back more silent and serious than before. Hanging about the teacher's desk, at times lingering, occasionally catching a teacher's eye, she said little.

Martha Jane had come back lost and unable to put her mind to her work. When Claire sat reading to the class, she often caught her staring out the window. Her needlework became careless as she sat with it at times untouched on her lap. She appeared too bruised to accept even the kind words and tenderness the teachers poured out to her in turn.

Tessie, who somehow blamed herself for having taken a holiday, tried to mother them all. She was especially mindful of Claire who, though she appreciated the care, could find solace only in work.

Claire felt ill disposed to share her feelings with anyone and her letters home were only of the most general nature. She dozed fitfully at night waking with a cold fear that she should be up and about. Sleep seemed a terrible waste. She poured herself back into her painting with a ferocity she had not known she had. Trading her skirts for trousers and boots, unmindful of what people thought, she set about the mountains in search of whatever gifts winter held. Undeterred by steel gray skies, she searched the wildness of the winter woods. Whatever she came upon whether squirrel tracks, hemlock cones, or partridge berries peaking out of the snow, she embraced them as signs of life and of hope. She brushed the snow from fallen tree trunks and set sketching forest vistas and icy mountain streams. Hands tingling, face burning from the cold, she reveled in her discomfort.

One day when the snow was deep, she pushed herself to go further along the trail. Caught up in the windfalls that blocked the trail, she struggled to climb over raw broken trees until she came to a thicket of rhododendrons. Unexpectedly she pushed through and came upon Rainbow Falls. From a great wall of stone hung jagged icicles some twenty feet or more in length and at the base of the falls were two frozen cones of ice over thirty feet high.

Her breath caught at the sight of the sun sparkling on the translucent blue ice. As she made her way over snow covered boulders sometimes stumbling to her knees, she was aware of the danger. When Shade had discovered her solo adventures, he had cautioned her once again about venturing out alone into the mountains but it was only at times like these that she felt truly alive. When she finally stood at the base of the tallest cone, the frigid air engulfing her, her heart raced. When beams of sunlight struck the ice, they seemed to pulse from deep within the cone sending out radiant waves of blue and purple that washed over her. She could almost feel a kind of warmth from it. The color was illusive and seemed to come and go as she strained to hold on to its beauty. Out of such beauty, a strange tenderness flowed and filled her with a deep sense of peace. In that moment she at last felt whole and healed.

She realized that for as long as she could remember she had been like a water bug skimming across the surface of life. As long as she was allowed to light briefly on the swirling complexity that was human life, remaining ever vigilante, alert always to the danger of her emotions, she felt safe and in control. Dealie's death had plunged her into the very rawness of life. She had looked into the eyes of a grieving mother and heard her pitiful cries. She had watched as the community had not turned away but had come to share in the suffering and to offer their love and support.

When she came to the mountains, it was for her own selfish purpose, never expecting to fall in love with the people. Never imagining that what had first appeared as ignorance, superstition and a resistance to change in the people would reemerge in her eyes as courage in the face of life's challenges, a deep well of warmth and hospitality, an eager intelligence and a pride in a heritage passed down through time.

She had never expected to fall in love with the mountains. How could she have known that it was possible to rise from sleep to see hoarfrost on the hemlocks sparkling like a million diamonds asking nothing in return but to delight the senses. Or that the soothing sound of a mountain stream tumbling over boulders could be as evocative as a symphony. How could she have expected her deepest secrets to be revealed in the frozen blue ice of a waterfall.

She had returned from the falls determined not to keep life at arms length. She would allow Tessie to comfort her, she would write truthfully to her sister of her hopes and fears, she would embrace the messiness that was life.

The feeling of wholeness she felt at the falls had soon given way to confusion. In the weeks since that transcendent moment, the experience had taken on more of a dreamlike quality. Slowly she had begun to pull her emotions back in check. Soon she had come to doubt it all together.

Claire hastened her step as she came to the cutoff to the cabin, excited by the thoughts of a new season, one she had not experienced in the mountains. She had already come to think of the ramshackle cabin as her own. Shade had patched the roof and secured the porch so that at last she might feel safe going inside to have a look. The cabin was as tiny as Aunt Lydia's with only one room. The low roof made it seem cozy and suited Claire's small stature. The years of being opened and exposed to the weather had done its damage but she thought it would do for now. Shade was right that someday she might want to build a house of her own but for now she was thrilled with her diminutive refuge.

She was surprised to see Shade standing with his back to her looking at the cabin. When she called out to him he turned slowly his thumb and forefinger still on his chin.

"What are you studying so seriously?" she asked.

He smiled to her and gave her a welcoming wave. "I've been working on the chimney."

Claire came and stood next to him. The first thing she noticed was that the chimney was now straight and once again attached to the cabin. "How on earth did you get it back in place?" she asked.

"It took a might of digging to get to the foundation. Uncle Hiram had set it deep enough," he said with a grin.

She could see smoke coming from the top. "You've made a fire," she said.

"I wanted to see if it would draw," he said. "I was worried it might not draw and fill that little cabin with smoke. Then you'd a seen me come out hollering. Me and whatever other critters have been livin' in there."

"Well that might have been a sight worth seeing," she teased.

One side of Shade's mouth came up in a lop-sided grin.

"What's that?" Claire asked pointing to the chimney. Smoke had begun to pour from hundreds of places in the chimney.

"Bees," Shade said shaking his head. He paced about for a minute examining the chimney.

Claire looked at him puzzled.

"They make a home in the chinking. That's the problem with mud. It hardly gets dry until bees start to drill holes in it. I was figuring on having to do some chinking when the weather warms some more," he said with a shrug.

"You must let me help you," she said.

"Well that might be a sight worth seeing," he teased, echoing her words. He laughed a quiet laugh.

She threw her hands to her hips but then she laughed along with him. Then she grew more serious. "I can't let you do all of this for me. You must let me help. You must let me pay you for your work."

"We made a deal," he said cheerfully. "I'm not letting you out of it."

She waved him off. "Of course, I haven't forgotten, I will paint you a dozen paintings, but I mean to own this place outright," she insisted. "I mean for it to be mine."

His face held a pained expression.

"It is not that I'm not grateful to you," she rushed to explain. "It's just that it means a lot to me to make my own way."

"I don't see how me fixing up this cabin is any different than you teaching Emily to draw," he remarked, "or you painting a picture for me. We'd both be doing with what talents we'd been given. That's the way it's always been done here."

"It's just that I hardly feel my talents are equal to yours," she said honestly.

"That's where you are wrong," he said matter-of-factly.

She found herself chuckling at his bluntness.

He grinned down at her. Then he grew more serious. "You're just afraid if you let folks do for you that somehow that will take away from who you are."

"Yes," she said weakly. "I have always been afraid that if I accept help, I will owe more than I can repay. I don't mean money…" she stammered.

"I will never make you feel beholden to me. I can promise you that much. Do you believe me, Claire?" he asked solemnly.

Her throat closed up. She nodded.

"Good," he said turning suddenly lighthearted. "Now come here. I want to show you something," he commanded as he walked toward the cabin.

She followed him curious at what he had in store for her next. She followed his eyes as he looked to the porch. A window sparkled where there had only been an opening before. "Shade you've put in a window," she said with genuine surprise.

"So you can have a little light and to keep out the critters," he said proudly. His eyes glistened.

Impulsively, she stood on her tiptoes and kissed him quickly on the cheek.

Blushing he said, "I put another one in the back."

She punched him in the arm.

Grabbing his arm he feigned terrible pain.

She looked at him surprised. "I didn't mean to hurt you."

He laughed. "I've had flea bites that hurt worse."

She huffed away. Throwing her satchel on the porch, she sat down. Pulling out a jelly biscuit, she unwrapped it from its napkin and passed it to him and then got one for herself. He sat down beside her. They sat eating the biscuits and alternately licking the jelly from their fingers. Claire leaned back against the porch railing, closed her eyes and turned her face to the sun. "It's so peaceful here," she said.

Shade did not reply.

She opened her eyes to find him gazing intently at her.

He looked away slowly.

"Let's go to the spring and get a drink," she said.

The spring house was long gone but water still trickled over the rocks that had been stacked for decades before and collected in a clear pool. Claire bent and scooped up a handful of water, letting it drip down her chin, wiping it with the back of her hand. She saw Shade following her hands. "The water is sweet here," she remarked.

"This place has good water," he agreed, dropping to one knee to scoop up a drink.

Suddenly springing to his feet, he walked to a place where the woods opened up and the sunlight filled the ground. He looked at her and held his arms open wide. "I thought come spring I might plow you up a little garden spot," he said.

His words sent her reeling and left her too stunned to speak. He was making plans for her to be here long enough to grow a garden. He expected her to stay through the summer, perhaps longer. He had no idea that her term ended in May and that she was expected to return home. What had she been thinking to let him to do all of this for her and to build this life for her here? The truth was she had allowed herself to be carried along like a leaf in a stream, through calm pools, over waterfalls, spinning into eddies without any thought to where she was headed. Thoughts had flitted about the edge of her mind, as she had cleaned the cobwebs from the cabin and swept the twigs and leaves outside, but she had brushed them aside like gnats without putting meaning to them.

Now as she searched Shade's face, it revealed the secret he had been keeping. How was it possible that she could have been so unaware, she thought? When his eyes met hers, it was clear that he knew he had given himself away.

"That is I thought you might want it just for your own pleasure. I know you wouldn't be living here. I know you take your meals at the school," he rambled on, growing evermore unsure of himself.

"Thank you, Shade. It's a lovely thought. It's just that I may not be here in the summer." She felt cowardly for even now not making clear her plans. "My sister is having a baby this summer. I promised her I would be there," she stammered. "My parents too are expecting me home."

Finally, she stopped talking and looked at him.

"Emily and me can tend to it till you get back," he offered.

Her stomach turned over as she realized that he still did not grasp what she was trying to tell him. "I've only contracted for the one year, Shade. I am not sure I will be back to teach." She watched as he took in her words.

"I reckon they would welcome you back," he said.

"It's not what I had planned," she said feebly. "When I came here, I mean."

He moved toward her and gently took her by the arms. "Sometimes you can hold on to a notion too hard Claire. Would it be so bad if you loosened your grip just a might?" he asked "and give something else a chance."

She realized that she had denied her own growing affection and respect for this humble and tender man because it did not fit into her imagined future—a future that required her to cast off all ties and to claim no place or person as her own. She had guarded herself so completely from the advances of men who wanted to claim her only to find that she had allowed her feelings for this man to grow unaware, just as her love of the community and the mountains had grown. The thought left her confused and unsure. Had she not always planned to go, she asked herself? When had she allowed this feeling of comfort, of safety here in the mountains to slip into her life? She felt pulled in different directions.

She looked up into his eyes searching his face for the answer. He took her deep into his arms and kissed her on the lips. The world spun around her and she braced her hands against his chest.

Releasing her from his embrace, Shade stood looking down at her. His dark eyes searched her face. She wanted to tell him of her feelings but she was too unsure of her voice.

"Maybe another summer when you come back to the cabin," he said, at last looking away.

As she slipped out of Shade's strong arms, she felt he was releasing her from all expectations. He looked at her as though to affirm his promise that he would never make her feel beholden. Whatever he had revealed about his feelings was his concern and he would not hold her to them. He was a man of his word, his eyes said, and he was freeing her to make her own decision.

"Yes, perhaps then," she said, "perhaps another summer."

Chapter 24

Frannie thought Clem Ollie Riley was the sweetest baby ever to be born. He had come into the world quickly and quietly on a bright April morning with only a tiny kitten like mew to announce his coming. Since that day two weeks ago, there had been no need for him to squall out, demanding to be fed, or held for the family doted on him. Someone stood ready to sweep him up into waiting arms before he had time to announce his needs.

The family had spent the winter hunkered down in sorrow. Frannie's pa had sat in his chair in front of the fire every night watching the flames until they had almost died out. Surprised to discover the room growing cold, he would look up and gaze about. After a time he would get up and add more sticks of wood to the fire and then go back to searching the flames. Frannie's ma would go about her chores wordless and blank eyed. Sometimes as her ma peeled potatoes for supper, Frannie would see her tears plopping into the dishpan. The house was quiet without Dealie's rambunctious nature. Even Frannie and Martha Jane, whose habit it was to go after each other over the least little thing, causing their ma to say, 'ain't that a fine way to act' could find no pleasure in fighting.

The guilt of what had happened to Dealie hung like a thick icy fog over them all. That morning, her pa had been in a hurry and rushed them through their chores. Martha Jane had wanted to go back and check the latch but she had not wanted to mention it to her pa who was already fussing at them. Frannie had told Martha Jane that if she spent as much time on her chores as she did fixing her hair they would have been finished with their chores before their pa got mad. Her ma wondered aloud if she had only warned Dealie about standing too close to the fire before she had gone out to check the cow. No one mentioned blaming another. There wasn't any need. They all wore it like a heavy winter coat.

Then the baby came.

When Dealie was born, Frannie had gone to stay with neighbors. It had taken two days for Dealie to make it into the world. She had spent the next weeks squalling, red-faced and angry about it. Her ma had been weak for months after, as though all of Dealie's liveliness had been grabbed from her on the way out. She had never slowed down for all of her six years and she had at times tested the whole family. Frannie had come to regret all the times she had been upset with her for what she called "her trifling little ways." She prayed each night that there was a special place in heaven for Dealie to play. She did so love to play.

Ollie could never replace Dealie. That was what they all said but the terrible sadness that had hung over the family lifted when they looked at his sweet face. When folks saw her pa holding Ollie they remarked, "He sure does think a sight of that boy." Other folks said, "I never did see a man make so over a baby." Her ma said, "I do believe he must be an angel done fell from heaven." Frannie knew her folks would never stop grieving for Dealie but they needed the joy of a new baby.

All manner of thoughts about dying had passed through Frannie's mind since she had watched them lower Dealie's coffin into the ground. Thoughts on what happened to a person after they died. Thoughts on heaven and hell and why God would see fit to take a little girl like that. She wondered if Dealie would have her beautiful hair back in heaven. She wondered if the angels knew that Dealie sometimes had bad dreams and would they sleep with her at night. She couldn't make sense of it and it had worn her out with the thinking of it. It seemed like a person could only dwell on something so long without an answer.

Ollie seemed content to be held or content to be put down. Frannie liked to hold him and sing lullabies. As she sat rocking him and singing, he would wrap his whole hand around her finger and make sucking noises as he slept. She especially liked it when her ma would be working in the kitchen as she was now and she could hear her humming along.

Sometimes when no one was listening she talked to Ollie about Dealie. Frannie thought that maybe a baby, having come so recently from God, might be more understanding than grownup folks. Maybe he could even get a message to Dealie about how sorry she felt for not being a better sister. She promised him that she would be a better sister to him. She had already told him how sorry she was about thinking that a new baby would be a burden. He had scrunched up his little face and puckered his little lips. She hoped that meant he was forgiving of her selfish ways.

Her pa had gone to take Martha Jane and Theo Campbell to the courthouse in Sevierville to get married. They were due back soon and her ma was making a wedding supper for the couple. They would spend the night and then go to live with Theo's folks until they could get a place of their own.

Martha Jane had been so sad after Dealie's death that Frannie had been worried for her. She had lost all interest in school and even Frannie could not find it in her to be mad about that. So it had come as no surprise when she had announced that she was quitting school to get married. Even her ma had not fussed about it. "The Campbell's is not a bad lot," was all she said on the matter. Her pa had made Martha Jane bring the boy around to meet them. He was tall and wiry with his dark hair greased back. Frannie had watched him playing baseball and acting all silly for Martha Jane. She thought him a poor trade for school.

He had stood blushing and shuffling his feet until her pa had taken him out to the barn for a long talk. In time, her pa went to talk to the Campbell family. It was all agreed upon. After that, Martha Jane seemed more at ease with herself. She had not even protested when Frannie insisted she go and tell her teachers that she was leaving school to get married.

Slowly, the family had latched on to a kind of happiness that no one was ready yet to speak about out loud. As rare and fine as a Lady Slipper in bloom, they were constantly alert to its fragileness.

"Come help me set the table, Frannie," her ma called. "They should be getting back anytime now."

Frannie laid the baby on the bed and kissed his little forehead. She ran her fingers over his downy head and whispered, "Sleep baby, sleep." When she went into the kitchen, her ma was moving a skillet of cornbread from the fire. Frannie took the plates down from the shelf and set the table.

Mary Riley went to the pie safe and opened it. Frannie came up behind her and they stood looking at the dried apple stack cake that Mary had made as a surprise for Martha Jane. "It's pretty Ma," Frannie exclaimed. Mary put her arm around her and gave her a squeeze. Frannie reached up and took her ma's hand, scarred and rough from the burns, and pressed it to her face. Frannie did not know why but she felt like bursting into tears. Choking them back, she smiled up at her ma.

A noise at the door made Mary Riley close the pie safe door. Frannie and her ma grinned at each other as though they had a great secret. Al Riley came through the front door followed by the newlyweds. Mary rushed forward to hug Martha Jane and then Theo in turn. Theo stood stiffly in his blue serge pants and white shirt, his arms by his side.

Martha Jane smiled shyly at Frannie who stood in the kitchen doorway. She came to Frannie and bent down kissing her on the forehead. "I'm a married woman now, Frannie," she said.

The words made Frannie sad for reasons she could not understand. She looked at her sister in her white, shawl-collared dress with the soft gathering above the wide waistband and thought how she looked somehow different from the sister she had always known. It was as though the trip to Sevierville had somehow changed her. Or was it that they had always been different and now with Martha Jane's growing up she could see it more plainly.

"We will still be sisters won't we," she said, letting the words slip out. It was the thought that had been worrying the back of her mind. It had only been in the last months that she and Martha Jane had grown closer. Now Martha Jane was moving away. For so much of her life nothing had changed. It seemed of late that things were always changing on her.

"Of course, you silly goose," Martha Jane said. She tousled Frannie's hair and cupped her under the chin. "I wouldn't change that for the world. When Theo and me get a place of our own, you can come stay with us all the time. Would you like that?"

Frannie nodded.

"Now you younguns come along. I've fixed a good supper," Mary said.

They watched as Al went to the bed where Ollie slept. Frannie felt like time stopped as they all stood looking at him gazing down at the baby. Then he looked up and grinned. "Let's eat," he said heartily. "I'm plumb starved."

They all let out a sigh of relief that nothing was about to spoil the good mood that had settled over them. They headed to the kitchen where they sat around the table listening to Martha Jane describe the day, as Mary dished up the supper. The bride and groom cast sidelong glances at each other.

"The courthouse is the biggest building you ever seen," Martha Jane said holding her arms out wide.

Theo nodded as he looked on adoringly at his bride.

The color rose up her neck. "Theo paid for the license with money he made trapping furs," Martha Jane said proudly.

"Martha Jane was the prettiest bride there," he said in return.

"We was the only folks there getting married Theo," she said. Then her hand flew to her hip as she realized the joke. She poked him hard in the arm.

They all laughed, even their pa. Frannie thought it was the best sound ever.

Frannie said grace and they set upon the food. When Ollie made a squeaking noise, her ma rushed to get him. After she had nursed him, she brought him in and handed him to Al, who held him on his shoulder, his hand against his head while he continued to eat.

After they had eaten their fill, the couple eyed each other shyly. Frannie wondered why her ma did not bring out the cake she had been so proud and excited about earlier. She made no move to get up even as Martha Jane and Theo squirmed restlessly in their seats. They seemed shy and unsure of what to do next.

Suddenly a great racket came from the yard and the sound of people shouting filled the air. "Mercy, who could that be?" Frannie's ma remarked. Frannie looked around the table to see her ma and pa grinning at each other.

Martha Jane caught their eyes. "It's a shivaree," she shouted. Grabbing Theo by the hand, she pulled him to the front door. The family followed them outside to be greeted by Miss Tessie, Miss Claire, Miss Agnes and half dozen students all shouting, banging pie tins together and shaking cow bells.

Frannie clapped her hands in delight at the sight of her teachers all dressed up in their crisp blouses and pressed skirts banging pots and pans, making the worst racket while they laughed along with the students. She had never in a day expected to see her teachers like this and she thought she might be dreaming.

The bigger boys picked Theo up and carried him around the yard. The girls pulled Martha Jane into the yard where they stuck flowers in her hair and danced around her teasing her in their sing-song voices.

Frannie could see Martha Jane pretending like it plagued her to have so much attention, putting her hand to her mouth, looking all embarrassed, but she couldn't hide her smile. Frannie was thrilled to have all of her teachers at her home. It pleased her that they were not upset with Martha Jane for leaving school and that they thought enough to come all that way.

Finally when they were all exhausted, Frannie's folks invited them in to have cake. They brought the chairs from the kitchen for the teachers to sit on and the girls took the bed where they took turns holding Ollie. The boys all sat around the floor.

"Martha Jane," Miss Tessie spoke up, "we wanted to give you a wedding present." She held out the tissue wrapped gift, tied with a soft pink ribbon. "The girls sewing class made these for you."

Martha Jane gingerly untied the ribbon to show the hand embroidered pillowcases. The girls screamed with delight and clapped their hands. "Thank you," Martha Jane said.

The boys began to tell stories on Theo.

Theo made like he was going to run off, but then he laughed good-naturedly and sat back down.

"Hey Theo, you remember the time we was havin' a corncob fight at your barn," Horace said. Horace was a short, muscular boy in overalls and white shirt with a decidedly rascally manner about him.

"And you bout got me killed," said Theo's friend Lee.

"Theo soaked the corncobs in water," Horace said laughing, "it made'em real heavy. If you got hit with one, it would raise a welt."

"The way I remember it, you was the one made up to soak the corncobs," Theo protested.

"It was you that told Lee to look out to see was the other boys out there," Horace went on. "That was when Lee got hit right square between the eyes. Raised a knot on his head the size of a walnut." Horace paused in his story to look about the room to see that his story was being appreciated.

Frannie looked at her teachers expecting them to be upset at the boy's shenanigans. Miss Tessie seemed concerned that someone had been hurt, a small line creasing her brow. Miss Agnes shook her head bewildered by the boy's roughness. Only Miss Claire hid a smile behind her hand. She caught Frannie looking at her and winked. Frannie pushed her glasses back on her nose and winked back. She could not contain her smile. Her heart felt so full of joy she thought it might pop right out of her chest.

"I was so stunned-like I didn't hardly know where I was," Lee volunteered cheerfully.

"When I stepped out to help him," Theo said, "I got hit on my arm. It stung like a packsaddle done got hold of me. You know how bad a packsaddle sting can hurt. It just won't quit."

"You mean when you stepped out to take a shot," Horace said, grabbing his sides with laughter.

Theo gave him a look. "Then Pa called out from the house," Theo said his voice full of awe.

"We figured we'd been caught for sure," Horace chimed in. "We was all supposed to be helping Theo pitch hay. I grabbed Lee by the arm and took off running through the field so Theo's pa wouldn't see the pump knot on his head."

"They run off like cowards and left me there to face Pa," Theo said.

"What did he do to you?" Martha Jane asked.

"I'll just say it hurt a sight worse than a wet corncob," Theo said flatly.

The boys howled with laughter. The girls giggled nervously. The boys continued their good-natured ribbing until it grew dark and the cake was long ago eaten.

"We'd better go and leave these folks to their rest," Miss Agnes announced as she stood up.

Reluctantly, the girls hugged Martha Jane good-bye and the boys slapped Theo on the back. The teachers took turns wishing the couple well. The family walked the group to the porch and waved to them as they walked down the trail guided by the moonlight.

Only Frannie lingered until they were long out of sight. The night wind was coming up from the valley and for a while it carried the sound of their laughter. Then she was alone with the night. She scanned the sky for stars. She pictured Dealie looking down from one of the night stars. She thought about what a fun day it had been and how she wished Dealie could have been there. It was that way with life now, always the joy mixed with the sad both swirling together so that you couldn't have one without the other.

Frannie could not imagine where her life would take her. So much had happened in the last year, it was a riddle she could not solve. As she stood in the cool April air, the sound of her family's voices mingling with the calls of the night birds, she remembered the joy of the evening and she thought it might just be enough for now.

April 17, 1921

Dear Claire

     I am only just back from a month long visit to my parents in New York. It was a delightful trip and wonderful to find my family in good health. I took along the basket that you and Tessie so kindly gave me on your visit to Knoxville. My Aunt Olivia was most taken with it as was my mother. When I told them about the school and all the fine work that is being done, they expressed an interest in purchasing items. As you know Henry will be in Gatlinburg before the end of the month for a Clinic. If I send along money would it be possible that you might put together some items you find most desirable. You have written of the weaving that is being done there. Might some of these items be available for purchase?

     Now for the real purpose of my letter, my dear. I could hardly contain my excitement to this point. I have spoken to the gallery in New York that has had such wonderful success with your art work. They are very much interested in having a show of your work if you consent to be so honored. It would, of course, require your presence for a few days to make the social rounds. A number of prominent collectors are interested in your work and they are demanding to meet you. As you well know, there is always a great deal of cultivating that must be done. Mr. Phillip Graves is the gallery owner. His thought is that autumn would be an excellent time of the year and would allow for printed programs and invitations to go out. I feel you might also need the time to paint, as Henry has managed to sell your work in Boston and will be bringing you a check. Please let me know as soon as possible as I am wild to set the wheels in motion. I am over the top with delight at your success and all the possibilities the future holds for you dear.

I so regret that I will not be able to come with Henry to Gatlinburg. I was so looking forward to seeing the school and the mountains. After so long away from home, Joseph demands my attention here.

With deep affection
Victoria

Chapter 25

Spring burst out abruptly. Trees that had seemed reluctant at last begun to unfurl soft new leaves. Every branch and twig became touched by the soft ethereal green of spring. The dogwoods were in full flower. The sky was clear blue and the warm air was luminous. It was as though natures hope had no end.

As the group gathered on the porch of the Mountain View Hotel, Claire thought it was a perfect day to hike to Mount LeConte. They were planning to camp overnight on the top of the mountain and return the next day. Tessie and Agnes chatted excitedly as they waited for Henry Wyatt to join them. As soon as the plans for the camping trip had been arranged, Tessie had begged to allow Henry to join them since he would be in Gatlinburg for the upcoming clinic. They had dined the night before at the hotel and it was obvious that their relationship had progressed since Tessie had been corresponding with the doctor. Any reluctance Claire felt about the doctor accompanying them disappeared when she saw them together.

Only when Henry had asked to speak to her alone had she hesitated but it had only been to speak of her art work and to give her the check he carried. The amount had taken her breath. She tried to express her gratitude but he had waved it away. "I am delighted that Victoria and I can be of service," he said. But then he added, "If I cannot be more, may I always be a friend?" She had assured him, with some relief, that it would always be so. Then he had taken her hand in his and stood looking at her long after there was anything to say until she had grown quite uncomfortable. Finally, he had smiled at her, let go of her hand and walked away. It had left her with an odd feeling, as though she had made promises she was unaware of, expectations she could not meet because they came solely from the other person.

Shade, who had offered his services as a guide for the group, had joined them for supper. He had not made mention of their conversation nor made any overtures towards her since that day at the cabin, but she found herself studying him now in ways she had not before. Here was a man so opposite in her temperament and background and yet oddly they complimented one another.

As he sat at the table discussing the upcoming trip with Henry, she found herself once again intrigued by his knowledge of the mountains and the many ways men had learned to survive in them. He had patiently answered the groups many questions. When he caught her watching him, he held her eye but said nothing. She had been forced to look away. Her stomach had churned like a swollen creek.

Shade had simply gone on talking. He spoke of the practical matters of their hike.

He advised them all to wear soft wool socks and to bring along a spare pair. "Make sure your boots are broke in and well oiled. Nothing worse than sore feet for a man who has still got miles to go," he admonished. He told them to bring along two wool blankets for sleeping and to prepare for it to be cold on the mountain once the sun went down.

Henry came out onto the porch followed by Andy Huff. They stood briefly taking in the fresh morning air.

"Good morning, ladies," Andy said greeting the women.

They all greeted him cheerfully.

"Good morning everyone, isn't it a marvelous day," Henry said.

"Did you have a restful night, Dr. Wyatt," Tessie asked and then blushed.

"Thank you for your kind inquiry, Miss Tessie. Due to the wonderful accommodations provided by Mr. Huff, I slept like a baby."

"That may be a good thing, Dr. Wyatt," Agnes said. "I fear you may not find sleeping on the ground tonight quite as hospitable."

"Then I am glad to take my comfort when I can, Miss Agnes," he replied cheerfully.

"First we must make it to the top," Claire teased.

They all laughed.

"You make an excellent point, Miss Claire," Henry said. "It is a most formidable mountain. Let me see if I remember correctly from what Shade told us, the mountain is some six thousand, five hundred ninety-three feet above sea level. The top of LeConte consists of four small peaks. The peaks from east to west are Myrtle Point, Maintop, Clifftop and West Peak." Henry stopped and looked about quite pleased. "How did I do Miss Agnes?" he asked.

"You appear to have paid admirable attention to Mr. Morgan last night. Your memory seems to have served you well," Agnes said.

"Mr. Morgan has informed me that every step will most likely be rocky, sometimes wet, most often steep, and at times precipitous," Henry added.

"You sound most eager," Agnes chimed in.

"I am most encouraged that Shade has made the climb in every season imaginable in daylight and once or twice in darkness and that he is none the worse for it."

"He most likely didn't tell you about the time he got caught out in a snowstorm and had to sleep under a shelf rock," Andy Huff said. " Or the time the wind got so high it was uprooting trees all around him as he was high stepping his way back down," he added chuckling.

They all looked at him. Tessie and Agnes stood mouths agape. Henry rubbed his chin with his hand.

"I'm just joshing you," Andy said. "Shades among the best guides I know. That is short of Wiley Oakley. Can't nobody beat him."

Claire could not believe that Wiley Oakley had agreed to come along and that she was at last going to meet the legendary guide. She had heard a great deal about the man and was eager to discover if half of it was true. It was said that his mother died when he was just a boy and that it left him quite lost. He had taken to roaming the mountains as a way of finding solace and before long he was familiar with even the most secret places. Because he had to help feed the family, he learned from his father, an old time mountain man, how to hunt and fish. He was soon regarded as one of the best hunters in the Great Smoky Mountains. His father also taught him the rich history of the mountain people and soon Wiley discovered a talent for the old stories and had became a storyteller himself. His easy going nature and his vast knowledge soon led to a reputation as a superb guide for hunters, writers and even botanist from all over.

"We best be off if you don't want to be taking your first hike in the dark," Andy Huff said.

"Mr. Morgan was insistent at supper last night that we must see the sunset from Clifftop," Agnes said.

"And the sunrise from Myrtle Point," Tessie added.

"Of course, the sunrise," Henry said.

Claire saw the look that passed between them. She was sure the doctor had almost said "dear." She looked away so he would not catch her smile. She was happy for them both for she loved Tessie almost as much as her own sister and Henry had been most kind to her.

Huff had arranged to take them to meet Shade and Wiley Oakley. They loaded their things into Huff's automobile and piled in for the four mile ride up to Cherokee Orchard, where hundreds of acres had been planted with apple trees and where they would meet their guides.

When they drove up, Shade and Wiley Oakley were already waiting, having ridden their horses to the stable where Andy Huff kept his pack animals. Shade leaned against the rail of the hitching post looking loose and at ease in his own skin. Wiley, who appeared to be telling a lively tale, clapped his hands and threw back his head in laughter. Shade smiled and slapped Wiley on the back. He held on to the man good naturedly by the scruff of his neck and led him to where the group had unloaded.

"Folks, I'd like for you to meet one of the most likeable fellers you'll ever know and the finest man you'll ever have the privilege of going into these here mountains with. Folks, this is Wiley Oakley."

"Howdy," Wiley Oakley said, stepping forward and taking off his felt hat.

They exchanged 'howdys' all around.

Claire had pictured Wiley Oakley as a large man, but he was of average size, slim and wiry. He had dark, curious eyes and a long lean face. He was dressed in a black work coat and blue cotton shirt.

His boots were worn and she could only imagine the miles he had walked in them.

"Wiley will be your guide for the trip," Shade said. "He knows every nook and cranny of these mountains. I'm just along to tote the load, chop fire wood, cook and enjoy the fine company."

"That is very gracious of you Shade," Henry said. "I will be most willing to carry a pack, however."

"Well, that's kind of you Doc. The way is mighty steep and you have most likely never carried a pack, so I best take the heavy load."

They watched as Shade strapped on the heavy pack that contained their food and cooking utensils. To the pack was tied a double-bit axe. Wiley put on a smaller pack to which he had strapped his rifle.

"I reckon the ladies would welcome your help with anything they brought along," Shade offered.

Claire had brought along a small packsack to carry their personal items. In addition, Agnes chose to bring her plant press so that she might collect specimens along the way. Tessie chose to bring along a Kodak and Claire her small sketch pad. Henry brought along newly purchased flashlights which he had ordered from a catalog.

Henry took the pack from Claire along with all of their woolen blankets. Shade helped him tie the load together and at last they were ready to leave.

"Take care of the horses Andy. We will be back before dark tomorrow night."

"I'll be here looking for you," Andy said.

The sky was a beautiful blue with only a few wispy clouds near the top of the mountains. The group headed out in high spirits as they followed the trail along the east side of Mill Creek. The creek got its name from the many grist mills that served the surrounding farm community. The first mile of the trail as they headed toward Rainbow Falls was little more than a path worn by fisherman and it followed the course of the stream.

The land around them had never been owned by the lumber companies and most of it had been cleared for farming. Piles of stones marked an occasional boundary and the stumps of large hemlock trees littered the fields. Some of the fields had been abandoned long ago for the soil was so poor it took only a few years of crops to wear it out. Where the fields had been abandoned; yellow poplar, maple, silverbells and dogwoods had taken over. The silverbells with their bell-like flowers were just coming into bloom. The dogwoods were in full flower.

The trail led them deeper into the forest, onto a hillside covered with rhododendron and mountain laurel. As the trial followed the creek it turned and Wiley stopped to let the hikers catch up. Smiling at Claire, Shade pointed to the hillside. She was astonished to see the entire hillside covered in white trilliums all with their heads turned in search of the sun. She let out a gasp and then laughed with delight. Agnes, Tessie and Henry gathered beside her to stand in awe. "Oh Shade, it's simply beautiful," Claire said.

"I'm proud you like it," he said.

"Miss Agnes, Shade here tells me you like seeing new plants," Wiley said.

"Yes, Mr. Oakley, I enjoy it very much," Agnes said.

"Have you ever seen wild ginger? Wiley asked. He squatted down and gently lifted a heart-shaped leaf in his hand. Beneath the leaf was a brownish-purple cuplike flower.

Agnes bent low to examine the plant, her face intent. "Why I might have overlooked this all together Mr. Oakley. How unusual that the flowers are hidden beneath the leaves."

"If you dig the root up, it smells right strong. Granny women boil it up for childbirth and to give baby's with colic."

"I suspect this is from the birthwort family," Agnes declared. "It's been used since the Middle Ages. Do you think they brought the knowledge of this plant with them from Europe, Mr. Oakley?" Agnes asked.

"Most likely picked it up from the Cherokee," Wiley said, simply. "They know more about the plants here in the Great Smoky Mountains than I could learn in a lifetime."

Claire left them to talk and wandered to the creek. The boulders were covered with moss and tiny white violets decorated the bank. Foamflowers carpeted the opposite bank. Shade came up beside her, took off his pack and rested it against a tree. They stood looking as the flowers danced in a gentle breeze.

"It is so beautiful. I did not know that such extravagance could exist in nature. It's as though the flowers, the trees, the shrubs, even the boulders and the cascading water are putting on a show just for us."

"I think they do it for themselves," Shade said. "We just happen to catch them at it."

"Like children at play, full of the joyous energy. I feel privileged to be allowed to see it. Thank you for bringing me here to see all of this," she said.

"I like seeing it through your eyes," he said, not looking at her.

"And I like seeing it through your eyes," she confessed. She had not meant to say it, but she had spoken the truth. Furthermore, she realized she had no desire to take it back.

He turned to her and his eyes widened.

She wanted to tell him that perhaps she had begun to 'loosen the grip on her plans' as he had suggested. She wanted to say that this year, which had seemed a by-road on the way to her true path, had led her to the unexpected love of the Great Smoky Mountains and the people who inhabited them. Moreover, it had led her to Shade Morgan, a man whose roots in the mountains ran deep through the rocky soil and back through time. The words spun in her head but before she could speak them, Tessie and Henry walked to the stream.

"We had better rescue Wiley from Agnes," Tessie said laughing, "or we could be here all night."

"When we left them they were in search of the Dutchman's-pipe vine," Henry said.

"I'll go fetch them," Shade said.

As he walked off, he gave Claire a backward glance.

She smiled back at him and then turned to Henry. "Are you enjoying the hike?

"Most enjoyable," Henry said. "I look forward to seeing Rainbow Falls. The painting you sent Victoria was extraordinary. She took it with her to New York. It was met with considerable appreciation."

"Thank you, Henry. You are most kind to say so." Claire looked about to see if Shade was within earshot. She was not sure why she had not told him about the possibilities that awaited her in New York.

"I am sure you will find the falls quite different this time of the year. I am most anxious to see it again myself."

Shade walked back with his party in tow.

Agnes was flushed with excitement. "Mr. Oakley has a wealth of herbal lore," she said breathlessly.

"I don't doubt Wiley's knowledge," Shade said. "He's been a student of these mountains since he was a boy."

"And I'm still learning all the while," Wiley said.

"They's just one thing," Shade said with a grin, "you might should ask him."

"What would that be," Agnes asked.

"Ask him about the yodel," Shade said.

"The yodel," Agnes quizzed.

"Well, you see I like to tell stories," Wiley said. "Some stories has more truth to them than others. If the story is true, why then I don't yodel at the end."

They all laughed, except Agnes who said solemnly, "Well, Mr. Oakley, I am satisfied I have not heard you yodel yet."

Tessie made them all line up for photographs. Then Agnes volunteered to take one with Tessie in the group.

Finally, Shade put on his pack and they headed up the trail. About a mile and a half above Cherokee Orchard a footbridge crossed Mill Creek. The forest grew denser with enormous hemlocks and silverbells.

"See that yellow buckeye, Miss Agnes," Wiley said pointing to a tree. "The one where the leaves look like a man's fingers spread out."

Agnes nodded.

Wiley pulled a buckeye from his pocket. At the end of summer that tree drops a buckeye burr. It has a brown nut in it that has a pale spot on it that looks like a buck's eye. That's where it gets it name."

"Why do you carry one in your pocket," Agnes asked.

"Well you can rub it for good luck," Wiley said handing it to her.

"Are they good to eat?" she asked examining the brown sphere.

"I reckon squirrels think so. They eat most of'em soon as they hit the ground."

"What about people. Do people eat them?"

"Inside this husk is a pair of buckeyes," Wiley explained. "One is poisonous and the other is not."

"How do you know which is which?" Agnes asked.

Wiley shrugged.

"What about the squirrels? How do they know?"

"They eat both of'em."

"Why doesn't the poison hurt them?"

"I reckon nobody never told'em that one of them buckeyes was poisonous," Wiley said.

Agnes studied the buckeye and then looked at Wiley. Suddenly he let out a loud yodel and slapped his leg.

Agnes' face split with a soft grin.

Wiley's eyes sparkled. "Now that you know, I reckon it won't be generated in you to eat a buckeye."

Agnes stood blinking as she tried to take in his meaning. "Yes, Mr. Oakley, I will most certainly not be generated to eat it." She handed the buckeye back to Wiley who, his body still shaking with laughter put it in his pocket.

They followed the trail on up to an exposed ridgeline and began a series of switchbacks and stream crossings until through the trees appeared a massive cliff face obscured by a thicket of rhododendrons.

Claire realized that they had reached Rainbow Falls and her heart quickened. She rushed ahead scrambling over the rocks to stand at the base of the seventy-five foot falls. The creek was narrow overhead and the water was forced outward over the falls as it fell. She stood arms outstretched with her face turned skyward, laughing as the mist sprayed her face. The falls seemed to have awakened from its winter slumber and was intent upon enjoying its new freedom as it fell with abandon and danced upon the rocks below.

Shade called to her.

She waved back and scrambled back to meet him laughing with delight.

"I swear, Claire, did you look up out of your cradle with those eyes," Shade said.

"Why what ever do you mean, Shade?" she asked.

"Wild, searching eyes, that's what you have, Claire Blackburn," Shade said teasingly. "Like a panther prowling the woods."

"If I did, I am sure it must have given my mother quite a fright," she joked in turn.

"What were you searching for in the falls just now," he queried.

A sign, perhaps, she thought but instead she said, "Don't they say if the sunlight strikes the mist just right it will cast a rainbow," she offered. "Isn't that why they call it Rainbow Falls?"

"That's what they say," he replied.

"Have you ever seen it?"

He shook his head. "You don't always see it."

She nodded, lost in thought.

When the group caught up with them, Shade announced they would take their dinner at the falls. He took off his pack and pulled out ham and egg sandwiches on biscuits. "Ma made these," he said handing them out.

"My favorite," Claire declared when she took off the cloth.

"I reckon Ma knows that," Shade said.

She ate as though she had not that morning had a large breakfast. As they sat about enjoying their food, Claire took out her sketch pad. She wanted to capture the ebullient nature of the falls in spring.

"I must say so far the hike has been easier than I had come to expect," Henry remarked. "Tell me Shade, was there some exaggeration on your part about the difficulty?"

"You might wish I had," Shade said as he bit into a Hershey bar. He held up a handful of chocolate bars and offered them to the others. Everyone took the candy but Henry who claimed that sweets were bad for the digestion. Shade shrugged and put it back in the pack. "All the same, you are going to need it, along with some stout arms and legs from here on out," he went on.

"Where does the trail take out of here?" Tessie asked as her eyes searched about the falls.

"About a hundred feet west of here you'll see a hemlock tree leaning against the cliff. It takes up that tree," Shade said.

Claire looked up to see the shocked expression on Tessie's face. Henry's eyes were wide with surprise.

"Don't worry," Shade said. "I'll help you up to the first limb. Wiley will go to the top and pull you up through the tree branches. After that it's mostly straight uphill to the top."

"You better eat up and get some rest while you can," Wiley mused. "I've seen grown men so tired they couldn't do nothing but fall over and go to sleep. They wouldn't even walk around to see the view. They couldn't bring themselves to walk the few hundred yards to the sunset they come all that way to see. That's a crying shame."

Henry studied Wiley's face and waited. Time passed and Wiley went on chewing his sandwich. Then he slowly tore the wrapper from his Hershey bar and bit off a huge chunk. He sat lost in the pleasure of it until he had eaten every bite.

Henry continued to watch Wiley, his face screwed up with concentration. He crossed his arms and then uncrossed them sighing each time he did.

Claire realized that he must be waiting for Wiley to yodel. She chuckled to herself and looked up to see Shade's body shaking as he held in the laughter.

In time Henry gave up all hope of Wiley yodeling and said, "I believe I will have one of those Hershey bars, Shade."

Chapter 26

Claire took the canteen from Shade and drank deeply. Her legs shook and her arms ached from the last scramble up the mountainside. She could feel the heat in her face. When she looked at Tessie, her ruddy complexion glowed deep red. Agnes, whose usual nature it was to flutter about like a bird, sat slumped on a boulder. Henry looked pale and drained. No one complained but she could see the relief catch up to them as they realized that they had at last made it to the campsite below Clifftop.

At the higher elevation, the air was cool and moist. The forest gave way to fir and spruce. The sweet aroma of balsam mingled with the earthy smell of nature returning to itself. Wood sorrel not yet in bloom appeared in the moss under the fir trees.

Shade and Wiley not stopping to rest set about the work of preparing the campsite. Hikers before them had built a crude lean-to and split logs for benches. The men cut balsam boughs and laid them in the small structure to prepare beds for the women. For the men, Shade cut more boughs which Wiley turned into crude thatched tents. Then the men turned to unpacking the provisions. While Shade cut and stacked the firewood, Wiley set about clearing the ground around the stone fire pit. He then built a fire while Shade went to fill the canteens from a nearby spring.

Claire could not believe that within an hour, as they watched, the camp was made tidy and comfortable. Trimmed brush had been driven into the ground and the cooking utensils hung from the stubs. A shelf had been made from straight sticks placed between two limbs and on it was a tin pan. "Shade the camp is so very nice," she said. "Thank you for all your work."

"I like to build a campsite so when I leave the wildness is still there," he said. "Pa taught me that."

"That seems very wise," she said.

"I made you a washstand," he said pointing to the shelf. "So you wouldn't have to go to the spring to wash up."

Realizing that the men left alone would give little thought to such cleanliness, she was touched by his kindness. "Its perfect, Shade, how thoughtful of you."

"I'm pleased you think so," he said, looking uncomfortable to have given himself away.

"Are you ready to see the sunset," he asked.

She nodded.

He looked about at the others. "If you folks are rested, we'll head up to Clifftop for the sunset. We can eat our supper when we get back."

"Oh yes," Agnes said, hopping up from her seat on the boulder. She was once again her efficient self. "We want to make the most of our time."

Henry gave Shade and Wiley each a flashlight and kept one for himself. They headed out single file up to the craggy rocks of Clifftop where the view opened up to the valley below. The mountains stretched out before them in a haze of blue and purple.

The hikers stood side by side, along the treeless outcropping. Henry and Tessie stood a little away from the group. Claire watched as Henry put his arm around Tessie. They whispered back and forth to one another. Wiley and Agnes discussed the veeries nesting nearby. Wiley said they were plentiful on the mountain along with chickadees and duck hawks and on occasion a pair of eagles.

Suddenly, they were struck silent by the boundless beauty of the vista as the sky turned to shades of pink and orange. The men turned off their flashlights, as the group waited expectantly. The veery paused in its ceaseless whistling call and the wind held its breath in profound respect for nature's display. A few clouds gathered like curtains on a stage before a grand performance. The beams of radiant violet and golden light shot down from the sinking sun to the valley floor below like God's stage lights.

Claire could almost taste the rich, intoxicating colors in her mouth. She wanted to hurl herself from the cliff and fly out into the evanescent beauty. She felt completely alive and wholly awake. "I never want to leave," she whispered to Shade. "I want to stay here forever."

She knew suddenly that she was not just speaking of that fleeting moment of a glorious sunset but that she wanted to stay forever in the Smoky Mountains. After resisting her heart for so long, she found herself trembling with a kind of expectant happiness. Shade reached out and touched her hand and their fingers entwined. They did not look at one another but kept their eyes on the sunset. There was so much she needed and wanted to tell him. But it could wait, for now they had time, she thought.

As the last rays sank quickly behind the mountain, the group let out a collective breath, the magic of the moment vanishing like a dream. They did not waste words trying to describe what they had seen for there were none to match the experience.

"We better head back and get supper started," Wiley said.

They stood about for a few moments reluctant to leave.

"We'll want to get to bed early if we are to get up before dawn for the sunrise," he added.

"How wonderful to have yet another treat for which to look forward," Agnes said.

"It will have to be grand to top this marvelous sunset," Henry said. "Don't you agree, Tessie?"

"I do indeed, Henry," Tessie said chortling.

The hikers headed back to camp, when Henry and Tessie suddenly stopped and called out. The others turned to see what was wrong.

"Tessie and I have an announcement," Henry said excitedly.

Everyone turned to face Henry and Tessie wrapped in the glow of their flashlight. Shade let go of Claire's hand and they stood next to each other feeling suddenly shy.

"Tonight, with this lovely sunset, I asked Tessie to marry me and she said yes," Henry said.

Claire stood for a moment in stunned surprise. Was this the reason Henry had stood before her so silent and awkward earlier in the day. Had he meant to tell her, surely not to ask her permission? What had he expected from her, a last minute confession of her feelings for him? Did he think she would feel betrayed? Whatever he had expected, he had mercifully left unsaid for she could bear no such admissions. She was concerned only for Tessie who spoke so often and earnestly of her love for Henry that Claire worried for her sanity as well as her own.

She rushed to hug Tessie. "I am so happy for you Tessie," she said and truly meant it.

"Oh Claire, isn't it all so wonderful," Tessie gushed. "It was a complete surprise. I would have told you, if I had known. Henry had it planned all along."

"Tessie, I am delighted. You deserve to be happy."

Agnes shook Tessie's hand. The men slapped Henry on the back.

"All this celebratin' is giving me an appetite," Wiley said.

They all laughed. Then remembering their own hunger, they headed back to camp with Wiley in the lead. The moon was rising and they were in high spirits as they walked along.

Claire was eager to find a moment alone with Shade to tell him that she was earnest in her intention to stay. She had been waiting for some sign, some sense of certainty about what she was to do and now she felt that it had been painted across the sky in a sunset. Claire pictured telling Tessie later that night as they lay in their beds of balsam talking over the day. Her decision now seemed overshadowed by Tessie and Henry's engagement. As they walked in the dark, she decided that she would keep her secret until morning and allow Tessie her moment.

As soon as they were back at the campsite, Shade dug the potatoes out of the fire that had been buried in the coals earlier. Claire unpacked the plates and forks and helped Shade fry the bacon and set the cold cornbread they had brought along on a stone to warm. It seemed as natural as anything she had ever done. In the time they had worked together at the cabin, they had worked out a rhythm and a fluid way of moving around each other. He taught her how to do proper measurements and how to hew and notch a log. She helped him shore up the floor with new sleeper beams. She would look up at times to see his special look of approval. He told her that a well-crafted log cabin was "a work of art." But, it was the child-like spirit and freedom of creating something beautiful that he brought to his work that she found most delightful.

Shade caught Claire's eye as he dished up the food and she smiled shyly at him. They ate with only the sound of their forks on tin plates breaking the silence. When every morsel was consumed, the group began to stir and talk again.

"That was the best meal I believe I have ever eaten," Henry said, "and I have eaten in some fine restaurants."

"Did you have to walk six or seven miles to get that restaurant?" Wiley asked.

"No, I don't think I ever have," Henry replied.

"That can put some special kind of flavor in your food," Wiley said.

"Then I hope to repeat this experience again someday, Mr. Oakley and I thank you for it."

"You might orta wait to thank me until you see how your breakfast taste after you get woke up at four o'clock to see the sunrise."

They all agreed that as tired as they felt, they looked forward to it and that despite the climb it had been a most enjoyable trip. One they hoped to repeat. They sat quietly watching the fire and musing over their good fortune.

"Dr. Wyatt might I ask, do you and Tessie intend to make your home in Knoxville after your marriage?" Agnes asked.

Tessie turned to Henry and waited for his answer. He smiled and took her hand in his, "I had wanted to tell Tessie this first but I am sure she won't mind if I say that I have purchased a home in Knoxville this very week."

Tessie clapped her hands with delight. "Oh, Henry."

"I suppose we will soon lose you as a teacher then." Agnes said.

"I am sure Henry intends to continue his work in Gatlinburg. He has spoken often of it," Tessie said. "I intend to be of service to him in that endeavor."

"Yes, I won't be taking her away forever. I plan on a day or two a month in the mountains," Henry agreed.

"And what about you, Claire? Agnes asked. "What are your plans? Are you planning on teaching another year?"

Claire watched as all eyes turned to her. She was at a loss for words for she had first wanted to talk to Shade before announcing her intentions. Before she could speak Henry spoke up.

"Has Claire not told you of the wonderful opportunity that awaits her," Henry said with excitement. He looked at Claire for confirmation.

"Well, it has only just come to me by way of a letter from Henry's sister, Victoria," Claire said.

"Claire has been offered her own show at a major art gallery in New York. It is a very rare and momentous event for someone so young and new to the art world."

"That is truly good news," Agnes said. "I know you must be delighted."

"Of course, I am," Claire stammered. She glanced at Shade whose jaw was set in a hard edge. She regretted not having told him about the letter. She wanted to catch his eye, to somehow explain but his face was hollowed by shadows and unreadable in the firelight. "Victoria and Henry have been so generous in their support," she stumbled on. "I am so appreciative of their help."

"It's Victoria mostly," Henry said proudly. "She is quite the mother hen about it all. She is beside herself at being a part of helping Claire. She is expecting big things from her little protégé."

"Well, there is no question then, you must go," Agnes said emphatically.

"No question at all," Henry agreed without waiting for Claire to respond.

The group went on talking and soon Wiley was regaling the hikers with stories of his adventures in the mountains. Shade stood up and began to clean up the campsite. She watched as he hung the packs high in the trees away from the bears and cleaned up all traces of their supper. She wanted to hold out until everyone had gone to bed so that she might speak to him and try to explain, but soon her head was nodding. Tessie reached over and took her hand leading her off to bed. She could only look back helplessly over her shoulder at Shade silhouetted against the moonlight.

She awoke to the sound of her name. As unaccustomed as she was to sleeping fully clothed, she was surprised to discover that she had dozed. Her body ached from the hard ground cushioned though she had been by the balsam boughs. Her mind had turned over just as her body had done.

"Claire," Shade whispered again.

She crawled out of her blanket. "Shade is that you? Is it time for sunrise?"

He put his finger to his lips and held out his hand for her. She took it and he led her away from the shelter.

"Here put this around your shoulders," he said, as he wrapped her in a blanket. "There is something I want to show you."

The night had grown cold and the air was damp with a light mist of rain. Claire pulled the blanket tightly around her. "Shouldn't we wake the others," she said, her voice hushed.

"It isn't time for sunrise yet."

"Then where are we going?"

He did not answer but pulled her along through the moonlight up a steep rocky path through a thick undergrowth of sand myrtle. They emerged onto an open protrusion of boulders.

Claire's heart was pounding, the sound roaring in her ears. The set of Shade's shoulders told her he was angry and she wanted him to tell her why he had brought her here. "Is this Myrtle Point? Why did you bring me here without the others?"

He turned and took her by the shoulders. The hurt was etched in his face as he looked down into her face.

"Why didn't you see fit to tell me about New York?" he demanded. "Did you not trust me to have the sense to know that you have a gift?"

"Shade, I…" she stammered.

"Do I not mean enough to you to share that part of your life?"

She stood stunned by his words. "Shade, you must believe me, it isn't that way at all. You are the finest man I have ever known and you mean the world to me."

"Then when were you going to tell me?"

She pulled away from him. The clouds covered the moon and she stood feeling the damp mist penetrate the depths of her soul. "I have had this dream for so long. I've dreamed of being an artist and of making my way in the world," she said. She could not see his face and the darkness gave her the courage to go on. "Then I came here to the mountains. I came because I was a coward. The time had come to go after my dream and I lacked the courage." She smiled a sad smile and she could not stop the tears that filled her eyes. "I did not come here because of some noble desire to be of service. I came to help myself."

"Don't you think it might just be possible that in helping yourself, you helped a few other people along the way? You helped Emily. She was a lost little girl after her mama died and you showed her a way back through her drawings. You helped the Riley family just by caring for them in their grief. Why, half the little girls in that school see the moon and stars when they look at your face. You showed them all the things they could be and do with their lives."

"They have given me so much more," she said.

"There is not a thing wrong with that, Claire. Life is not a scale you can balance. Sometimes it tips one way or another and you can't always know why."

"I have come to love the Great Smoky Mountains. I love the rugged beauty and how every season spreads a banquet of delight. I love the children and how earnest and giving they are and their families whose courage inspires me. I love the pride the people here have in their heritage and their love of independence," she said.

Then she hesitated. Softly she said, "Everyday I could feel the pull to stay here as it grew stronger."

"I have watched as you struggled," he said.

"I have fought it. I thought I would be giving up my dream. I thought I was once again being a coward and that it was easier to stay here where I felt safe."

"And then the offer came to go to New York."

"Yes, quite unexpectedly my paintings started to sell, paintings that I had done of the Great Smoky Mountains. It seemed that just when I had decided to stay," she said and waited before stumbling on, "my dream of becoming an artist, of living independently, and traveling the world seemed a possibility."

"So is that why you did not tell me?"

"I didn't tell you, because I didn't know what I was going to do. I've been looking for a sign," she said with a bitter laugh.

"Good lord woman, I thought I had given you sign enough without even meaning to," he said his voice hoarse.

"That was what I was trying to tell you tonight at Clifftop as we watched the sunset. I want to stay here in these mountains I have come to love. I want to stay here with you Shade Morgan. I love you. I think I have loved you for a long time." She turned and pressed her face into his chest and he wrapped his arms around her.

He pressed his lips against the top of her head and then he lifted her face and stared down into her eyes for a long time without speaking. Then he sighed and said, "I have waited a long time to hear that Claire Blackburn. Because I love you."

"How long have you known," she asked.

"I think I started to fall in love with you the first time I saw you on the road coming from the revival with your chin stuck out, your eyes' throwing off more sparks than a campfire."

Claire laughed. "Is that the way I looked to you? Whatever did you think of me?"

"I didn't know what to think of you. I had never met a woman quite like you. But in time I found myself thinking of you at every turn. It caught me unaware, at first. I never expected to fall in love again after Sarah. I had to make my peace with that. I thought I had made it plain to you a time or two without meaning to how I felt. I didn't want that."

"Because you weren't sure how I felt," she said.

"You have to admit you were pretty good at keeping it to yourself."

"So you woke me up in the middle of the night and dragged me up here to force me to admit I love you?"

He shrugged. He cupped her face in his hands and kissed her on the lips. "I reckon it worked."

"I reckon it did," Claire said.

A gentle breeze parted the clouds like curtains revealing the full moon. In the soft mist, an iridescent rainbow crossed the sky.

Claire gasped. "It's a rainbow by moonlight."

They stood transfixed by the fleeting beauty of the rainbow. Claire felt her body straining toward the soft, illusive light wanting to absorb the colors into her skin through the mist. In seconds the clouds closed and the rainbow disappeared as though it had never been.

"Shade, how did you know?"

"I didn't know, but they say it takes a rare and special person to see one. I always knew that would be you Claire."

"It was the most beautiful sight I have ever seen. I will cherish this moment forever, Shade."

Sadness crossed his face as she spoke the words.

"What is it Shade. What's wrong?"

"You have to go," he said.

"What do you mean," she pleaded. "I just told you that I want to stay here with you."

"You can't stay here. You are not a woman content to be in one place just yet, no matter how right and safe it feels to you now. You have a gift, Claire, a rare and special gift. You have to step out into the world and see what that brings or you may always wonder. You might come to regret it if you don't. I can't live with that and I won't be responsible for it."

She knew in his heart that he was right. "But Shade, what about you."

"I'll be here. I'll always be here, Claire."

They stood with their arms around each other until the moon started to settle in the west. Then they walked back to camp to wake the others to see the sunrise over Myrtle Point.

Chapter 27

They had agreed not to say goodbye. After the hike down the mountain, they had met whenever they could at the cabin. Sometimes Claire would paint while Shade sharpened his tools or did repairs. Often times, they walked the woods talking, but never about her leaving.

Henry and Tessie decided not to wait to wed. They married in the White Oaks Flat Baptist Church in a ceremony attended by the entire Gatlinburg community including the teachers and students of Pi Beta Phi Settlement School. It was two weeks before Tessie's younger sister was to marry.

Shade and Claire joined the couple for a wedding supper at the Mountain View Hotel. They knew, without speaking the words, that it would be the last time they would see each other before Claire left for New York, but they made no mention of it as they laughed and teased the happy couple.

When Shade walked her back to the teachers' cottage, they stood for a long time holding each other. Then Shade kissed her softly on the lips and walked away into the night.

She did not speak to anyone about the rainbow she had seen in the moonlight on Myrtle Point. It was an illusive and haunting experience, one that could not be explained but nevertheless changed a person forever. She thought of Granny Kate's mother who had spent a lifetime trying to recapture the moment through the threads of her weaving, wanting desperately to pass it on to her daughter.

Perhaps, someday she might find a way to show the world a moonlight rainbow. For now, it was something only Shade would understand. For now, it was something only they would share.

Looking out the window of the teachers' cottage, she glimpsed the mountains swathed in their blue haze and remembered that first drive into Gatlinburg over roads so rough they had taken her breath and bruised her body. How terrified and excited she had been looking over the edge of the road into the Little Pigeon River. Then she had glimpsed the bewildering beauty of the Great Smoky Mountains. That had been a moment for which she had been wholly unprepared. She knew that wherever she traveled no matter how far or for how long she would be forever tethered to this place by her love of the mountains and its people.

She sat down at her writing desk and took out her pen and began a note to Shade.

Dear Shade

You once asked that I paint something for you. It was to be my choice you proclaimed. I thought, what could be equal to your patience and your faith in me. Is there a symbol for love that simply is, that exist without demand or expectation.

In the end, the painting chose me.

With all my love
Claire

She took one last look at the painting, the deep purple mountains, the lavender sky lighted by a full moon and the arc of iridescent color that formed the rainbow. She wrapped the painting in paper and tied it with a string. Slipping the note behind the string, she laid the painting on her bed. Agnes had promised to give it to Shade after she was gone along with a note.

Taking one last look around the room, she took a deep breath. Everything in her heart yearned to stay in the mountains where she felt loved and comforted. In her mind, she wove together the spirit of the strong mountain women, the pride of generations of settlers and the joy and enthusiasm of the mountain children and put it about her shoulders like a protective coverlet. Then she went down the steps and out the front door. With one last look back at the mountains, she stepped out into her life.